Evelyn

Evelyn James has always been fascinated by history and the work of writers such as Agatha Christie. She began writing the Clara Fitzgerald series one hot summer, when a friend challenged her to write her own historical murder mystery. Clara Fitzgerald has gone on to feature in over thirteen novels, with many more in the pipeline. Evelyn enjoys conjuring up new plots, dastardly villains and horrible crimes to keep her readers entertained and plans on doing so for as long as possible.

Other Books in
The Clara Fitzgerald Series

The
Fossil Murder

by
Evelyn James

A Clara Fitzgerald Mystery
Book 15

Red Raven Publications
2019

Chapter One

Captain O'Harris dropped the newspaper down on the Fitzgeralds' dining room table.

"Finally, a bit of science comes to Brighton!" He said with a grin.

Clara pulled the paper towards her and read the headline.

MISSING LINK TO APPEAR IN EXHIBITION: TOWN HALL TO BECOME MUSEUM FOR A WEEK

"This is about the exhibition of fossils that has been touring the country. I believe the crates with the displays inside arrived today," Clara perused the text of the article. "I see Gilbert McMillan is sticking to his usual formula of writing a lot of words without saying very much at all."

"Gilbert McMillan?" O'Harris asked.

"He is a journalist at the Brighton Gazette," Clara explained, passing back the paper. "I assume by your excitement you want to go this exhibition?"

Clara was smiling.

"Of course I want to go! But the tickets are all sold for the private viewings. I'll have to wait until the public open day," he grimaced at the thought of having to fight through a throng of people all barging into the town hall to see the exhibits on the one day they were open to the public for free.

"That's a shame," Clara said with a twinkle in her eye. "Especially seeing as I happen to have three tickets to the exhibition myself. I can't possibly think who I shall share them with."

O'Harris raised an eyebrow at her.

"You have tickets?"

"I like science too, you know," Clara pretended to be offended. "I did have an education."

"I never doubted it, I just thought your interests lied more in the present than in the past," O'Harris teased her.

"I could always ask Colonel Brandt to accompany me. He has some rather fascinating views on evolution, or rather how it can't possibly have happened," Clara said folding her arms over her chest.

"All right, apologies for questioning your interest in science," O'Harris winked at her. "You'll take me, right?"

"I suppose I really should," Clara couldn't resist smiling a little. "Seeing as we are friends."

O'Harris made a pretence of sighing with relief.

"Who gets the third ticket?" He asked.

"That would be me, old man," Tommy Fitzgerald walked into the room and smiled at his sister and the captain. "I wouldn't miss seeing that Archaeopteryx fossil for the world."

"Imagine, the one fossil that demonstrates how dinosaurs became birds," O'Harris whistled to himself.

"My understanding is there is still a lot of debate about that," Clara interjected.

"Depends on whose book you read on the subject," Tommy said. "But most scientists who follow Darwin's Theory of Evolution agree that the Archaeopteryx is the missing link between lizards and birds. Here is what at first glance could be just another small dinosaur, except it has feathers and we have to assume it could at least glide, if not fully fly."

"Certainly gets my vote for being the clearest bit of hard

evidence around for evolution," O'Harris nodded. "What about you Clara?"

"I don't question evolution," Clara shrugged. "But, I do like to hear all the various sides of the argument concerning this fossil. I find it fascinating how even scientists can twist the facts before them to suit their own ideas. This exhibition has already caused quite a stir in other towns. In Manchester there was a protest about the Archaeopteryx being displayed at all. A Baptist minister condemned it as a hoax and an insult to God. All over a bird encased in stone."

"So, when do we get to see the culprit in the flesh," O'Harris was grinning from ear-to-ear.

"Monday," Clara announced. "First day of the exhibition."

Captain O'Harris was obviously delighted and his excitement made Clara happy. They had known each other for a relatively short space of time, but their relationship was strengthening by the day. The dashing former Royal Flying Corps captain and Brighton's first female private detective had yet to admit to themselves that their friendship was deepening into something much stronger, but it was obvious to Clara's brother Tommy and to the Fitzgeralds' friend and housekeeper Annie. Sooner or later, Annie had declared more than once, Clara and O'Harris would have to admit they loved each other. And if they didn't, Annie was going to have words with the both of them.

Annie failed to appreciate that her own situation with Tommy was a mirror image of that of Clara and O'Harris. If Clara ever nudged her about her feelings towards Tommy, she refused to talk about them. Annie was quite comfortable with things as they were, thank you very much. She would acknowledge her feelings towards Tommy in her own time.

"Well, I need to get back to the house," O'Harris picked up the newspaper.

"How is everything going?" Clara asked.

3

O'Harris had founded a convalescence home for servicemen suffering psychology problems after the war. There were a number of facilities that helped former servicemen who had been physically disabled during the war, but very little for those who had suffered mental trauma, and whose suffering continued in everyday life. O'Harris had experienced this for himself and was trying to make a difference. It was a drop in the ocean, when you considered how many men were carrying the scars inside of that time, but it was a start.

"On the whole things have been running smoothly," O'Harris nodded, his smile becoming a little fixed. "We have had a couple of gentlemen complete their time with us and return home. From what I have heard they are doing well. The only fly in the ointment is Private Peterson."

"Your subsidised soldier?" Tommy clarified.

O'Harris' home was a private operation and the patients paid to attend. However, there was provision for at least one soldier to attend without charge. These subsidised patients would be men who could not normally afford the fees for the home, but who it was felt needed the help the place could offer. Private Peterson was the first of these subsidised patients and O'Harris had taken a huge chance on him. His case was pretty severe; he was suffering from hallucinations when he thought he was back at the Front and he regularly dipped into paralysing depression. He was unable to work and barely able to live a normal life. Treatments had been attempted in the past but had failed to have a lasting effect. The truth was, O'Harris' home was his last option. If they could not help him, it was difficult to see where else he could turn.

Peterson himself had given up hope of recovery. He had come to the conclusion that he was as permanently damaged as if he had lost a limb. Only the determination of his family, namely his mother, was keeping him from giving up altogether and ending things. O'Harris thought the young man was on the precipice of suicide or possibly

4

complete insanity. There was a real risk he would end up confined to an institution for the rest of his life.

"Peterson is willing enough, but so far we have not been able to find the key to his problem. He has suffered three hallucinatory episodes since being with us, the last one we found him in the garden in the middle of the night attempting to dig a foxhole to hide from falling shells. He screamed when we approached him, thinking we were German soldiers," O'Harris' former excitement had evaporated. "I knew he was going to be a challenge. Maybe I was over-confident when I insisted we take him on. I thought we could help him. Perhaps I thought it would prove the validity of my project to some of my naysayers if I took in such a severe case and cured him. Now I fear I will fail him. I gave him and his family hope, and now my cockiness may cost us all."

"You've barely begun to help him," Clara pointed out. "These things take time."

"She is right," Tommy concurred. "It's only been a couple of months."

"Hopefully you are right," O'Harris smiled again. "Anyway, enough of that, best let you get on."

O'Harris wished them farewell and departed out the front door. A few minutes later, Clara was heading out herself, off to her office to see what cases the day might bring. She had taken a brief break from work to travel to Belgium to solve a murder and had returned home to find correspondence piled up on the doormat of her office and a number of people trying to get hold of her. Clara was well-known in Brighton for solving crimes the police could not get their heads around and so many people wanted her help, that Clara was finding herself in a position where she had to turn down clients – something that had never happened before. There was too much work and not enough hours in the day, she was almost considering taking up Tommy on his offer of becoming her assistant. It would certainly ease her workload and would give her brother something to do with his time. Tommy had never had an actual job, having left university and signed up for the army at the outbreak of war. He had returned home a cripple and these last few years had been a long road of recovery for him. He could now walk with only a slight limp and wanted to start doing something more than just wandering about the house. It was probably time Clara had a chat with him about whether he wanted to be more than an occasional helper in her business.

Clara was mulling all this over when she bumped, almost literally, into Mrs Wilton. Mrs Wilton had been the client who made Clara's name. Through the woman, Clara had become involved in her first murder case. It had been an anxious and exhilarating experience and had set Clara on her path as a real private detective. Even so, when Clara bumped into Mrs Wilton, she always felt a pang of dread. The woman had a way of involving her in things she would rather stay out of.

"Clara!" Mrs Wilton said in delight. "You look very well. I hear you have just been to Belgium?"

"Yes, it was for a case," Clara said, trying to shuffle along the pavement.

"How exciting!" Mrs Wilton had a knack for being overly dramatic when she talked. She waved her hands about, gesticulating as if she was on the stage. "I hear talk you were working for Mrs Priggins?"

"I can't discuss my cases Mrs Wilton," Clara said gently. "I have to respect the privacy of my clients."

"Oh, of course!" Mrs Wilton brushed aside the matter with a flick of her hand. "But now, how fortuitous I came upon you as I did, it saves me coming past your office again. I went there the other week and that was how I learned you were in Belgium. The nice man in the grocer's shop told me."

Clara was hoping that Mrs Wilton had not found another 'friend' to inflict on her. The woman seemed to think it was her duty to find work for Clara and routinely sent the most trivial matters in her direction. Clara was long past finding lost cats and discovering who was taking flowers off graves in the churchyard (that had proved to be Mrs McGinny's nanny goat, who occasionally got loose from the garden and wandered to the graveyard to gorge on fresh flowers).

"It is a very serious matter," Mrs Wilton insisted, dropping her voice and not apparently noticing that Clara was trying to inch away. "My neighbour is really in a pickle over it."

Clara stopped moving, resigned to the inevitable. Whatever she did, somehow Mrs Wilton would find her and insist that she take on this case. Mrs Wilton was the human equivalent of an unstoppable force and there was no point trying to elude her.

"Your neighbour," Clara said, racking her brain to think about who had the misfortune of living next to Mrs Wilton. "The gentleman with the very old Great Dane?"

"No, not him. My neighbour further down the road. Miss Holbein, she is the sole heiress of a rather nice fortune and is quite alone in this world. Need I tell you the perils a young woman must face when it is known that she has an awful lot of money?"

It sounded like a Victorian novel. Clara could imagine that a woman alone and with a lot of money at her disposal would attract all sorts of rogues.

"I have been keeping my eye on her," Mrs Wilton said with an air of pride. "I told my son he ought to watch out for her too, not that I was considering him and her…"

Mrs Wilton gasped at the sudden realisation that it might appear that she was after Miss Holbein's fortune.

"No, no, I only meant he should do so as a friend. He has his heart set on this other girl, anyway. But that's another matter," Mrs Wilton snorted a little bit and Clara had the impression she was not enamoured with the girl her son had chosen. "What really concerns me is that there is this fellow hanging around Miss Holbein. He dresses well enough, but there is something about him that makes me uncomfortable. I don't want to think the girl is being taken advantage of. I promised her mother, God rest her soul, that I would keep my eye on her."

"You want me to find out who this man is," Clara elaborated.

"Exactly Clara, you are so good at such things and you are a very good judge of character. If you find out there is nothing sinister about this man then I shall bite my tongue, but until that time I really am concerned."

Mrs Wilton suddenly looked tearful, which surprised Clara. She gently touched the woman's arm.

"Are you all right?"

"I was very good friends with Miss Holbein's mother," Mrs Wilton sniffed. "We were of the same generation and understood each other so well. I'm out of touch now. I'm a Victorian woman in a modern age. Oh dear, I am being silly."

Mrs Wilton pulled out a handkerchief and dabbed at her eyes.

"I promised my friend I would watch over her daughter and I stick by that," she said firmly. "I won't let any harm befall that girl. You will help, won't you Clara?"

Clara could already feel that she was going to regret her answer, but it slipped out nonetheless.

"Of course."

"Thank you," Mrs Wilton squeezed Clara's arm. "Now, where shall we start? Ah, yes. Come to tea this afternoon and I shall tell you all about it."

Clara found herself agreeing without protest. Mrs Wilton bid her a cheery farewell as she disappeared to do her shopping. Clara stood on the pavement wondering what she had done.

Chapter Two

Clara returned home early to explain to Annie that she would be absent at teatime. Annie crossed her arms over her chest as she heard this news. Annie disliked anything that interrupted mealtimes and was perpetually concerned that Clara would make herself ill if she skipped meals. Clara had attempted to point out to Annie that she could readily afford to skip a few meals, without success.

"Mrs Wilton again," Annie snorted after Clara had explained the situation. "That woman seems to assume you are her own personal private detective."

"The situation does sound important, however," Clara tried to offset Annie's annoyance. "If this girl is being manipulated by a money hunter, then a stop must be put to it."

Annie huffed to herself.

"Well then, Tommy," she glanced over to where Tommy was sitting in the armchair near the fire. "Looks like it will be just you and me tasting my fresh batch of scones."

"Actually," Clara looked uneasy, "I was going to ask Tommy to join me."

Tommy glanced up in surprise. Before Annie could protest Clara carried on.

"I have been thinking that, with all the work I have on,

I could do with an extra pair of hands to help me. And, as you are at a loose end, Tommy, I was going to ask if you would be interested in working for me?"

"Be a partner, in your detective business?" Tommy said in astonishment.

"I hadn't thought about going that far," Clara hesitated, looking uncomfortable. "I am the business, you see. But there is always so much to do and some of the cases just need a quick glance over…"

"I would be your assistant then?" Tommy's eyes sparkled even as he pronounced the phrase with a hint of distaste.

"I wouldn't call you that as such," Clara frowned. "More like the deputy to the sheriff. Still very important."

"You've been reading my American crime books again," Tommy smirked.

"It's just… you already help me out from time to time," Clara was trying to explain herself without making things worse. "So, I thought you might as well be paid to do it. And I really am up to my eyes with work."

Tommy started to chuckle.

"All right, I'll let you off the hook. I am looking to do more than mope about the house and if you think I can be useful to you, I don't mind helping out, but," Tommy held up a finger, "with the understanding that if I prove myself you will consider making me a partner in your detective agency."

Clara thought about the suggestion for just a moment and then nodded.

"Deal."

"And now you are both going to Mrs Wilton's for tea," Annie threw up her hands in the air and stalked out of the room. "Her scones will be no match for mine! Don't come home with indigestion!"

Tommy smirked.

"She'll get over it."

They set off just after three, as they would have to catch a bus to reach Mrs Wilton's villa on the other side of town.

They were early for tea but were welcomed in with gusto. Mrs Wilton was wearing a flowing, tea dress in a very modern style for a self-professed Victorian woman. It was decorated with an elaborate pattern of Chinese dragons and waterlilies. Mrs Wilton rather looked like a wall painting as she swooshed into her front parlour with Clara and Tommy just behind her.

"My son is out, which is just as well because he hates me going on about Miss Holbein," Mrs Wilton declared, plumping herself down on a sofa and motioning for Clara and Tommy to do the same.

Clara recalled the last time she had visited the Wilton's villa. Back then the place had an aura of ruination about it; Mrs Wilton had lost her husband in the war and it seemed he had left her no money, certainly there was no will. She had also thought her son lost and with no income and no means of supporting herself, Mrs Wilton had been slowly selling her possessions just to try to survive. She was reduced to an impoverished existence by the time she first spoke to Clara.

Everything changed when Clara found Mrs Wilton's son. He had a better idea of where his father might hide his assets and had been able to restore the family's fortunes. He now worked in a bank in London, commuting back and forth to Brighton five days a week, and working a half day on Saturday at home, catching up on paperwork. Mrs Wilton had been able to refurbish the house, repair the furniture and invest in new paintings and ornaments to replace those she had had to sell.

"I am so glad you came," Mrs Wilton flared out the skirt of her dress to prevent it getting creased. "I am very concerned about Miss Holbein. I came home this afternoon and saw that her young man was here again. They were going out for a picnic. I don't trust him, he looks shifty."

"Do you know his name?" Clara asked.

"Naturally!" Mrs Wilton looked appalled that anyone might think she had failed to gain this singularly vital piece of information. "He is Victor Darling. If that is his real name, of course. These men go by aliases."

"These men?" Clara asked.

"Crooks. Con artists. They have a woman in every town," Mrs Wilton tutted to herself. "I shudder to think about it. He could be a murderer, you know. I read in a magazine how a man in France married and murdered five women for their fortune before he was caught by the police in the process of marrying a sixth."

"And what does Victor Darling do?" Clara avoided getting into a debate about serial wife murderers. "Is he local to Brighton."

"Miss Holbein has been cagey about him," Mrs Wilton sighed. "I guess she senses my apprehension. I did try to ask about him, but she changed the subject. Her mother would be so upset."

Mrs Wilton became solemn.

"My dear friend, Adelaide Holbein, was something of a local celebrity in her day," she said softly, her mind slipping away to another time, another world. "She had a beautiful singing voice, it was truly remarked upon. She wanted to sing opera, but her parents were hesitant as they were not sure it was an appropriate thing for a girl of her station to do. Adelaide managed to persuade them otherwise. She secured a spot with a company in London, and sang for a whole season. Then she met her husband, Gustav Holbein, a Dutch businessman who ran a textiles company in the city. He was handsome and wealthy. Adelaide never looked back."

Mrs Wilton sighed.

"Tragically, he was killed in an accident. Run down by a coach while hurrying to an important meeting. They had only been married five years and Adelaide had just given birth to their daughter Nellie. She was named after the famous opera singer, Nellie Melba," Mrs Wilton paused for a brief moment, contemplating it all. "Adelaide moved back to Brighton to be near her parents and she certainly had the money to live well. Nellie was brought up cossetted and well-loved, the apple of her mother's eye. She had a fine education, always the best clothes and dresses, perhaps you might say she was a little spoiled, but it never truly showed."

"When did Adelaide pass away?" Clara asked.

"The summer of 1919. She had been ill sometime, the same complaint her mother had endured all her life. The doctors muttered various technical terms for it, but it made no difference to the outcome. She was in a lot of pain during her last days," a tear trickled from Mrs Wilton's eye. "It was a release in the end. She was suffering so much."

"And then Nellie inherited all her parents fortune?"

"Yes," Mrs Wilton nodded. "Nellie had just turned eighteen. She decided the house she had lived in with her mother was far too big to suit her. She moved to a smaller villa just down the road. It is a modern build, very stylish though a little sterile for my liking. No flourishes or decorative touches to make a place homely."

Mrs Wilton cast a loving gaze over her own home, with its highly elaborate wallpaper and statuettes and vases in every corner. She almost seemed to sigh with satisfaction as she admired her own space.

"When did Victor Darling come on the scene?" Clara brought her back to the matter in hand.

"About three months ago," Mrs Wilton dragged her eyes away from admiring her own taste in decoration. "Unfortunately, since the passing of her mother, Nellie has been the target of a number of disreputable suitors. Young men looking for an easy fortune. Nellie is not equipped with the wisdom or maturity to see them for what they are. She is also beyond the age when a guardian can have any marked influence over her. She is a young woman with a lot of money and not a lot of common sense, who is actively seeking a husband."

Mrs Wilton gave Clara a defeated look.

"I despair…" she paused as her maid appeared with the afternoon tea.

Among the traditional cucumber sandwiches and scones, there was also a chocolate tiffin cake and some homemade fudge. Mrs Wilton dismissed her maid and poured the tea herself.

"Has Nellie received any marriage proposals already?" Tommy asked, until that point, he had been quiet, listening attentively to what was going on.

"A couple that I am aware of. The first was the most serious and we barely were able to persuade her to turn down the gentleman in question."

"We?" Clara picked up on the term.

"Myself and Nellie's maternal aunt. The poor woman is beside herself too. She lives in the North and has her own young family to take care of. She can't be down here keeping an eye on Nellie as well."

"She has had two proposals and both were unsuitable?" Clara queried.

"The first was from a young man she had only known for six weeks. He gave me the shivers. Very charming, but in that calculating way some men have. Like a wolf grinning at you," Mrs Wilton demonstrated her dislike by shuddering. "He claimed to be the son of a brewery owner, in fact his father ran a pub, didn't even own it either. Just leased it from the brewery. That was just one of the lies the young man spewed. It took some doing, but we convinced Nellie he was unreliable and after her money.

"The second man was equally unsuitable. He was an Irish musician who had heard of Nellie's mother. Adelaide had been pretty famous during the brief time she was performing. I think he liked the idea of the accolade he could gain for his own career by being married to the daughter of a famous opera singer. Nellie went off him pretty quickly, luckily."

"And now there is this latest threat," Mrs Wilton shook her head forlornly. "I honestly don't know how Nellie seems so drawn to these disreputable characters. It is not as though she could not go to some really nice parties where there would be decent young men she could set her sights on. Instead she finds these... ruffians, who only look at her money and her vulnerability. I am very worried for her future."

"But you don't know much at all about Victor Darling?" Clara pointed out.

"Only that he has squirmed his way out of the woodwork all of a sudden," Mrs Wilton sniffed haughtily. "I know most of the eligible young gentlemen in the town who would be a suitable match for Nellie, but this fellow eludes me. I don't know who his parents are, or where he comes from. And Nellie won't tell me."

Clara thought that Nellie was probably sick of having her personal life interfered with by other people. She didn't doubt Mrs Wilton had the best of intentions for the girl, and she probably had saved her from making a disastrous match with the two other suitors, but Nellie would not see it that way. She would feel that her every move was being monitored and that her judgement was being questioned. Everyone reached an age in their life when they tried to stake their independence. And that had to be respected, even if it looked likely that Nellie was going to make some serious mistakes along the way.

"You will look into this for me, won't you Clara?" Mrs Wilton leaned forward in her seat, her face anxious.

"Of course," Clara reassured her. "But I am not personally in a position to change Nellie's mind about this man, nor will I take responsibility for such an action. I'll find out everything I can about Victor Darling and then you can pass that information along to Nellie."

"That is perfectly agreeable," Mrs Wilton was visibly relieved. "Yes, any information would be good. Currently I can offer no protest other than I do not like the man much. I need more."

"I'll see what I can do, but if he does turn out to be everything he says he is, then we can do nothing about that," Clara reminded Mrs Wilton gently. "I think, at some point, you are going to have to allow Nellie to make her own mistakes."

"A bad marriage is a very big mistake to make," Mrs

Wilton cringed at the mere thought.

"That may be what it takes, though," Clara explained. "Nellie has lived a closeted life, she has not experienced the dark side of humanity. Every time you tell her a man is unsuitable it must hurt her pride and her intelligence, for she has already picked him. There will only be so many times she will listen. Inevitably, she is going to fall so in love with one of these fellows that anything you say will be ignored and she will do as she pleases. Maybe she will pick wisely, or maybe she won't. The most important thing is that she knows she has a friend she can rely on if things turn out for the worst."

Mrs Wilton looked morose at this prediction, but Clara suspected it had already crossed her mind. After all, Nellie was already refusing to talk to her about Victor Darling.

"I do understand that Clara," Mrs Wilton said at last. "I just wish we could find someone more appropriate for Nellie. Why is it all these rogues are so charming?"

"It is the only asset they have," Tommy opined. "Every man has to play to his strengths when it comes to finding a girl."

"I hate it, I really do," Mrs Wilton frowned. "They ought to go out and make their own money. Why can't they go find their own fortune?"

"I think," Clara said drily, "that is exactly what they are doing."

Chapter Three

Monday came around very swiftly and Clara was eager to get to the exhibition and view the mysterious fossil that was causing such a fuss among those who cared about such things. The Brighton Gazette had published a special edition on Saturday evening, covering the exhibition in-depth and also going through the controversy the Archaeopteryx fossil was stirring up, not just locally, but globally.

The discovery of the first Archaeopteryx had occurred in Germany. The fossil had been unearthed in a quarry, where a number of other fossilised animals had been found in the past, though none as unique as this one. The original Archaeopteryx had at first been thought to be a pterosaur until it was carefully exposed from the stone it was encased in. The realisation that the stone also bore impressions of feathers was the starting point of a long, drawn-out battle between those who believed this was solid evidence that birds evolved from dinosaurs, and those who refused to believe that such a thing could happen and claimed it was just a feathered lizard, which probably could not even fly.

Darwin's Theory of Evolution had only just been published and had upset those who took the Bible as gospel and could not fathom that creatures existed on the planet long before the current catalogue of species developed.

Evolution defied the reasoning that God had personally created every living being. God had placed each animal, each bird, even each lizard on this earth as he intended them to be – there was no room for evolution in that understanding. Evolution implied that God's first creations were imperfect and needed to change themselves to improve, that in turn implied God was imperfect.

Others denied evolution because they believed that every creature that had ever existed had been around since the dawn of time. Therefore, at the time of the dinosaurs there were also house sparrows, cats, wolves and kangaroos. The fossil evidence for these animals had yet to be discovered, that was all. Some of these creatures had ultimately died out, leaving those that remained in the modern age. This theory excluded evolution, as there was no need for it – every plant, animal and bird already existed as it was and as it always would be at the start of time.

On the opposite side were those who were fully convinced of Darwin's theory and saw the Archaeopteryx as indisputable proof. Here was a dinosaur that was transforming into a bird. Some of the features of the fossil were clear proof of a lizard heritage, while others, not just the feathers, were equally clearly bird-like. In the decades between the discovery of the Archaeopteryx and 1922, more fossils had been found and further study had given weight to the argument that at least some of the smaller dinosaurs ultimately transformed into birds. Yet, controversy still raged and could fill a whole edition of a newspaper, as Clara discovered when she read Saturday's copy.

She found it all very fascinating, but deep down she found she was siding with the evolutionists. Their arguments seemed soundly based on science, while some of the conflicting arguments were rather more hazy and emotional. She was looking forward to seeing the centrepiece of this debate for herself.

Clara and Tommy met Captain O'Harris at the town hall. He was looking very dapper in a brown suit and bow tie. He grinned at Clara.

"I'm like a boy again," he said. "I haven't felt this excited since I first climbed into a plane, but back then I was sick with nerves as well. This time I'm just excited."

He offered his arm to Clara and she accepted. They stepped through the door and Clara handed their tickets to a man in the foyer. He was blocking a door into the main room of the hall. Having taken a good look at their ticket, he allowed Clara's party through.

There were already a number of people in the town hall, though the exhibition had opened just minutes earlier. Glass cases lined the walls and formed a central aisle down the middle of the room and in each was a large selection of fossils, everything from ammonites with their beautifully curled shells, to small dinosaur skulls. But there was no denying that these exhibits, though important to the understanding of the creatures of prehistory, were utterly overshadowed by the fossil in the special end case.

The Archaeopteryx did not have to share a case with any other fossil. It was perched upright on a specially-made stand, so that it was easy to see every facet of its detail. The case was at the top of the room and a curator sat on a chair beside it. He was there, according to the guidebook Clara had purchased as she entered the room, to answer any questions concerning the skeleton, but Clara suspected he was also there to make sure no one either attempted to steal the fossil or damage it. There was no doubting there were some people who would go to great lengths to destroy an item they felt called into question their entire belief system.

A crowd had already formed about the case and Clara, O'Harris and Tommy had to wait patiently behind those ahead, glancing at the cases of other fossils, before they could step forward and admire the Archaeopteryx for themselves. The dinosaur-bird's body was lying on its back (though some contended it was really laying on its front) and had its wings splayed out, displaying those controversial feathers for the world to see. The legs were twisted over to one side, while the long, feathered tail flicked up in a curve over the back. The fossil's head was facing the opposite direction to the feet and the tiny jaw was slightly open, revealing the tiny, sharp teeth that marked this out as no bird.

According to the guidebook, it was supposed the dinosaur-bird had died and fallen into a river, where it was quickly swallowed up by mud, thus preserving it from scavengers who would have pulled apart the skeleton in the process of consuming it. Over the centuries the river dried up and the mud hardened and was pressed by incredible forces to form sheets of soft limestone. When these were quarried, millenniums later, they revealed their hidden treasure. The Archaeopteryx had lived and died in a world it was hard to imagine, and it had never once thought about itself as the missing link, nor could it have known the controversy it would cause when it fell from the sky into a river one day.

"The impressions of the feathers are remarkably preserved," O'Harris leaned so close to the glass his nose nearly touched it. "I've seen drawings, but it is much more impressive in the flesh, so to speak."

"Without the feathers, the body is remarkably similar to other small dinosaurs of the period," Tommy quoted from the guidebook. "That's why they are so sure this fellow is a dinosaur trying to become a bird."

"Not trying, he succeeded," the curator sitting in his chair had been listening to their conversation with a twinkle in his eye. Now he spoke to them. "This fellow flew. The latest studies are revealing that these are flight feathers. He probably didn't have the grace of modern birds, he perhaps was more of a glider. But make no mistake, this chap was airborne."

"Do you go with this exhibition across the country?" Clara asked the man.

"I do," the curator smiled. "Dr Archibald Browning, at your service. Or rather, at the service of the Archaeopteryx here. I have spent a lifetime studying this creature and learning everything I can about him."

Dr Browning held out his hand to shake, even to Clara, which put him up a notch in her estimation.

"You must have some interesting discussions about this fossil," Tommy said with a wry grin.

Dr Browning understood his implication.

"There are those who are very narrow-minded and cannot see beyond the tip of their own nose. Sadly, I believe there will always be folk like them. They fail to appreciate that the Archaeopteryx does not deny God, rather it proves he is even more spectacular than we can comprehend. God designed an animal that under the right circumstances could change its very nature. Think about it, this was a land-based animal that learned to fly under its own power! How much more remarkable can a thing get? It's like man suddenly developing gills and learning to live under water, this dinosaur managed a complete change in its behaviour and even its place in the world," Dr Browning's eyes shone with his clear wonder for it all. "To me, this is proof positive of God's greatness. I can't fathom why others don't see it the same."

Behind Clara people were pressing forward to see the Archaeopteryx and there were mutters that her party were hogging the display. Reluctantly Clara, O'Harris and Tommy thanked Dr Browning and moved on. They paid half-hearted attention to the other fossils on show, but they all had their minds on the star attraction behind them.

"I'd like to get another look at it," O'Harris said, glancing about the room which was rapidly filling with people. "My word, they sold a lot of tickets!"

"It will be even worse on the public day," Tommy said. "I hope they have some brandy on standby, I can see people fainting if the place gets overcrowded."

Clara was already starting to feel uncomfortably confined by the people pressing around her. Everyone was trying to head to the top of the room to see the Archaeopteryx, which meant Clara, O'Harris and Tommy were fighting their way against the flow of people.

"You have to feel sorry for the other exhibits. No one is looking at them," Tommy muttered as they managed to ease out of the press and into a corner of the room. They were stood by a case of ammonite fossils. Ammonites were one of the most common finds in the quarries where the Archaeopteryx was discovered, and no one paid them much heed. You could find polished ammonite fossils in antiques shops. Familiarity had bred contempt.

"Our tickets are valid until five o'clock this evening," Clara observed. "I suggest we come back a little later when this throng has died down. Everyone is curious right now and has come early."

"Fair point," Tommy said. "Hopefully later we can have a proper look at that fossil."

He had turned his head up to the far end of the room where it was now impossible to see the Archaeopteryx case over the heads of the people gathered around it. They slipped out the front door and Clara was more than relieved to be away from the crowd.

"What shall we do now?" O'Harris asked. "We've got to waste time somehow."

"Fancy a walk along the beach? You never know, we might unearth our own fossils in the cliff soil," Tommy suggested.

They all agreed, it was a nice day and a walk along the beach would be pleasant. Tommy led the way and they were soon strolling on the soft sand. It was the tail-end of the holiday season and there were still plenty of people taking the waters. Brighton's sea water was supposed to be very healthful, and people bathed in it, drank it and even had themselves purged with it. Having grown up by the sea, and having swam in it regularly as a child, Clara was not entirely convinced by the claims, but as it kept the tourism industry alive, she was not going to complain. Brighton relied heavily on its summer visitors to sustain its economy. They had truly built the town on its water.

"Look up there Clara," Tommy motioned ahead of them.

"I do say that is Miss Holbein."

Mrs Wilton had shown them a photograph of Nellie Holbein while they were having afternoon tea. Clara had expected her to be a beautiful and rather poised young lady, considering what she had just heard about her parents. The photograph revealed that she was actually quite plain; she had thick black eyebrows that were masculine in nature and almost met in the middle of her forehead. Her jaw was square and though the picture was supposedly taken on a happy occasion – Nellie's birthday – she was scowling at the photographer rather than smiling. She was acutely thin, in the way some girls naturally are, which made her appear altogether boyish. That made her rather fashionable, according to the women's magazines being printed, and especially suited to the straight-waisted dresses which were rapidly growing in popularity. Those same dresses were anathema to Clara, and she had felt a slight pang of envy for Nellie's fashionable figure.

Though, as Tommy had stated after they left Mrs Wilton's, what the fashion magazines say is beautiful and what men actually find attractive in a woman are usually poles apart.

With her flat-chest, bobbed hair and mannish face, Miss Holbein could easily have passed for a boy. Not a handsome boy, for sure, but you could easily be forgiven for thinking she was a young man in a dress. And never a more crueller slight could be levelled at a woman than to say when she was dressed at her finest, that she looked more like a boy than a girl.

"I suppose that young fellow with her is Victor Darling," Clara almost raised a hand to point, then remembered herself.

Victor Darling was dressed in a checked suit that was decidedly brash and reminded Clara of the suits the bookies wore when the races were in town. He offset the checks with a red bowtie, which was not helping the ensemble at all. However, he was very handsome in a slightly oily way. He looked over-done, like someone had taken him and polished him up before sending him off to meet Miss Holbein. His hair glistened with oil and his face had the appearance of having been scrubbed to within an inch of its life. Clara also noted that his teeth were remarkably, and possibly unnaturally, white.

"Who are these people?" Captain O'Harris asked, eyeing up the young couple who were sitting on a blanket on the sand watching the swimmers in the sea.

"People we have to spy on," Tommy said with a joking wink.

"A crude way of putting things, but not entirely inappropriate," Clara countered. "Mrs Wilton is concerned that Victor Darling is a fortune hunter after Miss Holbein's extensive inheritance. She wants us to investigate who he is."

"He looks like a horse dealer I once knew, same sort of suit," O'Harris mused. "I didn't trust him at all."

"Well, we have some time to spare, shall we waste it 'spying' on the unlucky couple?" Clara suggested.

Tommy grinned.

"No protest from me," O'Harris chuckled. "I'm always delighted to be involved in a case. They tend to be interesting in unexpected ways."

"Let's hope that is not the case with this one," Clara rolled her eyes, then she led the way towards the unfortunate pair of lovers who were about to have their day interfered with.

Chapter Four

Victor Darling was a man trying rather too hard. Clara noted that at once. When Clara and her companions came to sit near the couple and made polite greetings to acknowledge that on the crowded beach they had been forced to perch themselves near perfect strangers, Victor looked relieved to have someone else to talk to. Before long he was embroiled in a lengthy discussion with Tommy and O'Harris on car engines and had completely forgotten about Nellie.

Clara was not entirely surprised. Nellie's surly appearance on her photograph was not unusual, it was her normal manner. She seemed perpetually annoyed at life, and Clara didn't think that was just because her beau had abandoned her to speak to Tommy and O'Harris. There was something in Nellie's nature that told Clara she was a person sullen by design, who didn't see the joy in anything, and was largely disappointed with the world around her. Despite all that, and the fact that Clara swiftly took a dislike to her, she remembered her task and endeavoured to engage Nellie in conversation.

"Boys and cars," Clara chuckled. "They can talk about them for hours."

"Hmm," Nellie grunted without offering anything to

further the conversation.

"Still, it's all very useful if you happen to break down in one. They usually know how to go about fixing the problem," Clara said, trying to draw something out of Nellie. "Not that I own a car. Does your young man drive?"

"No," Nellie answered with the minimum of effort.

"He seems to know a lot about cars," Clara prodded her, feeling the answer was inaccurate. Victor Darling was holding his own in a complicated discussion about piston engines and the best way to keep them working on top form. Tommy appeared somewhat left behind by the conversation, though was listening keenly as O'Harris and Victor talked.

Nellie gave no indication she had heard what Clara said. She was staring out at the water.

"Do you swim?" Clara asked, hoping for something, anything.

"No." Nellie answered in the monotone fashion she seemed to have perfected.

"I used to swim a lot, it's supposed to be very good exercise for you," Clara remarked. "And, of course, the waters around Brighton are supposed to be very invigorating. Not that I intend to try drinking them. Are you local?"

"Yes," Nellie replied.

Clara wondered why she was bothering.

"I find, when you are local, you don't take the time to appreciate the beach as much as you should, don't you?"

"No."

"So, you come to the beach often?"

"No."

Clara felt like giving up, she glanced over in the direction of the others. There was no help from them, they had moved on to gear boxes and Tommy had discovered his lengthy perusal of car magazines had supplied him with a surprising amount of knowledge on the subject.

"Do you care for ice cream? Maybe we should get

some?" Clara suggested to Nellie.

Nellie just shrugged.

"Do you care for anything?" Clara asked her in mild frustration.

Nellie turned her gaze on Clara for the first time. Her eyes were dark and intense, and she glared as if daring Clara to say that again. Then she turned her attention back to the ocean.

Clara was beginning to feel that if Victor Darling was prepared to live with such an unpleasant companion for the sake of her money, good luck to him. She would be surprised if Nellie could find a husband on the merits of her personality alone. Clara's attention wandered to a pair of old ladies who had taken off their stockings, hitched up their long Edwardian skirts and were bravely paddling in the waves. The old girls were holding hands and laughing as the cold water washed over their bare feet. Clara smiled at the sight, they were enjoying a simple moment of time together in a way that she felt Nellie had never experienced. To be able to take joy in such humble things was the means to having a happy and contented life, Clara believed. In contrast, Nellie seemed to find fault in everything around her and to glare at the world with disapproval. She would always be dissatisfied with her lot. Clara was in half-a-mind to join the old ladies. Instead, she pulled out of her handbag the guidebook from the fossil exhibition and started to read it again.

Out of the corner of her eye, Clara noticed that Nellie was watching her. She opted to ignore her. Two could play at that game.

Victor finally appeared to remember why he was at the beach and returned to Nellie's side, though he did not look entirely delighted with the prospect. He had been animated and enthusiastic when talking to Tommy and O'Harris. When he walked back to Nellie, his demeanour became quieter. His smile vanished.

"I would like an ice cream," Nellie told him, the words

coming out rather like an accusation.

Victor looked pained, the statement so aggressively stated that it made it obvious his disappearance had earned Nellie's disapproval.

"There's a stand up on the promenade," Victor said, holding out his hand to help Nellie to her feet.

"Buy me one," Nellie demanded of him, before stalking off towards the beach steps.

Victor gave an apologetic smile to Clara as he departed hastily, briefly tipping his hat to O'Harris and Tommy as he went past.

"Good luck to him," Clara said as soon as the couple were far enough away.

Tommy and O'Harris glanced in her direction.

"She is completely obnoxious. A spoiled brat with no ability to take pleasure in the world around her," Clara explained.

"You didn't like her then?" Tommy asked sarcastically.

"She offered me no more than monosyllabic answers, or at times a shrug, throughout our conversation. Perhaps she was just very annoyed we had interrupted her day, but, as I recall, it was Victor who spoke to us first after we had smiled and said hello."

"Victor seemed desperate for the distraction we offered," Tommy agreed. "If he is a fortune hunter, he is going to have to work for his money."

"Did you learn much about him?" Clara asked.

"He didn't say so specifically, but his knowledge of cars suggests he is extremely familiar with them," O'Harris said. "My hunch would be a mechanic or possibly a car dealer. He certainly had working knowledge, could be he has worked as a chauffeur or a driver in the war. Definitely he is someone who has spent a lot of time around cars."

"I noticed his hands were rough, like someone who got them dirty a lot," Tommy added. "I don't think he is a gentleman. He has worked for a living in manual labour."

"Anything else?" Clara asked, feeling they still knew

very little about Victor Darling.

"His accent hinted at a Northerner, but it was quite soft. I would say he has lived in a few different places over his lifetime," O'Harris added. "He didn't mention where he lives now, he was rather cagey about any personal details. I might get more out of him when he comes over to see the cars."

"He is coming to see your car collection?" Clara said in surprise.

"Technically, it was my uncle's collection, but yes, I have invited him to pop over and take a look. He seemed quite keen. I'll be able to pump him for details," O'Harris looked very pleased with himself.

"And I think he will appreciate the break from Miss Holbein," Tommy said with a smirk.

"He didn't strike you as being genuinely enamoured with her?" Clara asked.

"Not really, what about you?" Tommy replied.

"He looked like he was enduring her presence rather than enjoying it," Clara nodded. "Which suggests he is in it for the money. Oh well, Miss Holbein's demeanour does not make her easy to like, there has to be some advantage to spending time in her company."

"Harsh, Clara!" O'Harris chuckled.

"You didn't just spend half-an-hour trying to talk to her," Clara rolled her eyes.

They went for a walk along the beach after that and finished back at a stand on the promenade that sold hot tea and meat pies. The tea was strong, the pies just about edible and they spent some time debating what exact type of meat might have been in them. The standard candidates seemed unlikely from the taste. Then they headed back to the town hall to try to get another look at the Archaeopteryx.

"Uh oh, what's this?" Tommy muttered as they approached and saw a crowd outside the hall.

Some of the people in the throng were carrying hand-painted signs that said things like – God Not Darwin!

Evolution is a Lie! Find God Not Fossils!

"Oh dear," Clara said as they paused on the side of the street opposite the town hall. "Protestors."

The crowd numbered about twenty and was a mix of men and women. They were trying to prevent people getting to the doors of the town hall and entering the exhibition. They were also handing out leaflets and shaking collection boxes at people, though what precisely they were collecting for was unclear.

Clara approached the crowd and was quickly accosted by a woman in a black hat.

"God not Darwin!" The woman almost shouted at her and pressed a leaflet into her hand.

Clara glanced at the folded piece of paper, which appeared to be someone's attempt to defy the idea of evolution. The front sheet repeated the woman's slogan and then quoted various Bible passages, though Clara was not entirely clear on the relevance of the ones they had chosen. They seemed slightly random, though probably there was a logic behind them. Inside the leaflet was a detailed ramble about God having made the earth and the timeline offered by the Bible, which contradicted the evidence for evolution. The argument was long and laboured and suggested someone with a very limited understanding of science. Several of the arguments were contradictory. Intertwined with the writer's over-blown points against evolution were more passages from the Bible.

Clara guessed that some people, who were already religiously inclined, might find the leaflet convincing. But anyone else would find it an absurd waste of paper. Clara popped the paper in her handbag, nonetheless.

"Come on, I've had enough of this," O'Harris was scowling at the protestors and attempting to go around the group to reach the steps of the town hall.

Every time he reached a clear space, someone jumped in front of him and thrust another leaflet in his face. It wasn't long before he lost his temper.

"Look, I have no interest in your damn nonsense!" He declared to the next person who pushed a paper at him. "Evolution is a fact, so you can take your Bible passages and shove them at someone else. I don't go around yelling at you God doesn't exist, do I?"

O'Harris barged through the crowd and made it to the steps. Clara hurried behind him. Tommy was delayed as he was trying to be slightly politer about his refusal to accept the protestors' claims. He finally managed to make it to the top of the steps to join Clara and O'Harris.

"The police are coming," Clara pointed up the road.

The police were marching their way. Someone had summoned them, and a large body of police constables was heading for the crowd of protestors. Several people who had been going into the exhibition now stopped at the entrance to the town hall to watch.

The police surrounded the protest group and told them they had to leave, in no uncertain terms. There were cries of frustration and hisses that this was a denial of their right to free speech, but the police were firm. They could protest, but they could not stop the exhibition or prevent people from entering the town hall. After a short argument, the protestors backed down and were successfully dispersed.

"Well, that's a relief!"

Clara turned around and saw that the person who had spoken was Dr Browning. He gave her a sad smile.

"We usually get some form of protest," he sighed. "People find this exhibition very controversial."

Looking rather glum, Dr Browning headed back into the town hall. Clara watched until the last protestor was gone and then headed inside herself. O'Harris and Tommy were close behind.

"I don't understand how people can deny science," O'Harris grumbled, still rankling from being detained.

"Evolution scares people because they think it denies God. For some people, religion is their rock, their safety net. Take that from them and you leave them terrified,"

Clara said, surprising herself a little with her understanding of the matter. "For them, it is like the world is ending. Scared people do drastic things. I dare say some believe what they say wholeheartedly, while others are just trying to convince themselves through action, as the alternative horrifies them too much."

"Like Dr Browning, I don't consider a belief in evolution and a belief in God mutually exclusive," Tommy added. "But I do have sympathy for people who can't see things that way. Their views may be due to a lack of education, or too rigid a reliance on the text of the Bible. Why did you keep the leaflet they gave you Clara?"

Clara had not realised he had noticed her stashing the paper in her handbag.

"I want to understand these protests better," Clara said. "I want to understand why people are getting so upset. I thought I would read the leaflet properly at home and get a better idea of what is going on."

"I still think it is all nonsense," O'Harris snorted, though he was calming down.

"At least the town hall is quieter now," Clara tried to soothe him.

They walked to the top of the room and took another look at the Archaeopteryx. This time there was no one behind them forcing them to move on and they could examine the fossil at their leisure. Clara bored of the bones before the boys and walked off to look at some of the other cases. Her mind was wandering, thinking about Victor Darling. Who was he really?

They stayed at the hall for an hour and then headed for their respective homes. O'Harris took his leave of Clara at the door of her house with a tender kiss on her cheek and talk of how nice a day he had had. They promised to see each other again soon.

"One of these days you two will figure it all out," Tommy grinned at his sister as she stepped into the hall of the house.

"Figure what out?" Clara asked him.

Tommy winked.

"You'll see."

Chapter Five

Hours later, Clara was on the verge of heading up to bed when there was a frantic knock on the front door. She shook off her weariness and went to answer it, wondering, with some concern, who would be trying to get her attention at this time of night. When she opened the door, she failed to recognise the man on her doorstep.

"Can I help?" She asked him.

"Clara Fitzgerald?" The man asked. He was in his thirties, a workman from the looks of his clothes and he was holding his cap in both hands, threading the edge through his anxious fingers as he stood before her.

"Yes?"

"Could you come to the town hall at once, miss? There has been an incident and Dr Browning heard you might be able to help with such things. He don't care for the police, miss," the man had nearly spun his hat in a complete circle as he worked his hands around the edge.

"All right, I'll come," Clara rubbed at her tired eyes. "I'll just get my coat and hat."

A short time later Clara was back at the town hall and being shown into the foyer. Her escort had revealed that his name was Wallace Sunderland, and that he was one of the workmen who went with the exhibition across the country.

"I put everything in crates when we leave, and I take it out again when we arrive," Wallace explained as they travelled to the town hall.

"What has happened, Wallace?" Clara asked him.

"I ought not to talk. Dr Browning is terribly upset," Wallace refused to say anymore.

Once inside the town hall, Clara noticed that there was a sizeable police presence. Several constables were in the foyer and she could see more through the doors to the exhibition room. Among them was Inspector Park-Coombs and Clara's heart sank a little as she realised that something serious had occurred to bring the inspector out at this hour.

Dr Browning was sitting on a chair just inside the doors, right next to the ammonite display case. When he saw Clara, he was startled.

"You are Clara Fitzgerald?" He asked, then he shook his head. "Excuse my astonishment, it is just that I recognise you from earlier."

"I thought that was why you had sent for me?" Clara said.

"No," Dr Browning managed to smile, though he still looked sad. "I summoned you because that gentleman said you were the best private detective in town."

Clara looked in the direction he pointed and recognised Oliver Bankes, a friend of the Fitzgeralds and part-time police photographer. Whenever a serious crime was committed, Oliver was called to take pictures of the crime scene for future reference. His presence at the town hall was further indication that something dreadful had indeed occurred.

"Dr Browning, why do you need a private detective?" Clara could see that Inspector Park-Coombs and Oliver Bankes were gathered near the top of the room, in front of the Archaeopteryx display case, but the other displays blocked her view of what they were looking at. "Has someone tried to steal something?"

"No," Dr Browning said in a hollow voice. "A man has died."

The academic shook his head miserably.

"And the police think I might have killed him!"

Clara looked over in the direction of the inspector. No one appeared to be paying a lot of attention to Dr Browning, there were no constables keeping a watch on him. She suspected he was being overly dramatic, certainly no one seemed in a hurry to arrest him.

"I need you to find out who has done this thing," Dr Browning said desperately. "The repercussions are awful to think about. It could cause so many problems for the future of this tour, and we must continue to travel and display the Archaeopteryx, so that everyone has the opportunity to see it!"

"Let me have a chat with the inspector," Clara said, moving away from Dr Browning and further up the room. She paused near Oliver.

Oliver Bankes ran a photography shop in town but moonlighted as a police photographer. His services were not needed often enough to warrant the force employing him full-time for the purpose, so he made his bread and butter by taking photographs of the living. He was a little soft on Clara, but the arrival of Captain O'Harris had dashed his hopes. They had, however, remained friends.

"You suggested Dr Browning hire me?" Clara asked Oliver with a smile on her lips.

"He was rather fraught when I got here, and when the police started questioning him about where he was at the time of the incident, he became quite distressed. He is convinced he is about to be arrested. I thought you might be able to help him out," Oliver shrugged.

"We'll see," Clara said without committing herself. "He may not need my help if the police do not consider him a suspect. What has happened?"

Oliver moved a step to the side, enabling Clara to look around the edge of a display cabinet and to the floor before the Archaeopteryx case. A man was lying face down on the wooden floor. His hands were splayed alongside his head and a hammer had seemingly fallen from his hand as he crashed down. The hair on the back of his skull looked dark and wet. Clara guessed this indicated blood.

"Clara," Inspector Park-Coombs nodded to her. "You've managed to get here quickly."

"I was asked to come," Clara replied.

She motioned with her hand to the glass case.

"Dr Browning appears rather distressed and seems to think you are about to arrest him for murder," she added.

Inspector Park-Coombs was amused.

"Does he now? Well, I am not ruling him out just yet, but I don't have the evidence to arrest him. Has he hired you?"

"I haven't accepted the case yet," Clara answered, glancing down at the body. "I wanted to see what was going on first."

"Well, it is a murder," Park-Coombs said drily. "I don't know the fellow's name yet, but we believe he may be with a group of protestors who were making a fuss outside the town hall earlier today."

"I encountered them. Anti-Darwinists," Clara hefted her shoulders to demonstrate what she thought of their views. "Looks like he was up to no good?"

"As far as we can tell, he broke in via a back window and it looks like he was going to try to destroy or steal the Archaeopteryx fossil. Unluckily for him, Dr Browning sleeps on a camp bed at the back of the room for security purposes. He claims he heard a muffled cry which woke him up. The room was pitch black, but he keeps a torch by his bed. He shone it about the room and spotted this man on the floor. He quickly realised the fellow was beyond help and ran outside to find a constable on patrol and summon us," Inspector Park-Coombs gave a flick of his fingers which was meant to indicate the police force at large. "By the time we had arrived, Dr Browning had managed to get word to the boarding house where the rest of the exhibition team were staying, and they were on the scene. It was a real muddle when we got here, with people all about the place."

"One of the workmen for the exhibition fetched me," Clara added. "From what you are saying Inspector, it would seem that Dr Browning is your only suspect. He was alone in this room when the man was killed."

"It would appear that way," Inspector Park-Coombs nodded. "But I have my reservations. For a start, the murder weapon is nowhere to be found and the constable who first encountered Dr Browning and raised the alarm tells me he was in a terrible state and looked fit to collapse from the shock. He didn't have the appearance of a man who could think rationally enough to hide a murder weapon.

"Then I find myself thinking about the circumstances. Dr Browning was in here alone, everyone knew that. He has stated it himself. Why bother to hide the murder weapon when he is the only one who could have killed the man anyway? If he killed the man in a fit of panic when he found him trespassing, the law is on his side. He can claim self-defence. Hiding the murder weapon looks suspicious."

"Only, Dr Browning does not claim he struck and killed this man," Clara pointed out.

"Exactly, another reason I have my doubts about him as our killer," Inspector Park-Coombs waggled his thick moustache thoughtfully. "Only an innocent man would claim something so preposterous as that he did not kill a man who died when he was alone in a room with him."

"I see your point," Clara smiled. "A truly guilty man would have either claimed self-defence or stated there was someone else in the room."

"And Dr Browning does not strike me as a deeply cunning man trying a double-bluff," Park-Coombs glanced over at the scared academic, who was hunched up in a chair looking miserable. "Which leaves me with a right pickle, because the only other man I know to have been in the room with this fellow, claims he had nothing to do with his death."

"Did you call my name?" Wandering towards the inspector, between the cases of fossils, was Brighton's police surgeon, the appropriately named Dr Deáth.

"You took long enough to arrive," Inspector Park-Coombs scowled at the surgeon in jest.

Dr Deáth was nothing like you would expect of a man who spent his days with corpses. He was jovial and constantly smiling. He was in his late forties and not very tall, with dark-rimmed glasses and a passion for sporty waistcoats that seemed entirely out of place at a crime scene. He took the inspector's ribbing in good humour.

"The wife was hosting a dinner party," he said. "We had just started a game of bridge. I had to wait until I could be replaced as a fourth hand. The wife gets very cross if I upset her bridge game."

Dr Deáth peered past the end of the display cabinet on his left, at the body on the floor.

"Ah, a blunt trauma incident!" He said with the sort of enthusiasm other people reserve for works of art or pretty butterflies. "I do like the cut and dry ones, nothing elaborate or complicated."

The surgeon knelt by the body and dropped a doctor's bag on the floor. He drew out a notebook, pencil and ruler, before beginning to inspect the corpse.

"Big wound, lots of trauma over a wide area. I would suggest a wide, heavy tool like a mallet," Dr Deáth took measurements of the wound. "Crushed the skull, but no deep lacerations. The shock of the blow would have caused grave injury to the brain and death would have come quite quickly. I suspect there are shards of bone embedded in the brain too, looking at the centre of this wound, but I'll need to study that further in the morgue."

"A mallet," Inspector Park-Coombs mused. "Haven't seen one of those lying around. Just that hammer."

"The hammer has no blood on it and has not been used to harm anyone," Dr Deáth said without looking up. "No, you will need to look for a big mallet or something similar.

Like the ones used for driving metal posts into the ground."

"Right," Inspector Park-Coombs scratched his head.

"It was swung with some force too," Dr Deáth was prodding the back of the dead man's skull with his pencil. "To do all this damage in one blow requires either some serious strength or a great deal of fury. It really is a heavy blow."

"Not the sort of thing a quiet academic might do, then?" Inspector Park-Coombs was looking over at Dr Browning once again.

"What?" Dr Deáth asked, glancing up from his examination.

"No matter," Inspector Park-Coombs told him, waving off the comment.

"Where would Dr Browning get a mallet anyway," Clara said. "It is not the sort of thing you have lying around an exhibition hall."

"Yet it is the sort of thing you might bring with you to smash a glass case and its fossilised contents," Inspector Park-Coombs frowned. "There has to have been another person here."

"I agree, Inspector, but if you are not intending to arrest Dr Browning, I think I should get out of your way and inform him he does not require my services."

"Very well, Clara," Park-Coombs nodded to her. "Sorry you got called out this late."

"Oh, hardly your fault," Clara replied, turning away and walking back to Dr Browning.

The academic looked up anxiously as she approached.

"The inspector does not think you killed this man Dr Browning," she told him.

Dr Browning gasped with relief.

"Thank goodness!"

"It appears you will not be requiring my assistance," Clara masked a yawn. "I shall therefore get out of the way of the police."

She started to head to the doors, but Dr Browning

jumped up and caught her arm.

"No, please, I still want you to investigate this," he said.

"But, you are not a suspect," Clara told him.

"I know, but this horrid mess could put an end to the exhibition," Dr Browning looked appalled at the thought. "And there is something else. I have been fearing something like this for weeks now."

"A murder?"

"No, someone breaking into the exhibition and trying to destroy the Archaeopteryx. There have been threats. Its why I sleep near the exhibit," Dr Browning had gone very pale. "I'm very worried about the intentions of these people. I have reported it all to the police, but they say they can do nothing. The threats are anonymous. But now it looks like these people are prepared to kill. What if that blow was meant for me?"

Dr Browning looked over at the corpse with some horror.

"In the dark, what if they thought I was stood by that case."

"No, Dr Browning, whoever did this probably came in with the dead man. He would have known who he was striking."

Dr Browning looked unconvinced.

"They are killers, Miss Fitzgerald, monsters," Dr Browning trembled from head to foot. "I need you to find out who these people are and stop them. I know the police will do nothing, so I must turn to you. I don't think this is the end of things, I think it is only the beginning."

He clasped her arm tightly, looking like a man who has stared into a nightmare and is terrified it won't leave him when he wakes up. Clara said the words before she had even given a thought to what she was doing.

"All right Dr Browning. I'll take the case."

Chapter Six

"We shall have to divide our efforts," Clara explained to Tommy over breakfast. "I need to work on the Archaeopteryx case, while you could investigate Victor Darling. Honestly, I think you will succeed better there than I will."

"Really, old girl?" Tommy said with a twinkle in his eye. "Not admitting I am better at something than you, now?"

"Victor will speak to you more freely than he would to me," Clara said smiling. "I would have to interview him formally, you can chat with him when he comes to see O'Harris' car collection. I also think you might have more luck with Miss Holbein. She didn't want to speak to me at all, but she might speak to a gentleman who shows a little interest in her."

"What is this?" Annie looked up from her breakfast plate of toast and marmalade.

"Don't worry, Miss Holbein is a sour-faced creature who's only redeeming feature is proving to be her vast fortune," Tommy grinned. "I'll see what Victor Darling has to say about her, maybe she has some qualities that have not as yet been apparent."

"She doesn't have any female friends, from what I can tell," Clara added. "She struck me as jealous of other women and didn't want to know them. In any case, she has met me and brushed me off. But Tommy can talk to her as a friend of her boyfriend. All we really need to know is if Victor Darling is a money hunter."

"I am not sure Miss Holbein would much care if that was the case," Tommy postulated. "She seemed to enjoy the power she had over him. That power came from her money."

"Sounds a rather unhappy person," Annie munched on toast. "If the only way you can draw people to you is by your wealth, or rather, that's the only way you think you can draw people to you, it's not going to make you content in life."

"She is difficult to like," Clara said, then added diplomatically. "Maybe she was having a bad day."

"We did interrupt her picnic and snatch Victor away from her," Tommy laughed. "No wonder she didn't want to talk to you."

Clara rolled her eyes.

"Anyway, I need to delve into this mystery at the town hall. Something serious is going on and Dr Browning seems justified by the events of last night to be worried."

"How awful that he sleeps alone in that place with all those bones," Annie gave a shudder. "It's not right, there should be a proper watchman on duty."

"Costs money," Tommy shoved half a slice of toast into his mouth in one, then mumbled through the crumbs. "This exhibition must be costing a fortune as it is."

"Who puts the money forward for such a thing then?" Annie asked.

"Various sponsors," Clara guessed. "This exhibition is not about making money, though it will recoup some of its costs with ticket sales. It's a philanthropic endeavour to spread knowledge across the country. I believe the Gazette stated that it was backed by a lord, or something. Dr Browning is officially employed by the Natural History Museum in London and has been loaned for the tour as much as the fossils in his care."

"Hmm," Annie considered this. "So, all the publicity the

exhibition can get is good? Even the controversial stuff?"

"Well spotted, a good controversy draws in the crowds and sells tickets," Clara was amused to see how much Annie was thinking like a detective these days. "It is why the Archaeopteryx is the star attraction. Without the controversy, it would just be another fossil."

"Well, I think it is a lot of fuss about nothing. Still, people do find all sorts of things to get hot under the collar about. Just remember to be home for dinner, I am making a steak and kidney pudding," Annie picked up her plate from the table and departed the room.

Clara eyed up her brother.

"When are you and Annie going to admit to liking each other?" She pinned him.

"When are you and O'Harris?" He shot back.

"That's different."

Tommy raised an eyebrow to indicate he did not think it was. Clara let the matter rest.

"I am going to see if the inspector has figured out who the dead man is, and then I need to speak with everyone involved in the exhibition," Clara rose from the table. "Any idea when Victor is coming to see O'Harris' cars?"

"He seemed keen, I doubt he'll want to leave it long. With any luck he has already arranged to go over today. I'll give the captain a call and find out. If not, I might just pay a call on Miss Holbein. I do believe she dropped her handkerchief on the beach yesterday," Tommy produced a handkerchief from his pocket, it was prettily embroidered around the edge.

"That's my handkerchief," Clara pointed out.

"Is it?" Tommy feigned ignorance. "I could have sworn it dropped from Miss Holbein's pocket."

"I am slightly concerned this detective business is bringing out the worst in you," Clara teased him. "When did you become so deceptive?"

"I learned from the best," Tommy winked at her.

~~~*~~~

Clara had no trouble finding the inspector at the police station, for he was just coming down the stairs as she arrived.

"Briggs? Where is my tea? Ten o'clock sharp there is supposed to be tea on my desk!" Inspector Park-Coombs bellowed into the rooms behind the front desk. He looked up at Clara. "Good morning. Did you get some sleep?"

"Yes, did you?"

Park-Coombs snorted.

"Do I look like I slept?" He turned and shouted through a doorway again. "Briggs! Tea!"

"Dr Browning hired me after all," Clara explained her presence. "He is concerned that last night's incident is just the start of something more. He says there have been threats against the exhibition."

"Yes, he said that to me too," Park-Coombs yawned. "I think he is getting worked up about nothing."

"A man is dead."

"Yes, a man who was clearly an idiot for wanting to smash the cases, but that does not mean that there is this great threat hanging over the exhibition in general," Park-Coombs looked exasperated. "It is one isolated crime that Dr Browning is taking to indicate a great conspiracy. Most of these protestors are old men and married women who enjoy making placards and leaflets, but don't intend to take things further."

"I can imagine something along those lines was said about the suffragettes, and look what trouble they caused," Clara said.

Park-Coombs gave another dismissive snort. Clara could see he was too tired to pay full attention to her concerns.

"You don't mind me poking around, do you?" She said.

"Not at all, if it means Dr Browning does not keep pestering the police with his concerns, all the better," Park-

Coombs frowned and lowered his voice. "Between you and me Clara, I am not sure how I will solve this murder. It looks like a crime of opportunity and I have no clue who could be behind it. I am not hopeful."

"Have you discovered who the dead man was?" Clara was undeterred, she felt that getting to the bottom of this mystery would be tricky, but not impossible.

"Ah, we did find that out," Park-Coombs scratched his nose and looked exhausted. "John Morley was his name. There was nothing on his body to give us an identity, but about an hour after we found him Mrs Morley came into the station to report that her husband had not come home that night. The desk sergeant was bright enough to pay attention and ask her questions about the clothes her husband was wearing. Then he came to see me. Just after midnight, Mrs Morley identified her husband's body."

"Poor woman," Clara sighed. "Did she know why he had gone out that night?"

"She said she thought he had gone to the pub, as he often did in the evenings. He was a keen darts player, apparently, and was on the local team. They had a match coming up, or something, and he was putting in extra practice. Anyway, he did not come home when she expected and that was not like him."

"Was he a drinker?"

"His wife was cagey on the subject," Park-Coombs' expression indicated he thought it very likely John Morley enjoyed a tipple or two.

"Had he taken part in the protests outside the exhibition?"

"His wife said he had not. He works during the day. Morley was a carpenter."

"Easy access to a hammer."

"Exactly," Park-Coombs slammed a fist onto the front desk. "Is that cup of tea coming?"

"I suppose I should speak to Mrs Morley and to John's friends," Clara said, thinking it might be wise to leave the inspector in peace. "Could you give me her address?"

The inspector fudged around in his pocket and found a piece of paper to write on, before scrawling out the address of Mrs Morley.

"Oh, before you go, we found a considerable sum of money in John's pocket. His wife was surprised at the amount and said he had not had it when he went out. Perhaps someone paid him to commit the crime?" The inspector shrugged, then went back to trying to summon up his tea.

Clara found the address down a quiet road, halfway between poor-but-respectable and down-at-heel. The address the inspector had given her led her to a terrace in the middle of a row. It looked as though the occupants had been experiencing some troubles; the door had a hole in the bottom half, as if someone had kicked it in and the pane of a window had been smashed and covered with newspaper. Broken glass littered the garden path and crunched under Clara's feet. She looked around her and wondered what to expect when Mrs Morley opened the door, she wasn't hopeful.

John Morley had been big and strong, even in death that was obvious. His wife was the complete opposite. When she opened the door to Clara she was hunched up, her skin a nasty shade of grey and her eyes and hair dull. She had an old bruise on her cheek and the worn expression of someone so used to trouble they hardly care about it anymore.

"Clara Fitzgerald," Clara introduced herself. "I am very sorry for your loss, Mrs Morley."

Mrs Morley gave a mumble, it was not plain what she said. She pulled an old cardigan tighter across her body and Clara noticed there was a hole in the elbow.

"I am helping the police with their enquiries," Clara edged around the truth. "Might I interrupt your day for a moment or two?"

Mrs Morley muttered something again, it might have been an invitation for Clara to come in or it might not.

Clara found herself leaning closer to the woman to try to hear what she said. Fortunately, Mrs Morley punctuated whatever she had mumbled by opening the door a little wider, and Clara surmised she was welcome.

Clara walked straight into the front room, which like most front rooms was reserved for special occasions and had the starched air of a space little used. Mrs Morley led her through a door at the back of the room which entered a corridor running horizontally across the width of the house. A staircase ran up to the first floor on Clara's left, while dead ahead was another door leading into a kitchen. A fire was burning low in the range and the supper things from the night before still sat on a table in the middle. Two armchairs squeezed against the wall nearest the door, almost blocking entry. This was the space where the Morleys spent their time. They ate and sat in this tiny room, on top of one another, because for the sake of form the front room was reserved for Christmas, weddings and funerals. Clara had always been practical over fashionable, which was why she utilised all the rooms in her house and did not keep one sealed up for important events.

Mrs Morley walked into the room ahead of Clara and paused by the table. Resting a hand on the wooden top she sharply coughed, the sound more of a bark than a polite clearing of the throat. She had her back turned, but Clara could guess the strain on her face the exercise had just caused. Mrs Morley's head drooped for a moment, then she recovered.

"Take a seat," she said in a hoarse voice that was at least loud enough to be audible.

Clara slipped into the nearest armchair, noting the arms were black with dirt and grease from fingers and arms. Cloths on the top of the chair back had been put there to try to keep the fabric clean from the oiled hair of men sitting in them. Clara spotted that they needed washing and opted to perch at the front of her seat.

"I could make tea," Mrs Morley had turned to face the table, now she had both hands resting on it and was still hunched up as she made the offer.

"Please, there is no need," Clara assured her. "I would just like to talk."

Mrs Morley nodded sadly. She coughed again.

"Such a bad night," she said, mostly to herself. "I shan't be much help at all."

"Maybe I could make a cup of tea for you?" Clara asked, feeling concerned about the way the woman was leaning over the table. "Mrs Morley, are you quite well?"

Mrs Morley coughed hard into her hand.

"Would you be so kind as to fetch my brother?" Mrs Morley said weakly. "I feel rather unwell."

Suddenly Mrs Morley collapsed forward onto the table and then slipped to the floor. Clara jumped up and ran to her.

"Mrs Morley?" She touched the woman's skin, which was clammy and taking a blue tinge. She was unconscious.

Clara wasn't sure what to do at first, but she did have to get the woman up off the cold floor. She pulled at her arms and was surprised at how light Mrs Morley was. It did not require great amounts of strength to lift her into one of the armchairs, though it was awkward to get the woman to remain in it. She seemed determined to slump back to the floor.

Clara tapped her cheek gently, but Mrs Morley was not coming around any time soon. Her breath was coming in and out in nasty rasps and her lips had become very pale. Clara felt sure she needed a doctor, but wasn't convinced the woman would thank her if she went for one. People like the Morleys did not have money for luxuries like medical care. Yet she did need help.

Clara made a decision, Mrs Morley had asked for her brother and someone in this road must know where he was. She hurried outside to fetch help for the poor woman.

Chapter Seven

Tommy knocked at Miss Holbein's door. Captain O'Harris had informed him that Victor Darling was going to look at his car collection that morning, which gave Tommy the ideal opportunity to catch Miss Holbein alone. When he was done, he intended to head to O'Harris' house and talk to Victor too. O'Harris had extended a luncheon invitation to the man, so he was going to be there a while.

Miss Holbein's maid opened the door.

"Hello, I was hoping to see Miss Holbein," Tommy told her with his best smile.

The girl eyed him thoughtfully. He had the impression he was not the first strange man to turn up on Miss Holbein's doorstep. The maid appeared used to such arrivals. She disappeared into the house, closing the door behind her, and without saying anything. He assumed she intended to return, and that he was not standing there like a fool before a closed door.

A few moments passed and then the door reopened; this time Miss Holbein was stood before him.

"You?" She said curiously, she had a sullen look on her face, but Tommy caught a hint of interest in her eyes.

"Sorry to disturb you, but I believe you dropped this yesterday?" Tommy produced Clara's handkerchief from his pocket and offered it to her.

"It's not mine," Miss Holbein said instantly.

"Oh, I apologise, I'll not trouble you any longer," Tommy gave her a smile and then turned away. He was only a couple of paces down the garden path when she spoke to him.

"You can come inside for a drink."

It sounded more like a command than a request, but Tommy wasn't going to argue, she was after all talking to him, which was more than Clara had achieved. He turned back around and walked to the door.

"A drink? Would that not be disrespectful to your young man?" He asked.

Miss Holbein shrugged.

"Do you care?" She asked him.

Tommy did not, and plainly nor did Miss Holbein.

"A drink would be nice," Tommy answered.

She led him through to a sun lounge at the back of the house. Big picture windows overlooked a beautifully kept lawn that had been recently rolled into a chequer-board pattern. Soft, over-padded sofas faced the window and Miss Holbein motioned carelessly to one.

"Sit."

Tommy obeyed her command. The room was very modern in style, quite minimalist in appearance. A gracefully elongated ceramic greyhound throwing up its head as if to howl was the only work of art in the room. It stood in a corner, catching the sun. Otherwise the walls were bare apart from a large mirror on the wall behind the sofas. A large drinks cabinet stood in the corner of the room and when Miss Holbein opened the doors, she revealed a vast selection of spirits. Tommy was somewhat surprised, and then he spotted the cocktail shaker on the top of the cabinet and realised Miss Holbein was following the latest fad from America for mixing spirits into new drinks with unusual names.

"Whisky?" Miss Holbein called out to him.

Tommy glanced at his watch, it was only a little past

ten o'clock.

"Just a small one."

Miss Holbein appeared a second later with a large tumbler of whisky and a gin and tonic for herself. She handed the alcohol to Tommy and he took a polite sip. The whisky was neat, and it was far too early for Tommy to be in the mood for drinking. He tried to appear nonchalant as he placed the tumbler on the nearby coffee table.

"Well," Miss Holbein said. "This was unexpected."

"I thought the handkerchief was yours," Tommy repeated.

"You said," Miss Holbein told him bluntly. "I wouldn't carry a handkerchief like that, too frilly. I like things clean-cut, modern, simplistic."

Miss Holbein took a big sip of her drink.

"You're in luck," she said.

"Am I?" Tommy asked.

"Victor called off our trip out today," Miss Holbein pouted. "He said he was unwell, some sort of stomach upset. Really inconvenient of him. I was just feeling quite despondent, and then you turn up."

Miss Holbein graced him with a smile, which seemed so out of character that it almost startled Tommy. He would have liked to have said that a smile improved Miss Holbein's face, but it was clearly not a natural thing for her and rather reminded him of a leering gargoyle.

"Quite lucky then," he said awkwardly. "Are your parents not about?"

"They are dead," Miss Holbein said bluntly. "I live alone, and I have a lot of money."

She reached over and placed her hand on top of his.

"People say money can't make you happy, what do you think Mr…" Miss Holbein paused. "I don't know your name?"

"Tommy," Tommy said, trying to remove his hand from hers without looking obvious. "That is quite a fine garden."

"Oh, yes," Miss Holbein looked disinterested. "I avoid the sun if I can help it. It does nothing for the complexion.

Now, tell me a little about you. You look like the sort of man who would have been in the war?"

Tommy had failed to remove his hand from beneath Miss Holbein's and now she was edging herself nearer to him. She shuffled up until her hip bumped against him and she was pressing against his arm.

"Were you a soldier, Tommy?"

"I was," Tommy said uneasily, trying to think how to escape. When Clara had said Miss Holbein would probably speak to him more readily than she would to her, he didn't think this was what she had in mind.

"Do you still have the uniform?"

"Er, yes?"

"Oh, then you must come around wearing it one time. I simply cannot resist a man in uniform," Miss Holbein purred into his ear. Less and less Tommy was feeling that Miss Holbein was a naïve young lady in danger of being seduced by a money hunter.

"Wouldn't Victor mind that?" Tommy asked her.

"Victor is beginning to bore me," Miss Holbein snorted. "He was exciting at first, I even considered his marriage proposal, but now I am not so sure. I've had several marriage proposals, you know. I've been engaged twice, but broke it off because those men proved to be so... unworthy."

Miss Holbein gave a sigh.

"It is all so tiresome. I want a husband, I do. But I want them to be fun, interesting, not dull. People all prove to be dull in the end. But you won't, will you Tommy?"

"I, er…" Tommy cleared his throat. "I think you probably see more in me than I do. I'm afraid I am rather boring."

"Don't say that Tommy!" Miss Holbein beseeched him playfully, slipping her arm through his. "We could have a lot of fun together. Do you work Tommy?"

"No, not really…"

"Victor works, but he tries to insist he doesn't," Miss Holbein laughed. "He won't say what he does, but I know he only pretends to be a playboy."

"He is lying to you," Tommy tried to sound affronted on her behalf.

"Oh, I don't care, not really. All men lie to get what they want," Miss Holbein rubbed her shoulder against Tommy's. "My mother used to say that all the time. You know, my father promised her she could continue singing on stage after they were married, but that was a lie. No sooner was the ring on her finger he crushed her dreams. She never forgot that. She used to praise the day he was run over by a carriage."

Tommy did not know what to say, the statement was so blunt.

"Do I shock you?" Miss Holbein chuckled. "I speak my mind, I consider it a virtue. Too many people can't speak their thoughts. They smile when they are sad, laugh when they hate, say they are your friends when really they only want to control you."

"That is a harsh assessment of the world," Tommy said.

"But truthful. I'll admit, when I first started being pursued by admirers, I was blind, I listened only to their words and thought they loved me. Now I understand," Miss Holbein was hugging his arm to her chest. "They wanted my money and they would say and do anything for it. I was upset, at least at first. I know I am not pretty or accomplished, I can't sing like my mother, or dance, or do anything that is considered enchanting in a woman. I suppose I am unattractive and that would be an awful disadvantage if it was not for the fact that I have money, a lot of it."

"I don't see…"

"Oh, you do see Tommy, its why you came here today, its why all the men come and fawn over me. I have a fortune and men want my fortune. That made me unhappy until I realised it gave me power. Power over my admirers and over my future husband. I am being honest with you, Tommy, so you won't be surprised later on."

Tommy abruptly rose from the sofa and disentangled

54

himself from Miss Holbein. He walked to the window, trying to put space between himself and her.

"I'm not one of those men," he said firmly. "I didn't come here to court you."

"What then?" Miss Holbein said with a smirk on her face. "Why did you come?"

"To return the handkerchief…"

"Don't lie."

"All right, I was curious," Tommy shoved his hands in his pockets and paced before the window. "I wanted to know why a girl like you was with a man like Victor Darling."

"You think he is not good enough for me?" Miss Holbein laughed.

"He didn't seem… a good fit," Tommy replied.

"And you are right, he isn't good enough, far from it. But, oh, he does make the neighbours curl their toes when they see us together. Why, my mother's friend lives just down the road, and I do delight in giving her the terrors by parading him before her," Miss Holbein laughed even harder. "They all think they are protecting me, when I really don't need their protection. I know what Victor Darling is after. He wants my money and he has been very accommodating to try and get it. I like that. Most men would not give me the time of day, if it weren't for my wealth."

"You sell yourself short," Tommy frowned at her. "You should be looking for a man who wants you with or without your money."

"No man exists!"

"Why not? Because you have not met him yet?" Tommy could not fathom how Miss Holbein was so content to accept that her money was the only thing attractive about her. True, her personality and looks were not easy to get past, but he was sure if she tried she could find someone who wanted her because they liked her, not because she had a fortune.

"Tommy, you act as though it even matters," Miss

Holbein gave him a pitying look. "It doesn't bother me. If a man wishes to please me because I have a big bank account, that is just as good as if he wants to please me because I am pretty."

"What about love?" Tommy asked her.

"Love doesn't exist outside novels!" Miss Holbein found that most amusing. "Many of the girls in my social circle say they married for love, but within a year, maybe two, they hate their husbands. No one knows what love is, maybe it is just being nice to someone because they can give you something back."

"I think that is an awful thing to believe," Tommy shook his head. "You are too young to be so cynical."

"Are you saying you are not here for my money?" Miss Holbein leaned back on the sofa.

"I can honestly say I am not," Tommy told her firmly. "That was never my intention."

Miss Holbein was quiet for a moment. She spread her arms out along the back of the sofa and tilted her head to one side.

"You are a strange kettle of fish."

"I'm ordinary," Tommy replied. "I don't need your money and I would never marry a woman for that reason. I intend to marry for love. I want my future wife to be my friend, first and foremost. We shall be companions, happy in our lot whatever that is. We may be poor or rich, but we shall have each other."

Tommy paused and his gaze went to the window and to the lawn outside. His mind had drifted to Annie.

"And people call me a fool," Miss Holbein scoffed at him. "I have never heard such nonsense. But, if that is the way you feel…"

"It is," Tommy said.

Miss Holbein smiled.

"I dare say I like the challenge. A companion, a friend. All right, if that is how you want it."

"What?" Tommy said uneasily.

"I shall be interested to see how this goes, especially if

you are genuine about not wanting my money. I wonder if you will be so amenable as the others who did want my fortune? You might argue with me, now that would be novel!"

"I think you have the wrong end of the stick," Tommy said hastily. "I was not implying I was here to court you."

"I've blown your bluff," Miss Holbein mused. "You'll need to save face, naturally. Men can't bear to be caught out. I like your tease with the handkerchief though, so genteel. Victor was far more brazen, he turned up on the doorstep with a picnic hamper and told me he was going to sweep me off my feet. I much prefer things this way."

"I really need to be going," Tommy headed for the door as fast as he could.

"You never finished your drink," Miss Holbein pursued him. "Why, I have never run after a man before! This is quite fun. Are you coming back tomorrow?"

"I don't think so," Tommy had his hand on the handle of the front door, but Miss Holbein had caught his arm.

"You must, you know. Don't be a tease!"

"I never meant for this," Tommy extracted himself from her grasp and stumbled out of the front door, hurrying for the road as quickly as he could.

"Ta-ta!" Miss Holbein waved at him. "Until tomorrow, my sweet."

She blew him a kiss. Tommy was too horrified to respond, he just wanted to get as far away as fast as he could. He had no idea how he was going to explain this all to Clara. He wasn't sure he could explain it to himself. Tommy felt a new respect for Victor Darling. Anyone who could survive whole days in Miss Holbein's company, even if they were only out for her money, surely deserved a medal!

Chapter Eight

Clara knocked hard on the door of the house next to Mrs Morley's. This property was in better repair; the door had been recently painted and the front garden had been mown and weeded, with pretty Busy Lizzies in a bed before the window. An older woman opened the door and looked at Clara with slight apprehension. Clara imagined she looked rather urgent and dishevelled, she was certainly feeling agitated.

"Sorry to disturb you, but Mrs Morley has been taken very ill. I am trying to locate her brother."

The older woman peered around her door to her neighbour's house, a knowing look on her face.

"I said she wouldn't last the year out," the woman tutted to herself. "Harry Beasley lives five doors down. You'll probably find him there, he works nights at the railway station. He won't appreciate being woke up."

The woman's expression suggested that Clara was really making a fuss over nothing, and ought not to bother people further. Clara opted not to listen.

"Thank you," she said, deciding she had got as much help from the woman as she was going to give.

Clara had not even reached the garden gate before she heard the woman slam shut her front door. So much for neighbourly love, the woman was clearly not going to interfere in Mrs Morley's affairs any more than she had to. Clara shook her head, slightly angered by the woman's cool disregard for someone else, then she hurried to find Harry.

The Beasleys lived in a house that had a very similar appearance to the Morleys' home, except the door was intact and none of the window panes were broken. But the front garden needed attention, the grass of the lawn growing high and encroaching on the shingle path up to the front door. The garden gate was rotten on its hinges and nearly fell off when Clara opened it. She did her best to shut it after her, out of politeness, then remembered she was wasting time. Her mind seemed to have gone fuzzy after Mrs Morley collapsed and she was fixating on the most minor of things, rather than the problem at hand. She snapped herself out of her daze and hurried to knock on the Beasleys' door.

Mrs Beasley opened it to her. She was about Clara's age, with very curly hair and a delicate face you could have imagined on a china doll. She smiled at Clara brightly, the first person that morning to be welcoming. Clara felt awful that she was about to rain bad news on the woman.

"My apologies for interrupting your day, but Mrs Morley has been taken very ill."

Mrs Beasley's eyes grew large as she took in this news.

"Oh dear! She will want Harry then. Is she at home?" Mrs Beasley was hurrying into the house as she talked, Clara followed her, the layout of the house was the same as the Morleys.

"Yes, I've left her in the kitchen. I wanted to call a doctor," Clara said.

"Oh, you mustn't do that. Doctors are so expensive. I'll get Harry and we shall come over at once. I have some medicine in a cupboard we can bring," Mrs Beasley disappeared through the door at the back of the room and Clara could hear her heading upstairs.

The woman had seemed so calm and in control of the situation, which was more than Clara felt right then. She could not help thinking that without a doctor Mrs

Morley's condition would prove fatal. Truthfully, even with a doctor there may be no hope. And then there was the situation with her husband. Did Harry Beasley know that his brother-in-law was dead? Clara felt there was so much to explain to these people, so much grim information to impart. She tried to distract herself by looking about the front room. It was in a better condition than the Morleys', there were a number of porcelain ornaments on the mantelpiece and a painting on the wall. There was even an old piano sandwiched into a corner. It had a gaping hole in the side of its case, but appeared in working order.

Clara's brain was flitting again. She was not normally like this in an emergency, but there was something about Mrs Morley's situation that made her feel desperate, as if every second she wasted was one less the poor woman had. Clara paced and wished she could go for a doctor, maybe if she offered to pay… But people could get very upset about such perceived acts of charity, it could hurt their pride.

Mrs Beasley reappeared in the room.

"Harry will be there as soon as he can. He has to get dressed. We should go ahead. I have the medicine," Mrs Beasley had a bag in her hand, she seemed unnecessarily cheerful about the whole thing.

The two women headed back down the road at a brisk pace. Across the street a couple of neighbours were talking in their respective front gardens and watched them pass. Clara sensed there were a lot more eyes on them than just the ones she could see. People would be peering from windows, peeping between the curtains, surreptitiously monitoring what was occurring. Clara knew the same would happen in her own road if there was some emergency occurring. People were all the same, always interested in the misfortune of others, though not always prepared to help them.

Clara was relieved when they were back in the Morleys' house and the front door was closed behind them. Mrs Beasley had slipped ahead and hurried to the kitchen. There, thankfully, Mrs Morley was still sitting in the armchair, though she was all flopped over to one side.

Mrs Beasley crouched before her.

"My gosh, she do look blue!" She gasped, before opening her bag and producing a bottle of smelling salts.

Mrs Morley had taken on a duck egg hue since Clara had left her. Her cheeks looked as though someone had painted them with the colour and her lips had turned grey-blue. Clara understood, from her time as a nurse during the war, that this implied she was not getting enough air into her lungs. Since she was not being artificially suffocated, by a cloth or a rope, for instance, the cause must be a medical complaint. Clara had seen men who had been gassed and left with such badly damaged lungs that they struggled to breathe and slowly suffocated to death. There were diseases of the lungs that could cause something similar. Equally, if the heart was not strong and could not pump blood around the body sufficiently, it could cause the patient to lack oxygen and turn blue.

Only a doctor could say for certain what was wrong with Mrs Morley and if there was any hope of curing it. Clara feared, from the look of the woman, that her condition was far advanced and there was no chance of saving her in the long-term.

Mrs Beasley wafted the smelling salts under Mrs Morley's nose and the unfortunate woman roused slightly, enough at least for Mrs Beasley to open a big brown bottle of sticky yellow medicine and place a spoonful in the woman's mouth. Mrs Morley swallowed with difficulty and her eyes fluttered weakly.

"Ruby, dear, stay with us. Harry is coming," Mrs Beasley clutched the hand of her sister-in-law. "Gosh, she is cold."

Clara was feeling useless up until then. She suddenly sprang into action and pulled a crochet shawl from the back of a chair and placed it over Mrs Morley, tucking it around her.

"What if I make a cup of tea?" She suggested.

"We can try to get her to drink it," Mrs Beasley

frowned. "She has had these episodes before, but never quite this bad."

Mrs Morley's head had flopped to the side again and it was hard to know if she was conscious or not. She did not look in a fit state to drink tea. Clara sighed.

"Has she been ill a long time?" She asked.

"Years now," Mrs Beasley answered, her voice quiet as she packed away the bottle of medicine. It appeared to have had some effect as a little colour was returning to Mrs Morley's cheeks. "As long as I've known her, anyway, and that is now five, no, six years. I was friends with Ruby before I knew Harry. She introduced us."

Mrs Beasley smiled to herself.

"I was luckier in love than poor Ruby. Harry is a good husband, loyal and kind."

"Unlike John Morley?" Clara asked in a hushed tone, just in case Mrs Morley was still awake.

Mrs Beasley's frown deepened. She looked at Mrs Morley for a while, then she rose and took Clara aside.

"John Morley is a brute when he is drunk," she said. "Harry has squared with him more than once over how he treats Ruby, but it never does any lasting good."

"Are you aware that John Morley was killed last night?" Clara asked softly.

Mrs Beasley's startled look was all the answer Clara needed.

"Someone hit him on the back of the head with a mallet," Clara explained. "He was at the town hall at the time. It appears he broke in to smash some of the display cases that are there as part of a touring exhibition."

Mrs Beasley whistled through her teeth.

"Well, that's a turn up for the books," she took a moment to contemplate what Clara had said. "Smashing display cases? Whatever for?"

"The police found a lot of money in John's pocket. It appears someone had paid him to do the job."

"Well…" Mrs Beasley glanced over at her friend and her gaze hardened. "Good riddance. That's all I can say."

"What would Mrs Morley say?" Clara asked.

Mrs Beasley became sad and sighed deeply.

"She loved him, that's for sure. I can't say as how she could love such a man, but she did. She forgave him everything and it weren't just the punches he threw when he had had a skin-full. It was the other women, the tarts he went off with," Mrs Beasley shook her head, disbelieving of her friend's tolerance. "John said he had needs and Ruby weren't fit to fulfil them. We all knew what he meant, disgusting pig. He should have been here of an evening looking out for Ruby, instead he was out drinking and picking up women. I dare say he paid for a few of them too, he would have had no shame about it. Had he been any sort of husband, he would have saved his money for a doctor for Ruby. Now look at her."

Clara followed the command. Ruby Morley looked like a corpse slumped in the chair, her chest barely rising and falling. Her face was turning blue again.

"Is there no chance of a doctor, or to send her to the hospital?" Clara asked.

"We can't afford the bills," Mrs Beasley shrugged her shoulders. It was a fact, not a complaint. "Ruby wouldn't want to die in a hospital, anyway. She can come and be with us. She'll go in the spare bedroom. Not like she'll be able to keep up the rent on this house now John's gone."

"Did he work?" Clara asked.

"Sometimes," Mrs Beasley rolled her eyes. "He had no fixed profession, but he did a lot of grave-digging for the local churches. He was big and strong, and didn't fuss if he accidentally came across some bones from a former internment. He brought home a leg bone once, you know? Ruby was appalled and said he must take it back at once, could be that the spirit of the person whose bone it was would follow it and haunt their house. John kept waving the bone at her and scaring her. He was mean like that."

Mrs Beasley looked at her friend.

"Do you think we could get her up to bed? And then, when she is better, she can come to my house."

Clara didn't like to say that she was not sure Ruby Morley was going to get better. Once they had her upstairs, she could not see how they would get her down again alive.

"It might be better to carry her to your house straight away," she said gently. "She can't be left alone, after all."

"No, of course," Mrs Beasley dabbed at an eye, small tears slipping down her cheeks. "Harry will help with that when he comes. Let's make that cup of tea, shall we? Oh, and I never caught your name?"

Clara realised she was a perfect stranger to this woman and must seem completely out of place.

"I'm sorry, I forgot myself. I am Clara Fitzgerald, I work as a private detective and I have been asked to investigate why John Morley was in the town hall last night."

"Oh," Mrs Beasley took a moment to absorb this information. "What is a private detective?"

"Someone a person hires to investigate a problem for them rather than the police," Clara explained. "I do work with the police, however, and they are looking into the murder of John Morley."

"I don't much care about that," Mrs Beasley gave a sniff to indicate how little it concerned her that John Morley was dead and that someone had killed him. "Who hired you?"

"Dr Browning, he is the expert who travels with the exhibition that is currently in the town hall. He is concerned about threats made towards the items on display. After last night, he is rather frightened."

Mrs Beasley was puzzled.

"Why would people make threats against an exhibition? Are there valuable items on display?"

"One of the items is very valuable, but also controversial," Clara nodded. "It is the fossilised skeleton of a dinosaur with feathers. Many believe it proves that some dinosaurs evolved into birds and that it is proof that Charles Darwin's theory of evolution was correct. But other people are angered by this, because they feel it contradicts the teachings of the Bible."

Mrs Beasley listened politely but was clearly baffled by all this.

"Don't people have better things to do than worry about some bones?" She said. "They must not have to work for their bread, or worry about the rent going up, is all I can say. If they did, they wouldn't have the time for such nonsense. And John was involved in all that?"

Clara did not have a chance to respond as just then Harry Beasley appeared in the house. He had washed and dressed as fast as he could and was now there to see what could be done for his sister. He arrived just as the water in the big kettle started to boil. He glanced at his wife and then at Clara, before looking at Ruby Morley.

"Can someone explain to me what is going on?"

Chapter Nine

Clara went through the story again for Harry. She explained how she had come to be there, and that John Morley was dead, and she was investigating why he had been at the town hall, though not specifically his murder. No one had hired her to find his killer, that was the job of the police. She had been hired to resolve who was behind the attack and threats on the exhibition and whether there was a possibility of further violence.

Harry Beasley listened intently, and Clara sensed that he was an intelligent man whose only limitation on his learning had been his circumstances. He was also very good looking, in a rugged way, and a perfect match to his pretty wife. She busied herself making tea while Clara enlightened Harry.

Harry, meanwhile, sat in the armchair next to his sister and held her hand as he took in everything Clara said.

"Funny business," he said when Clara was done. "John was not a religious man, or one to take to political causes. He had no strong beliefs, as such. John was only interested in himself and his own pleasure. That meant drink and women."

Harry glanced at his sister, as if he had forgotten she was so near while he was bad-mouthing her husband. Ruby Morley was unconscious, and Clara was not convinced she was ever going to wake again. There was something deathly about her pallor. She had seen too many patients fall into such stupors and never rouse to be confident that Ruby's condition was only temporary.

"I didn't much like John, it's no secret," Harry continued. "He was an oaf who didn't deserve the devotion my sister gave him. He was always looking to earn some quick cash, seeing how he spent everything he earned legitimately and had no real job. I once tried to get him work at the railway station, but he was too much of a danger to himself. He would turn up drunk. You can't have that around trains, anything could happen."

"Can you think of anyone who might have put John up to smashing the display cases in the town hall?" Clara asked.

"No. But I didn't move in John's circles, for good reason. He could have met the person anywhere," Harry looked at his sister again and squeezed her hand. "I wanted better for Ruby, now... now I think it is too late."

"Don't say that John, with a few good meals and a warm bed she'll perk up," Mrs Beasley said with remarkable optimism.

Clara kept her mouth shut, but she could see that Harry was as acutely aware as she was that Ruby Morley's sickness was terminal.

"Mrs Morley said her husband was a carpenter," Clara recalled something Park-Coombs had said.

"John certainly had the training. He was apprenticed as a carpenter and when he first met Ruby that was his profession," Harry explained. "I'll give him credit, he was not bad at it, either. But he was lazy and didn't want to work, and then he took to the drink. Within a year of the marriage he had lost his job as a carpenter and he never worked properly again. He kept some of his tools, however, and from time-to-time, when the mood took him and he wanted the money, he would do work for people. But it never lasted for long. Each time he pulled out his tools Ruby would get her hopes up, say that this time she was sure he would make a good go of things. She always clung to the notion he was a professional workman who had just fallen on hard times. Never could get her to understand he was a loafer with no interest in working."

"His death must have hit her hard," Clara looked at the sick woman, feeling so sorry for her. "She clearly loved him a good deal."

"They say love is blind," Mrs Beasley remarked, bringing over cups of tea for them all. "In Ruby's case, that was very true."

"If you want to know about John, you might want to speak to his friends at the Hole in the Wall. It's a terrible pub, serves the worst ale you can come across, but it was where John went all the time. They might know who paid him to do the job."

"Thank you, I'll try that," Clara said. "Did John go to church?"

"Never!" Harry laughed. "I think he feared he might be struck by lightning if he stepped into a house of God! No, if you are thinking he might have been motivated by a religious fever of some description, you'll be disappointed. I reckon the last time he was in a church was on his wedding day, and he looked mighty glad to leave."

Harry snorted.

"What John knew about evolution and Darwin you could write on the back of a postage stamp and still have room for more," Harry's eyes took on an amused twinkle. "I once asked him what he thought about humans being descended from apes, he thought I was implying his mother had run off with a gorilla."

"He was a very stupid man," Mrs Beasley added. "He thought cows cocked their legs, like dogs do, and wondered how the farmer got around such behaviour when he milked them!"

"If ever an education was wasted on a man, it was wasted on John Morley. He was lucky he could read and write. I blamed that on chance rather than any great aptitude for learning," Harry snorted. "I was planning on going to that exhibition, as it happens, on the public day. Will it still be open?"

"As far as I know," Clara said. "I can recommend it, if you are interested in fossils. Dr Browning is very informative on the subject."

"I borrowed Darwin's book from the public library," Harry said slightly shyly. "I like to read."

"Harry is a great reader," Mrs Beasley said with affection in her voice. "He is always trying to improve himself."

"You'll enjoy the exhibition, they have put together a fine collection of fossils. And I do recommend speaking with Dr Browning if you have the chance," Clara said, she had warmed to the Beasleys and liked them a good deal. She was saddened that Ruby had had the misfortune of marrying John Morley, but then everyone made their choices in life, for better or worse.

"Harry, if Miss Fitzgerald is going to go to that pub, I think you ought to go with her. It isn't a place for a woman alone," Mrs Beasley looked anxiously at her husband.

"I really am quite self-reliant," Clara responded politely. "I don't need to inconvenience you."

"No, Emma is right," Harry Beasley sat a little straighter in his chair. "That is not a place for you to go alone, besides, I can probably point out the right people for you to talk to. I'm not sure if many will talk to a woman though."

Clara was used to such obstacles in her investigations. After a moment to consider, she thought it would be prudent to have Harry at her side. Whichever way she looked at it, there were occasions when a woman alone was at a disadvantage. She could not afford to be precious about her pride when it came to making headway in a case.

"When does the Hole in the Wall open?" Clara asked.

"Early afternoon," Harry glanced around for a clock in the kitchen to judge the time and spotted one on a shelf above the stove. "Not for a while."

"We need to get Ruby to ours," Emma Beasley spoke

up. "Then, once she is settled, I shall make us some lunch and you can help Miss Fitzgerald."

"I don't like to put you to all that trouble," Clara was thinking she could go home, collect Tommy or O'Harris and then go to the pub.

"It's no trouble," Mrs Beasley insisted. "If you had not been here Ruby would have been all alone when she collapsed, and you came to fetch us and have interrupted your day to assist us. No, we are just returning that kindness."

Mrs Beasley was firm, she would not be swayed. Clara was liking her all the more and felt that Ruby could have no better sister-in-law taking care of her.

"Then allow me to help you make arrangements for Ruby," she said.

Mrs Beasley was agreeable to that. Ruby remained unconscious in her chair. Harry said she would be no bother to carry back to their house, she was as light as a feather. He remained with her, almost dozing off in the chair himself, as Clara and Emma Beasley went upstairs to pack some clothes and belongings for Ruby.

"Your husband must be exhausted," Clara said, feeling bad that she was going to be keeping Harry Beasley away from his bed.

"He works nights," Mrs Beasley explained. "He can doze for a bit while we pack."

They entered the back bedroom of the house. Being directly over the kitchen it was the warmest room upstairs in the winter, the heat from the stove rising through the floor and taking the chill off an otherwise unheated room. It was also rather barren. An old bed with an iron bedstead sat in one corner unmade. It looked like Ruby had briefly slept in it, or rather tossed and turned waiting for her husband, and had then abandoned it. The blankets were grey with age, the mattress sagged and was in places darned with thick thread. There had been no money to replace it; like so many others, Ruby Morley made do.

A rough wardrobe looked fit to fall to pieces in the

opposite corner of the room. The doors sagged painfully on their hinges as it was opened to reveal a handful of clothes. Mrs Beasley removed all those that belonged to Ruby, pointedly ignoring the two spare shirts and a pair of trousers that had once clothed John.

"They would rent out the front bedroom," Mrs Beasley explained as they wrapped up Ruby's clothes in a blanket. "But lodgers never stayed long. John was always accusing them of having designs on his wife. It made everything so difficult."

"He was very jealous then?" Clara had picked up a hairbrush that belonged to Ruby and handed it to Emma.

"Ironic, isn't it?" Emma Beasley sighed. "Ruby could not see him for who he really was. She could have left any time. I would have taken her in. We have the room. I use the front bedroom for my work. I embroider things for people. Wedding gifts, christening gowns, handkerchiefs for Christmas. That sort of thing. Some of it goes to shops to sell, other pieces I make specifically for someone. The front room has the best light all day, but we keep a bed in there also. Harry always liked to think there was a safe place for Ruby if she needed it."

Mrs Beasley drew up the edges of the blanket and looked at the sad bundle of items inside.

"Not much, is it?" She frowned.

Clara opened the drawer at the bottom of the wardrobe and produced a pair of stockings and a couple of handkerchiefs. They had been finely embroidered with the letter R and roses. Clara passed them over to Emma who smiled to herself.

"I made these for Ruby's wedding. I wasn't so good then, I can see every error I made," she placed the handkerchiefs in her bundle. "Not even a cardigan or a hat to call her own. I guess they are in the pawn shop for the summer."

A tear slowly crept from the corner of Emma Beasley's eye. She wiped it away crossly as it started to trickle down her cheek.

"I'm glad he is dead," she said softly.

Clara was not sure she was meant to hear the statement.

They went downstairs and woke Harry. After looking about the kitchen for anything else to take with them and discovering a pair of outdoor shoes and a coat, though how much use Ruby would get from them now was questionable, they prepared to leave. Harry lifted up his sister easily. They walked out of the house, Mrs Beasley locking the front door as they departed. Clara motioned to the broken window and the damage to the door.

"Has there been trouble?"

"John often owes people money," Harry answered, he was waiting by the front gate for someone to open it for him. Clara hurried forward to help him. She did not correct his statement. John's debts were past tense now.

Those eyes were on them again as they headed for the Beasleys' house. Clara felt them stinging into her back. It was like an itch you couldn't scratch. Clara would have liked to have asked those same neighbours, who now peeped at them and secretly gawked, how many had helped Ruby when they could. She suspected many of them had watched the activity at the Morleys, but kept themselves to themselves. It made Clara a little angry, especially when she realised Ruby's neighbour, the one who had refused to come out of her house and assist when Clara was trying to find the Beasleys, was standing on her doorstep watching them as bold as brass. Clara had to bite her tongue to avoid saying something rude.

They arrived at the Beasleys' house and Harry carried Ruby upstairs, his wife following. Clara decided not to intrude further and loitered in the kitchen, feeling that awkwardness of a guest who is left unattended and does not know what to do with themselves.

It was a short while before Emma joined her.

"Harry is taking a nap, while I start lunch," she said,

looking weary herself.

She stroked a strand of hair back from her forehead.

"I'm glad you came today, Miss Fitzgerald."

"Please, call me Clara."

Emma smiled. Then she rubbed at her eyes, as if rubbing away her tiredness.

"I have cold meat and I was going to boil some potatoes and beans to go with it," she said. "I made fresh bread this morning too. You will join us, Clara?"

"If I am not imposing," Clara said.

"You are most welcome," Emma pulled out a chair for Clara to sit in. "I know you are not looking into who killed John and, honestly, I don't much care who was responsible, but I think Ruby would like to know. Could you keep an ear open for any information regarding that too, while you are solving Dr Browning's mystery?"

"I will," Clara promised. "As will the police."

Emma Beasley looked relieved.

"Ruby doesn't know how lucky she was you knocked at her door this morning," Mrs Beasley leaned on the back of a chair with her hands. "Sometimes, everything works out for the best."

Chapter Ten

After lunch, Clara and Harry Beasley headed down the road for the Hole in the Wall. Harry had explained that it was the sort of place where people who had nothing better to do hung around. Even though it was early, Harry was sure they would find some of John's friends there. The customers at the Hole in the Wall rarely had jobs.

"John liked easy money," Harry elaborated as they walked along. "He would do anything as long as it did not require much effort. I always suspected he dabbled in illegal activities, but I couldn't ask."

They reached the pub, which was stuck on a corner and resembled its name rather appropriately. It was a dirty, brown-brick building, with large dark windows and a gaping door. Next to the red-brick houses, it looked like a mucky smut. It made Clara think of a missing tooth in an otherwise pleasant smile. There was something about the grim looking pub that seemed to suck people in, like a bottomless pit. Passers-by made the effort to give it a wide berth, if they were not intending to actually go in.

Clara could see why Harry had insisted on coming with her. It was not a place where women would be welcomed as fellow drinkers. The women who went into the Hole in the Wall were there on business, but not the sort of respectable business Clara did. She suspected she would get a cold reception, and her questions would fall on deaf ears, but one had to try.

They walked through the door and Clara was instantly struck by a strong smell of alcohol and tobacco. The aroma was so dense, it almost had a physical presence. She also had not realised how dark the interior was until she stepped through the doorway and had to take a moment to get used to the dim light. When her eyes did adjust, she saw a small room with a bar against the back wall and round tables and chairs dotted about. There were a dozen drinkers filling the tight space. They were all men and looked at Clara with either disdain or lechery.

The landlord was behind his bar, picking up the pieces of a broken glass. He scowled as Harry and Clara approached.

"No women in the bar," he said. "I've made it a rule. Too many tarts kept coming in. Police were starting to take an interest."

"Do I look like a tart?" Clara asked him coolly.

"Takes all sorts," the landlord sneered. He was in his later years, balding and with crooked, stained teeth. He also had a lazy eye, which was slightly off-putting, as it seemed as if he was looking two ways at once. "Some of them dress fancy."

"Mind your tongue," Harry rumbled.

"This your pimp?" The landlord regarded Harry without concern. "You two ought to be ashamed."

Clara did not bother to get angry, the landlord was not worth the effort.

"I am a private detective," she explained. "And I am here because of the murder of John Morley."

She had raised her voice a fraction to ensure she got everyone's attention. In the small pub, it was not hard to be overheard.

"John Morley is dead?" The landlord was thrown for a second. "He was only in here last night."

"And now he is in the morgue, someone clobbered him

over the head," Clara added.

"Then why are you here and not the police?" The landlord sneered again.

"Would you prefer I fetch the police?" Clara challenged him. "I'm sure that would do your business the world of good."

"Are you threatening me?" The landlord pointed a dirty finger at her.

"I haven't even worked up to threatening you yet," Clara grinned at him. "But if you insist, I shall gladly go get the police."

The landlord was starting to bluster, he shook a piece of broken glass at her, at which point Harry grabbed his wrist.

"I am really taking offence to your manner," he told the landlord in his deepest tone. Harry was big and muscular, working on a railway did that for a man. "Be nice to the lady, or must I teach you some manners."

The landlord was a bully and, like so many men in his position, the second he was accosted by someone tougher than him he backed down. He dropped the shard of glass into a bucket behind the counter and moved back from the bar.

"You want to ask questions, fine. Don't expect anyone to talk to you. And I ain't serving you a drink, neither!"

Clara was relieved about that. She had no desire to drink the beer the landlord kept on tap. Instead she glanced to Harry.

"Any of these men friends of John's?"

Harry looked around him and then motioned to a table to the side of the bar, where three men were sitting.

"I've seen him talking with those lot before now."

Clara approached the trio, who eyed her with suspicion and clutched their drinks a little closer as if she was about to steal them.

"I am trying to find out what happened to John Morley

last night. Did any of you see him yesterday?" Clara asked.

The men exchanged looks but remained sullenly silent.

"It is odd how a man's friends can be so utterly uncaring about his death," Clara remarked in a loud aside to Harry. "It is not as if I am accusing them of anything. Nor, for that matter, am I the police. All I want to know is if they saw John yesterday, not to get them into trouble, but to discover what happened to him."

The men seemed to drop their heads in unison. One took an uneasy sip from his pint mug.

"You'll have no luck," Harry told Clara, shaking his head. "These men weren't friends to Harry, not in the way you mean. They knew him, drank with him, but they don't give a damn that he is dead."

Clara tried to catch the eye of the men, but none were interested.

"Well then, this is a pickle. Let me lay out what I know for you, and maybe you will be inclined to help me then," Clara placed her hands on the table and leaned forward, making it hard for them to ignore her. "John Morley came here last night for a drink. Someone approached him and offered him money to do a job. The job was to break into the town hall and smash the glass cases holding a certain fossil. Now, something happened while John was there, someone smacked him over the head with a mallet and killed him. Then they vanished into thin air. I'm not saying any of you were involved, but I want to know who hired John."

The men were silent. Clara guessed they were all around John's age, it was hard to tell in the semi-dark. She could only surmise why they were here drinking instead of working. Though one had lost an arm, which easily explained his circumstances. Clara wondered if he had been in the war, or whether the missing limb was a deformity.

"Really? You don't want to help?" Clara was losing her patience. "What sort of friends are you?"

She rose up and looked to Harry.

"I give up, with this lot around there is no hope of

getting any justice for John. I guess his killer will get to walk free, crowing about what he did."

"I figured as much," Harry shrugged. "This isn't the place to make loyal friends."

"You want to make a man feel guilty to his soul," a voice behind Clara snarled.

She turned and saw that she had been addressed by the man with the missing arm.

"It's not as though I killed him, how could I?" The man waved his singular hand. "I was right-handed before the war, can't get used to being left-handed. I definitely can't lift and swing a mallet."

"I already said, I am not accusing any of you of murder," Clara replied.

"Why not?" The one-armed man declared. "Could be any of us done it. Maybe we went on the job with him? Well, not me, but one of these two."

He waved a hand between the two men sitting either side of him.

"Shut up Frank!" The man on his right barked. "None of us left the pub until it was late, you know that. John was long gone by the time we went home."

"I'm just saying," Frank lifted up his pint and held it to his lips, "we all saw John pocket that money. We all thought about what we would do with it, if we had the chance."

"Speak for yourself," the man on his left grumbled. "I didn't begrudge John that money."

"I never said that, not as such," Frank was holding forth now, enjoying tormenting his companions. "But we all thought about it. That was a lot of cash, and none of us are wealthy men."

"Where did John get this money?" Clara interrupted.

Frank glared at her as if she had suddenly appeared before him and demanded he hand over his wallet.

"How do we know you ain't something to do with it all? Maybe you are trying to get that money back?"

Clara laughed.

"The police have the money. Its locked up, considered evidence in their case," she shrugged. "I am truly here to discover what happened last night and who hired John Morley."

"Who are you working for, then?" The man on Frank's right asked her. He was missing his front upper teeth and stuck his tongue out a little when he talked.

"Dr Browning," Clara answered.

The men all looked blank, as she had expected.

"He is one of the people in charge of the exhibition of fossils in the town hall," Clara added.

She received further uncomprehending stares and almost groaned aloud.

"John Morley was murdered trying to smash one of the cases in the exhibition. Looks like someone paid him to do it."

The three men exchanged looks.

"It was that fellow in the dark suit," the man to the left of Frank whispered to his companions. He didn't do a very good job of masking his words from Clara. "He was talking to John for ages, and then John pocketed that money he gave him."

"I reckoned he was trouble as soon as I saw him," the man on Frank's right added. "He looked too smartly dressed to be coming in here. I thought he was up to no good."

"Are you saying that fellow killed John?" Frank asked aloud.

His companions glanced at one another.

"Well, none of us went with John, did we? So, who else?"

Frank looked morose for a second, then he glanced at Clara.

"You just want to know who hired John?"

"Yes," Clara said.

"Well, it was a man in a dark suit," Frank repeated what he had just discussed with the others. "He had a pencil moustache and black hair."

"You don't know his name," Clara tried not to sigh in exasperation. What a waste of her time!

"He wasn't for introducing himself to us," Frank took offence at her tone. "He looked like someone who works in an office, or something."

"He wore a really nice pin," the man to Frank's right recalled. "It looked like a bird. He wore it on his lapel, like it meant something. It was gold, I reckon."

"More likely gold-plate," Frank scoffed. "He weren't that rich looking."

"He spoke odd, strange accent," the man on Frank's left remarked. "Sounded foreign. But not like the foreign accents of the French or Belgians I met in the war."

"No, he weren't from there," the man opposite concurred. "If you ask me, he was Irish."

"No!" Frank looked at his friends in horror. "That accent was South African, sure of it. I knew a man from South Africa in the war. He had faced the Boers."

"South Africans have a lot of gold," the man who had mentioned the gold pin muttered this under his breath.

"What's a South African doing here?" The man on Frank's left snapped. "Thinking about it, he could have been Scottish."

Clara was becoming exasperated. Instead of helping her, the men were causing only further confusion. Whoever this man with the gold pin and peculiar accent was, she was going to get no more from the gentlemen in the pub about him.

"Let's go," she said to Harry. "Thank you gentlemen."

She nodded to the drinkers around the table and turned away with Harry.

"Do you think that fellow killed John?" Frank called from behind her.

Clara turned back.

"It would be odd to hire a man just to kill him," she observed.

The three men put their heads together and talked in

low voices. Then Frank looked up.

"You see, we heard the man tell John that he would only give him the rest of the money for the job after it was over, and that he would come back to the pub the next day, which would be tonight, to meet with John and settle up," Frank seemed pleased with this nugget of information. "Seems to me, that fellow ought to be back here tonight as he agreed. He probably don't know John is dead, right?"

"What time might he be here?" Clara asked.

"He came over around nine, last night," Frank said. "And, if you ask me, John knew he was coming. He was looking out for him. They had met before. I should have been more alert to that at the time."

Frank's face fell.

"John has drunk with me these last five years. Who am I going to drink with now?"

"You got us, Frank," his companion on his right said.

"You? You can't hold your drink! Anyway, soon as you get another job you will not be here, will you? You have that wife of yours nagging at you to make money. Never thinking about me, about how lonely I get."

"Now Frank…"

"Don't 'now Frank' me. I know how it is. I can't work, can I? All I've got is this pub, but you all want to up and leave me!"

Clara moved to Harry and nodded her head to the door. "We're done here."

As they left the pub Harry spoke.

"Will you come back tonight?"

"Yes, but I shall bring company with me, don't worry," Clara smiled at his concern. "Thank you for helping me today."

Harry shrugged.

"I did it for Ruby, not for John. I knew he would always come to a bad end. Quite frankly, I wish it had been sooner," Harry doffed his hat to her and then walked away, heading for his home.

Clara watched him go, mulling over his last words.

Railway workers had access to some very hefty mallets.

Chapter Eleven

Tommy had arrived at O'Harris' house in time for lunch. Victor Darling was already there and had had a full tour around the car collection, followed by being shown around the house. O'Harris' Convalescence Home for Wounded Servicemen was slightly revolutionary in its methods for healing the mental scars of its patients. For a start, they weren't called patients, they were guests and the house could almost be mistaken for a very upper-class hotel. There was no hint of a hospital about it. No bleached floors, or stark rooms. Everything was cosy and homely. That was part of the therapy. These men needed to integrate back into the real world, not be further removed from it by being treated in a ward with white-coated orderlies and nurses.

Each guest had their own room which was well appointed and furnished. They could spend as much or as little time within it as they wanted. The only exception was at mealtimes, when everyone was to come together in the elegant dining room. O'Harris worked on the basis that the men who came to him wanted to be helped and would work with him, they had not been forced there, they were paying to be healed. He didn't think they would opt to spend their time at the home in their bedroom, but he wanted it to be a place of sanctuary for them, so they could retreat to it at any time they needed to.

The men's day was arranged around a schedule of therapy and personal time. This was unique to the individual. Men booked appointments with the doctors at the home, who would sit with them and go through their problems to find solutions. These doctors had been deliberately chosen for their forward-thinking attitudes, and their skills as psychologists. Ideally guests would arrange regular sessions with the doctors, but it was their choice, like everything at the home. Throughout the day there were opportunities to participate in various activities. Work therapy was considered especially helpful, and the men could work in the garden, or learn new skills in the workshops O'Harris had built behind the house. Various lecturers came in over the course of the week to teach everything from carpentry to physics, exercising the men's minds as a way of overcoming their demons.

O'Harris had opened his car collection up as part of the mechanics and engineering courses on offer. The men could tinker with an engine, learn the science behind its functionality, or just how to change the oil. There was also plenty of leisure time for the men to play cricket or tennis on the old courts. Men could just go for a stroll, if they wished, or spend time in the library reading. O'Harris had plans for starting other activities, especially for the winter months when outdoor sports were going to be less of an option. He was hoping to turn the old hangar where he had once housed his aeroplane, The White Buzzard, into a theatre and have the men rehearse and put on plays. It would be a good way of inviting the public into the home and learning more about its function. For O'Harris was not blind to the fact that some of the local population were worried about his establishment. They thought it was full of madmen, lunatics who knew how to fire a gun, and that they were all destined to be murdered in their beds. It was a challenging assumption to overcome.

O'Harris was happy to regale Victor with all this information and his future plans as they walked about.

Victor, in turn, was intrigued and had had his head turned by all the cars in the big garage behind the house. He could hardly imagine what it was like to be able to tinker with them all day, every day. He was still looking a little star-struck when Tommy arrived.

"Hello Tommy, you know Victor?" O'Harris greeted his friend, pretending they had not concocted this plan together, or that he was aware of where Tommy had been that morning.

"Mr Darling," Tommy greeted Victor. "We met on the beach yesterday."

"Oh yes," Victor nodded happily. "Call me Victor, I can't get used to 'Mr Darling'."

"Lunch will be very soon, Tommy. You will be staying?"

"Certainly," Tommy grinned, keeping up the charade that he had just casually dropped by. "I was coming over to see if you had that book you mentioned I could borrow?"

"Ah, of course, the manual on car engines," O'Harris played along with their little ruse. They had arranged it over the telephone that morning. He turned to Victor. "Tommy is keen on cars too. He's learning about the way they work, aren't you old boy?"

"Always interested in broadening my mind," Tommy agreed. "I don't have a car of my own yet, but one day I plan to."

Victor nodded enthusiastically.

"I don't own a car. I want to, but the cost," Victor stopped himself. He had been cautious about revealing information all day, but it was hard to keep on top of yourself when you were bubbling with excitement.

"They are a price," Tommy pretended not to notice Victor's reticence. "They will get cheaper, I believe. What we all need to do is to marry someone wealthy!"

Tommy laughed at his jest, hoping he had not pushed it too far. Victor joined in, apparently not taking offence.

"Except O'Harris, of course," Tommy added. "He inherited his fortune. When it comes to money you have to either make it or marry it, unless you have a rich family."

Tommy grinned at Victor.

"I'm afraid I fail on all counts."

"You don't work?" Victor asked.

"Not since the war. I was badly hurt," Tommy glossed over that part of his history quickly. "I only recently recovered my health and I have to consider my future a bit harder. For a while I didn't think I had one, now I feel things are looking up. But I missed out on going to university and I struggle to think what skills I have that are actually useful in a work environment. It's all a bit depressing, sometimes."

"Tommy sells himself short," O'Harris interrupted. "I believe there are plenty of opportunities out there for him, if he just had the confidence to take them."

Somewhere in the house a gong rang out.

"That is the dinner bell, this way gentlemen," O'Harris ushered them towards the dining room where the other men were gathering.

"What sort of work would you like to do, Tommy?" Victor asked as they walked in.

"I really would like to work with engines, or at least cars in some capacity," Tommy explained. "I know it is not expected of a man of my station to get his hands dirty fixing engines, but why not? And even if that was not possible, I could sell them, maybe?"

Victor was thoughtful as they approached the table and took the two chairs O'Harris indicated for them.

"The car industry is growing rapidly," Victor spoke again once they were seated. "I have a friend, for instance, who works for an engineering firm. He helps to test new engine designs in this great workshop. There are all sorts of tests you have to do on engines to see how efficient they are, how fast, how reliable. Engines are the heart of a car and manufacturers are constantly trying to improve them. It can take years to perfect a new engine, but if you get it right you can make a fortune."

"That sounds interesting," Tommy was genuinely

intrigued. He wondered if Victor's 'friend' was really himself. "But I haven't studied engineering."

"Oh, that's not necessary. You just need a good head for figures and the ability to follow instructions. A lot of it is watching dials or operating a stopwatch," Victor was becoming enthusiastic again. "Timing the firing of pistons, that's an interesting one. Pistons can be a tricky business. If they misfire or don't work at all, that's an engine messed up at once. There is a lot of work going into pistons right now."

Tommy was now certain that Victor was talking about himself. He was too knowledgeable on the subject to be referring to a friend's line of business.

"Where does your friend work?" Tommy asked.

"Red Lion Engineering, in London," Victor answered without hesitation. "The company does not make cars, but conducts research on engines for car manufacturers. If someone has designed a new engine they send it to Red Lion to have it fully tested. Red Lion have facilities for all manner of tests. Equally, if an engine develops a fault and the manufacturer wants to know why, they might send it to Red Lion to be taken apart and examined. Red Lion has a lot of top experts in its employ. They don't just test car engines either, but plane and ship engines. Plus, just recently, they secured a contract with the military to test any future engines they may use in tanks and armoured vehicles."

Victor dropped his voice as he said the last bit. He tapped the side of his nose to indicate he was giving Tommy top-secret information.

"That sounds fascinating," Tommy didn't have to work hard to be interested. "Do you think I could get a job there?"

"It would depend if there was an opening," Victor suddenly became a little cagey.

"You could ask your friend for me?" Tommy suggested.

Victor smiled but did not say anything more. He had become wary and Tommy surmised that he now realised he had said too much. He was probably worrying that if Tommy made enquiries at Red Lion, his name might come up and it would be revealed that he worked there. What was curious was how this engineering assistant, who tested engines for a living, got to know about Nellie Holbein in the first place.

They were distracted by lunch being served. It was a cold plate of ham, cheese, thick bread and salad. There was a good variety of homemade pickles to accompany everything. For a while Tommy and Victor were absorbed in their meals and that gave a sufficient break in the conversation for Tommy to change the subject.

"Was that Miss Nellie Holbein you were with yesterday?" He asked, throwing in the topic carelessly.

Victor concentrated on his food.

"Yes."

"I thought so. Not that I had seen her in many years. In fact, she was just a girl last time," Tommy used his knife to put a blob of pickle on his cheese. "It was sad about her mother."

"Yes, terrible," Victor's conversation had all dried up.

"Having lost her father too when she was young, can't be easy. She has an aunt, though."

"She lives away," Victor mumbled. "But Nellie has mentioned her."

"I'll be honest with you Victor, I always thought Nellie was a little bit spoiled when she was a girl. Didn't always make her the nicest of company. Bit too used to getting her own way," Tommy toyed with a salad leaf. "I hope she treats you all right, old boy!"

"She is fine, really," Victor was keeping his eyes down, his spark had gone. Tommy almost felt bad bringing up the subject.

"I'm surprised she doesn't own a car, actually," Tommy hoped to drag a little something else from Victor. "She has the money for one."

"I don't think she cares for them," Victor said. "Or maybe she is just not interested."

"At least she now has you to keep an eye on her," Tommy remarked lightly. "Rich girls all alone can be terribly vulnerable. Have you been walking out long?"

"No, just a couple of weeks," Victor tossed the comment aside, as if it didn't really matter.

"Be honest now, old boy, is she hard work? She always struck me as the sort."

Victor did smile a little at that.

"She can be strong-willed," he conceded.

"Her mother was too," Tommy said without really knowing if that was true, but he was confident Victor had no clue what Mrs Holbein had been like. "Did you know she was an opera singer? Just for one season, but apparently she was very good."

"I had heard," Victor nodded. "Nellie makes no mention of it, though."

"Really?"

"Yes, never mentions it. Barely mentions her mother at all. I don't think they always got along. Mrs Holbein sounds like she was very protective."

"Mothers can be," Tommy agreed. "Especially when they only have the one child. If Mrs Holbein were still alive, I would say you were a very brave man taking on Nellie."

Victor did laugh at that. He had relaxed somewhat, and no longer seemed so tense about the conversation.

"I say similar things about my own sister, though," Tommy chuckled. "In her case, it is she who is the challenging one. Stubborn, strong-willed, dogmatically independent. Captain O'Harris is taking his life in his hands with her."

"Oh, are they…?"

"Yes," Tommy winked at Victor. "But they haven't figured that out just yet. It's obvious to everyone else, not to them."

Victor was amused.

"Isn't that always the way?"

"Always," Tommy found his gaze wandering to

O'Harris who was at the far end of the table. "I like O'Harris, however, so I hope it works out for him and my sister. I think they would be good for each other."

"And what about you?" Victor asked.

His question was so direct that it startled Tommy for a moment and he actually blushed. His thoughts had jumped back to Annie, but he also had a pang of guilt over his recent encounter with Miss Holbein.

"I have someone, I ought to make my intentions clearer to her."

"Why don't you?" Victor persisted.

"I don't know. Fear, maybe? We are happy as we are, I don't want to destroy that. Marriage is such a big thing."

"It doesn't have to be," Victor continued. "Not if you listen to your heart."

Tommy found it was his turn to pause. He felt confused, a little unsettled by their talk. What did his heart say about Annie? That he knew all too well, what he could not be certain about was whether Annie felt the same. They were great friends, of course, but would she want to marry him? It occurred to Tommy that was why he was reluctant to ask her, in case she said no.

"I didn't mean to offend you," Victor had taken his silence as a sign he was upset.

"You didn't," Tommy assured him. "You made me stop and think, that's all. Not such a bad thing."

Tommy decided that he had had enough of playing detective and just wanted to enjoy his dinner. He glanced up as further plates were brought into the dining room and a smile returned to his lips.

"Look at this! Pudding too," he nudged Victor. "Spotted Dick, you can't say fairer than that."

Chapter Twelve

Clara decided she ought to report what she had learned about John Morley's last hours before he died to Inspector Park-Coombs. Her professional relationship with the inspector was based on mutual trust and reliance on the sharing of information. She would not like to think he would withhold something important from her, and she had to show him the same respect in return.

Park-Coombs looked morose when she was shown into his office. He had the first two fingers of each hand pressing into his temples, while his elbows rested on the top of the desk.

"Clara," he said dully.

"You look unwell," Clara said with concern.

"I have a terrible headache. Would you mind drawing the curtains on that window?"

Clara walked across the room and pulled the dark curtains, blocking out the bright sunlight.

"Thank you," Park-Coombs said quietly.

"Have you taken anything for it?" Clara sat before his desk and opened her bag. "I have aspirin."

"I will be all right, thank you," Park-Coombs drew in a deep breath then sat back in his chair. "I get these terrible headaches when I am stressed, and nothing is more stressful then getting no sleep and then being harassed by the Director of the Natural History Museum for an hour on the telephone."

"Oh," Clara didn't know what else to say.

"You know the Natural History Museum is behind this exhibition and has loaned a number of the fossils, including the bird-lizard one?"

"The Archaeopteryx."

"Honestly, Clara, I've tried getting that mouthful out enough times today already. From now on it is the bird-lizard or the lizard-bird, depending on my mood," Park-Coombs closed his eyes for a moment and sighed. "Anyway, the Director of the museum is irate that someone nearly destroyed a precious artefact and is threatening to have it removed from the exhibition, which of course is creating a backlash from Dr Browning and the other sponsors of the tour. So, I get it in the neck from the Director for not providing adequate security for the exhibition. No matter that it is not my responsibility to provide guards for his display of stones. If he wants security, he can pay for it. But, no, I get an ear-lashing first from him and then from my Chief Inspector, who the Director called after talking to me. Right at this moment in time, Clara, I hate that bird-lizard."

"Understandable, Inspector," Clara said sympathetically. "I'm sorry to hear that. I don't know if this helps at all, but I have spoken to some of John Morley's friends and it appears he was hired by a man who met him at the Hole in the Wall last night. Depending on who gives the description the man was well-dressed, with a thin moustache and an accent that has been described as Irish, Scottish or South African."

"Well that narrows it down," Park-Coombs managed to laugh.

"There is some good news," Clara added, smiling herself. "According to John's friends, this man is to return tonight to pay him the rest of the money for the job. It is possible that he does not know John is dead. If that is the case, he should appear, and we can nab him."

"Nab him?" Park-Coombs raised an eyebrow. "You are spending too much time here. But that does sound promising. At least we could find out who hired him, though it doesn't tell us who killed John Morley. Unless we suppose the chap who hired him was involved in his death."

"In which case, he will not come to the pub tonight, he will have no need to."

"True. Let's hope he wasn't involved and that he has not heard about the murder. We have been keeping it quiet."

"As far as this fellow knows, the police presence at the town hall could be because John Morley was successful in his destruction of the Archaeopteryx," Clara pointed out.

"Let's hope that is what he is thinking. I don't have much else to go on. You know, if it did not seem so improbable, I would have to assume Dr Browning killed him."

"Except for the missing murder weapon," Clara said.

"Exactly," Park-Coombs nodded his head and then regretted it. He cupped his forehead in his hands and groaned.

"You need some of Annie's finest Madeira cake," Clara felt sorry for him.

"Does that cure headaches?" Park-Coombs mumbled.

"According to Annie, as long as she soaks it thoroughly in sherry first. I suspect it is more a case that you just don't care about the headache so much after eating it."

"I'll bear that in mind," Park-Coombs had not raised his head. "Unfortunately, I am not allowed alcohol while on duty."

"I've disturbed you too long," Clara started for the door.

"Wait a minute," Park-Coombs stopped her, cautiously tilting his head in her direction. "Are we going to this pub tonight together?"

"It would seem a good idea," Clara smiled. "You may need to arrest this man for conspiring to destroy a valuable national treasure."

"What time?" Park-Coombs asked wearily.

"I suggest we get there just before nine, the time the man is probably going to arrive," Clara winked at him. "And then you can have that drink."

She departed the inspector's office and headed for home.

~~~*~~~

Tommy was a little stuffed after his meal with Victor. He took his time walking home, enjoying the fact that he could walk these days. He entered the front door and was greeted by the ever-jubilant Bramble, a small black poodle with springs in his heels.

"Hello boy," Tommy rubbed the dog's head.

He had just managed to negotiate himself around the prancing dog when Annie appeared from the kitchen. He looked up and smiled, before coming to a halt. He had never seen Annie looking so angry.

"A message came for you," she said, and her tone was like ice. "It's on the table."

Tommy noticed that there was a slip of paper on the half-oval table that stood in the hall near the coat rack. Tommy picked it up and saw at once that it was from Nellie Holbein;

"My Darling Tommy, do not neglect to come to me tomorrow. I shall prepare lunch. Victor is a thing of the past, you are the future! My everlasting love, Nellie xx."

Tommy cringed as he read it. No wonder Annie was fuming.

"It's part of the case, Annie," Tommy turned back to her, but Annie had stormed off to the kitchen.

Tommy took a deep breath and followed.

"Annie, this is all to do with Clara's latest case," Tommy said as he found her peeling potatoes.

"Really?" Annie glared at him. "This Nellie person seems to think you are her future!"

"I have not said that to her, I only met her yesterday!"

Tommy threw the paper down on the kitchen table. "She is a wealthy heiress and Mrs Wilton believes she is being pursued for her money by a man named Victor Darling. Mrs Wilton wants Clara to find out who Victor is. We lured Victor over to Captain O'Harris' home today, so that I could speak to Miss Holbein and discover what her intentions were with Victor. Somehow the girl got it into her head that I was attracted to her."

"You must have given her reason," Annie sniffed, a hint of emotion coming into her demeanour.

"I gave her nothing Annie, she is really quite frightening," Tommy shook his head. "She has it in her head that I am going back to her house tomorrow, which of course I am not. I barely got out with my life earlier today. Victor Darling is very welcome to her!"

Annie did not look convinced. She peeled a potato and threw it so hard into the pan of water that droplets splashed onto the table.

"Since when did you begin seducing women to assist on Clara's cases?" She demanded.

"Since she asked me if I would like to work with her," Tommy insisted. "Look, Annie, have I ever given you reason to doubt me?"

"No," Annie admitted, mellowing a fraction.

"Then trust me now. Anyway, I'm not going anywhere near Miss Holbein again. She scares the living daylights out of me. And not in a good way like you do," Tommy moved forward and squeezed Annie's shoulder. "The only future I want is one with you. You know that, old girl."

"Do I?" Annie asked petulantly.

"Of course you do," Tommy kissed the top of her head. "You're the only one who would put up with an old crock like me. I'm not letting you go."

A slow smile crept onto Annie's lips.

"Ok Tommy, you are forgiven."

"Thank goodness," Tommy put his arms around her and hugged her. "Because Clara would kill me if I upset you."

Annie elbowed him playfully.

"Go away, I have potatoes to peel."

~~~*~~~

Inspector Park-Coombs arrived at Clara's door just after eight o'clock. He still looked tired and bleary-eyed from his headache.

"Feeling any better?" Clara asked him.

"I managed to take a nap after my supper, which helped a little," Park-Coombs shrugged. "I could do with this case being over, however. I have a hunch I shall be forced to put in a lot of extra hours by my superiors. All over a bloody stone."

"Language, Inspector," Annie said lightly, coming to the door with a slice of cake on a plate.

"Annie's headache cure," Clara explained.

"Madeira cake soaked in sherry and a couple of aspirin," Annie winked.

"Well, I am now off duty," the inspector took the plate and began to eat while Clara fetched her coat.

"I hope this gentleman turns up," Clara said over her shoulder as she prepared. "Otherwise it is going to be a long job getting to the bottom of all this."

Inspector Park-Coombs said nothing, he was munching appreciatively on Annie's cake.

"Still, there is always some way to solve a puzzle," Clara appeared back at the door dressed in her coat and hat. "Ready Inspector?"

Park-Coombs handed the now empty plate back to Annie.

"I feel fully restored Annie, thank you," he told her.

Annie looked pleased with herself. She was always satisfied when someone appreciated her cooking.

"Inspector?"

"Ready, Clara," the inspector returned his hat to his head. "Now, for the purposes of this evening, you best call me Arthur. You call me 'Inspector' in that pub and everyone is going to run a mile."

Clara laughed.

"All right Arthur," she tested out the name. "What would your wife say?"

"Oh, she is fully aware of what I am up to!" Park-Coombs chuckled. "I told her, I am going out to the pub with young Clara. She said 'fine, as long as you remember to take your key'."

Clara shook her head, amused. They walked off into the night. Inspector Park-Coombs offered Clara his arm.

"Well, Inspector!" Clara said in surprise.

"Arthur," he reminded her. "But if you are too independently minded to accept a gentleman's offer…"

Clara smirked and slipped her arm through his.

"What must we look like!" She said aloud.

"I hope, when we get to the pub, we look ordinary and not like a police inspector and a private detective."

"Good point," Clara agreed.

They arrived at the Hole in the Wall just before nine. It was busier than it had been in the afternoon, the tables packed with the sort of people you might watch carefully around your wallet. Clara and Park-Coombs entered and found a space at the end of the bar. From there it was possible to look across the room and spot anyone entering. Park-Coombs ordered them drinks from the landlord, who glanced at Clara with a look of suspicion. She assumed he recognised her from earlier and hoped it would not cause a problem.

"Those three men playing draughts at that corner table were John's friends," Clara whispered in the inspector's ear.

He looked over discreetly and then nodded to Clara.

"Noted," he said. "Any chance they knew more than they were telling you?"

"Who can say? They seemed shocked John was dead, at least."

The pub was growing busier. Men were pushing in through the door and trying to find a space to stand, there was certainly no place to sit. Clara and Park-Coombs relinquished their spot at the bar and retreated to a corner near the window, where they could watch the front door unobtrusively. Clara was uncomfortably aware of how close she was standing to a table of drinkers, the men casting lecherous glances in her direction from time to time. She hoped their suspect arrived soon.

Abruptly, a commotion broke out at the far side of the room. Someone swung a punch at someone else, though it was not plain what sparked the fight. There was a brief scuffle and several people surged to the scene, some to cheer, some to break it up. By the time it was over, and the culprits were being thrown out the door, a new man had arrived at the pub. Clara had been distracted by the fight and had taken her eyes from the door. The new arrival had slipped in unseen. He paused for a second just inside, looking around the room for someone. When he failed to see them, he started to turn away. It was at that moment that Clara spotted him.

The man was wearing a nice suit and light summer overcoat. He had a bowler on his head that had been recently brushed and was certainly not an old cast-off as so many of the drinkers in the pub were wearing. As he looked around him, his thin, pencil moustache was noticeable on his otherwise clean-shaven face. Clara also noticed the glint of a gold pin on his lapel.

She nudged Park-Coombs.

"That's him!"

Park-Coombs glanced up. The man was leaving again, pushing past men who were then entering.

"Come on!" Clara hissed and she started to thread her way through the crowd.

It seemed to take forever to extract themselves from the pub, and the man was already outside and walking up the road as they exited. Clara pointed him out and she and the inspector hurried behind him.

"Excuse me!" Clara called out.

The gentleman turned around. He looked surprised at

being accosted by a smartly dressed woman. He frowned.

"May I help?" His words were spoken with an obvious accent. Clara was not certain if it was South African, but it was definitely not Scottish or Irish.

"I think it is more a case of us helping you," Clara stopped before him. "You are looking for John Morley?"

The man hesitated and glanced between the pair.

"What is this?" He said.

"We hoped we could talk with you." Clara explained. "It's about John."

The man frowned.

"Where is he?"

"Well, that's where the problem lies," Clara held the man's gaze. "John Morley is dead."

Chapter Thirteen

The man was clearly surprised by this news and for a moment looked as though he was going to bolt. Maybe it was because he wanted to know what had happened to Morley, or maybe it was Park-Coombs' presence, but he held his ground and finally agreed to talk with them. There was nowhere really to go, except back to the pub, and none of them fancied that. What they had to discuss was private and not to be shouted about over the din of a public house. They settled on going to a nearby park which was still open at that hour. Clara was playing her cards close to her chest. She wanted information, and she didn't want to put the man off from talking by intimating that she knew he had paid John Morley to commit a crime. Park-Coombs was also being very restrained, letting Clara do the talking while he just listened.

They acted as if they were concerned friends of John Morley, though whether the man bought this pretence was debatable. They didn't look like the sort of people John Morley would be friends with. However, the man was curious and that prevented him from thinking too hard about who Clara and Park-Coombs really were.

"What happened to John?" The man asked after they had walked into the park.

They were stood on the bank of the duck pond, the

ducks splashing about nearby and looking hopeful for bread.

"We are not entirely sure, but it appears someone attacked him." Clara explained. "It happened last night while he was at the town hall."

The man stopped and stared out across the water of the pond. His silence made Clara wonder if she had said too much. She was just going to say something more when she caught a glimpse of the pin on his lapel. She stared at it in surprise.

"A gold Archaeopteryx!" She declared.

The man suddenly looked at her and then touched the pin.

"But…" Clara frowned. "I thought you paid John to destroy the fossil?"

"Destroy it? No! Nothing could be further from my mind!" The man looked appalled at the suggestion.

"Then why did you pay John Morley to go to the town hall with a hammer?" Clara asked him.

"You don't understand," the man shook his head. "I belong to the Golden Archaeopteryx Society. We are devoted to the study of these unique specimens and ensuring they obtain their proper place in science. We believe that the Archaeopteryx is not a dinosaur turning into a bird. It is already a bird, an ancestor of modern birds. The Archaeopteryx developed separately from the dinosaurs, possibly, at some point, they shared a common ancestor, but after that they split apart. To state that the Archaeopteryx is a dinosaur is to diminish its obvious importance as a primitive bird. We have experts who can prove that these fossils are birds with lizard-like features, but not lizards becoming birds."

Park-Coombs scratched his head.

"That sounds pretty much the same to me."

"It's not!" The man said, a little fiercer. "If we believe dinosaurs became birds, then we are suggesting that birds did not have their own unique evolutionary path. We are effectively saying birds are dinosaurs. My Society disagrees with that. Birds developed on their own, they did not start out as dinosaurs."

"Whatever your interpretation of the fossil, that does not explain why you hired John Morley to go to the town hall last night and break in," Clara interjected.

The man became uneasy, he took a pace away from them.

"That was due to stupidity on my part," he said. "The Society was not party to my plan."

"What was your plan?" Park-Coombs discreetly moved around the man, blocking his escape.

"Look, this fossil is precious, we all agree with that. And to have it carted about the country is pure recklessness. Anything could happen. We don't want that," the man clasped his hands together. "The society wrote letters protesting, saying the fossil is too valuable to science to risk it being damaged or stolen. No one would listen. I grew frustrated. When I saw the fossil was coming to Brighton, the place I lived, I made a decision. I would do something that would force the Natural History Museum to remove the Archaeopteryx from display.

"I paid John Morley to break in and smash the case. To make it look as if someone was going to damage or steal the fossil. I knew Dr Browning was sleeping in the town hall and would wake up at once. John was to escape the old man, leaving him worried that someone had attacked the Archaeopteryx. I hoped that would be enough to get the Natural History Museum to insist it came back to them."

"Well, you have nearly achieved that," Park-Coombs said grimly. "The future of this exhibition is now questionable."

"I had to do something to wake people up," the man insisted. "There had been threats against the exhibition and you saw those protestors, utterly insane the lot of them. You just don't know what such people will do. I only wanted to make it plain how vulnerable the fossil was. No one was supposed to get hurt."

Clara frowned.

"Who are you, anyway?" She asked him.

"Sam Gutenberg," the man answered her. "My parents were South African. I still run the family mines over there. I had the money to pay John Morley handsomely. I understood he was taking a big risk. He could have been arrested."

"Instead he was killed," Clara sighed. "Did you hire anyone else to go with him?"

"No, just John," Sam assured them.

"How did you meet him?"

Sam Gutenberg shrugged his shoulders.

"I had been asking around for a while. For a man willing to do a job that was slightly illegal. Someone pointed out John to me. We first met down on the pier. I explained what I was after and he said he would think about it. We agreed to meet at the pub the following night. I would bring half the money I intended to pay John for the work with me," Sam patted his pocket. "I promised he would have the rest after the work was done. That's why I came tonight. I saw the police at the town hall. I thought John had been successful."

"So, there were a few people who knew you had hired John to do this?" Park-Coombs asked.

"I guess," Sam looked downcast. "No one was meant to get hurt. I specifically told John that Dr Browning was not to be harmed. I never thought John would be the one to end up…"

He froze, contemplating what he had said.

"Are you going to tell the police?" He asked.

Clara glanced at Park-Coombs. He said nothing.

"My role is to discover who was making threats against the exhibition," Clara told him. "Dr Browning has hired me to investigate the matter."

"That's easy, look to those protestors outside the town hall!" Sam snorted. "They belong to a group called The League for Christians Against Evolution. They refuse to believe in evolution. To them it is the work of the Devil to even speak of it."

"You've met them?" Clara asked.

"Bumped into them once or twice," Sam concurred. "They have members all across the country and everywhere the exhibition goes they have organised protests. Their leader has been following the Archaeopteryx and has caused trouble at each stop of the tour. His name is Reverend Parker. He has Austrian ancestry, which makes him doubly suspicious to me."

Sam Gutenberg touched his pin again.

"The Archaeopteryx is not safe with that man around and I intend to protect it. I am very sorry about John Morley. I really don't know what happened to him."

"I think you best give us your address, Mr Gutenberg," Inspector Park-Coombs said sternly. "We may need to speak with you again. Your intentions might have been noble, but you conspired to commit a crime and now a man is dead."

"I didn't kill John!" Sam looked stunned at the suggestion.

"No, I don't think you did," Park-Coombs admitted. "But I will need to keep track of you. We may have further questions."

Sam looked miserable, then he told them his address.

"I was only trying to save the Archaeopteryx," he insisted. "I wanted people to see the danger. That was not wrong, was it?"

Park-Coombs did not offer him a reply, but he did move out of the way so Sam could leave. Mr Gutenberg looked very relieved to get away from them.

"If I am not completely baffled," Park-Coombs groaned as soon as Sam was out of the way. "Now there are people who think this bird-lizard is a dinosaur growing feathers, and others who think it is a bird with lizard-like features and then there is this Anti-Darwin lot who say it is... what? A hoax?"

"It is certainly complicated," Clara agreed with him. "I wish I could say I understood it all myself. Honestly, as soon as I think I know and comprehend all the various arguments surrounding the Archaeopteryx, something new crops up that throws me again."

Park-Coombs glanced up as the park keeper wandered around the edge of the pond, ushering the last of the visitors out before he locked the gates.

"What remains a mystery is whether there was a third person in the town hall that night John Morley was killed," Clara said as she walked with the inspector out of the park. "There is no evidence for them."

"Yet, no real evidence Dr Browning committed the crime," Park-Coombs concurred. "Though, if things carry on this way, I am afraid I will have to arrest him. He was the only other person we know to have been there when Morley died. He would have had motive, considering he was protective of the bird-lizard and he was not to know that Morley was only pretending to try to damage it."

"Surely no jury would convict a man on so little?" Clara countered.

"You tell me Clara. Two men are in a room together. One dies by means that were not natural and could not have been self-inflicted, what is the obvious assumption?"

"Yes, but as you say, it is an assumption," Clara held her finger up as she made her point. "It would be a terrible thing to hang a man on so little. There is no murder weapon, and Dr Browning summoned the police."

"A good prosecutor would argue he threw away the weapon as he went to find a policeman. That he acted panicked and scared to cast suspicion from him. We come back to that same point; there is no evidence of a third man."

Clara sighed. She could not deny anything the inspector had said. To a jury who had not been on the scene and seen Dr Browning's obvious confusion and shock, it would seem entirely plausible that he had killed Morley. In fact, it would seem preposterous that someone else was there and had vanished before Dr Browning saw them.

"I don't like the way this is all going," Clara admitted.

"I have this nasty feeling that an innocent man is going to take the blame for a very serious crime."

"It would not be the first time," Inspector Park-Coombs said darkly. "Look, I don't want to arrest Dr Browning. I agree with you, he does not strike me as the killer, but if I can find no alternative, I shall be forced to. My superiors don't much like hunches, especially in murder cases. They want a suspect arrested sooner rather than later. Not to mention the pressure we are being put under from the authorities at the Natural History Museum, and some of the other sponsors of his exhibition. I believe there is an earl among them, and he is itching for a conclusion to this drama."

Park-Coombs groaned to himself, looking miserable.

"You know, if I don't have the killer under arrest by the time this exhibition closes, I shall have to insist everyone involved remains in Brighton. I can't have the murderer waltzing off to another part of the country, and that means the exhibition will have to stay here. I don't like to think about the reaction to that."

Clara felt very sorry for Park-Coombs. He was in a difficult position.

"I shall do everything in my power to help, Inspector," she promised. "I think it is time we expanded the scope of our search. Supposing this is not about the exhibition at all, but about John Morley? Maybe someone took an opportunity to kill him."

"Inside the town hall, while he was sneaking about?" Park-Coombs looked unconvinced.

"We have to try, and we need to look at the town hall again," Clara suddenly paused and glanced at her wristwatch. "It is approaching ten o'clock, about the time John Morley broke into the town hall."

"And?" Park-Coombs looked puzzled.

"Why don't we follow his route? Recreate the crime as it would have happened? That might give us an insight into how the murder was committed," Clara explained. "It may even clarify that it was impossible for anyone else to have murdered Morley, then we shall know we have to look to Dr Browning, as remarkable as that may seem."

"Very well," Park-Coombs uncertainty had evaporated, he stood up a little taller. "I'm game if you are."

Clara turned and started to head in the direction of the town hall. Abruptly she came to a halt, so the inspector nearly stumbled into her.

"We can't be arrested for this, can we?" She asked him.

"Who would do the arresting? I am the senior police officer in Brighton," Park-Coombs snorted. "Anyway, the town hall is part of an ongoing investigation and I can enter it at any time I wish to look around. I have been given my own key."

Clara relaxed.

"Yes, of course," she smiled. "I just wondered for a moment."

"And since when have you been concerned about breaking and entering into somewhere while trying to solve a case?" Park-Coombs remarked.

"Since I am breaking and entering with the police inspector watching," Clara laughed in response.

"That's all right," Park-Coombs said with a glint in his eye. "I'll just keep my eyes shut, then I can't see you breaking the law."

"Really, Inspector!" Clara said in mock indignation.

Chapter Fourteen

The town hall was dark, not a single light glowing behind the windows. It looked shut up and empty. Anyone passing would not be aware that a worried academic was sleeping inside, one uneasy eye on his most prized exhibit.

Clara and Park-Coombs approached from the front. The town hall was flush with the road and on one side it abutted a large building that consisted of offices for various businesses, including a dentist and an accounting firm. The building was also unlit and apparently empty.

On the other side of the hall there was a narrow alley that led to a yard at the back. There was no gate and it was a simple matter to slip down the side of the building. At the rear of the town hall there was another set of doors, smaller than those at the front. The yard was fenced, with large gates locked with a chain leading onto the road at the back. Clearly the intention was to prevent vehicles being driven into the yard without permission rather than people, since the alleyway provided easy access on foot. When events occurred at the town hall, any deliveries would come to this yard and be unloaded here.

"It was that window Morley broke," Inspector Park-Coombs pointed to a small window close to the corner of the building. It had been boarded over where the pane had been smashed. "Unfortunately, the ground beneath the window is covered in concrete. No trace of a footprint or something useful like that."

Clara took a look at the broken window.

"Where does this lead?"

"Into a cloakroom," Park-Coombs explained. "It is used to hang up coats and store cleaning materials. I think there is a sink in there too. Nothing exciting."

Clara turned her back to the window and looked around the yard.

"What are you up to?" The inspector asked curiously.

"Wondering about witnesses," Clara replied. "No one from the road could see what was happening, the fence is too high. They might have heard a noise, if they were passing."

Clara was scanning the buildings behind the town hall. Most of them looked empty like the offices to her left. They were shops or business premises that at this time of night were deserted. As she looked to her right, she was suddenly distracted by a light flickering on in a top storey window.

"Look at that building, Inspector," Clara pointed it out to him. "Someone is in that top floor."

The building had three storeys and the top had a miniature bay window, where the light now glowed. Clara thought she saw someone moving about in the room.

"What are the odds they were looking out of their window at the right moment?" Park-Coombs said pessimistically.

"Greater than you may think, Inspector. There is something in that window, like a chair. I can't properly make it out, but let's hope the person in question sits at that window a lot."

"Hmm," Park-Coombs was sceptical. "Shall we go inside now?"

He pulled a key from his pocket and unlocked the back door. Clara placed a hand on his wrist before they went in.

"Let us be quiet and see how alert Dr Browning really is," she whispered.

The inspector nodded.

They went in and Park-Coombs silently motioned to the cloakroom where Morley had entered. Clara crept to the door and peered inside. The smashed glass from the broken window had been cleared up and, apart from the board across the missing pane, there was no obvious sign that anything had happened. Clara stepped back out and pushed the door closed. She noted it moved perfectly on its hinges, not a single creak or squeak that might have otherwise given them away.

The cloakroom led onto a back hallway with the rear doors at one end. In the other direction the hallway led off on the left to various small rooms related to the functional side of the town hall – offices, a kitchen, a larger storage room for chairs and tables. On the right was a set of double-doors which led into the main room, the heart of the hall. This took up the majority of the right side of the hall, with a smaller foyer at the front. Clara walked to the double doors and noted that they did not have a lock, no one had ever considered it necessary to secure them. It was simple to depress the handle slowly and push open the door. The hinges here were well-maintained too. The caretaker at the hall was obviously a very thorough man, which was rather unfortunate in some regards.

The main room had no curtains over the tall windows, therefore moonlight streamed in and provided enough illumination to enable Clara and Park-Coombs to see where they were going. They slipped past the glass cases and found themselves before the Archaeopteryx within moments. Clara stood in the spot she thought Morley must have been before he died. She could see the camp bed Dr Browning was using against the wall behind the display case. She could also hear him snoring.

Clara nudged Park-Coombs and nodded in the direction of the sleeping academic. For a while they stood observing him, then the inspector gave a quiet cough. Dr Browning did not even stop snoring. Park-Coombs coughed louder. There was still no reaction from the sleeping man. Clara tapped lightly on the case of the Archaeopteryx, then she stamped her feet a little. Dr Browning mumbled in his sleep, but did not rouse. Clara shrugged at the inspector and he motioned that they should leave. They slipped back out into the hallway without Dr Browning rousing.

Outside again Clara paused to consider what they had learned.

"You know, it seems to be that if John Morley slipped in here with just a modicum of caution, Dr Browning would not have heard him."

"The man sleeps deep enough," Park-Coombs nodded. "You know, I once had a fellow who slept through a murder. He was a little deaf and once he was out for the count, that was it. He was in this railway carriage, when two of his fellow passengers went for each other and one ended up stabbed. The other fled. The sleeping man never knew a thing about it until he woke up and saw the mess. Lucky for him we caught up with the murderer, because he looked like the killer for a while."

"Just like Dr Browning," Clara noted. "It strikes me, Inspector, that we can't be sure how long John Morley had been dead before Dr Browning realised. Morley was struck from behind and probably made little in the way of noise. If the killer caught him as he fell, then he would have made hardly a sound. All that being so, it must have been some other noise that roused Browning and in his startled state he spotted John Morley's body and assumed it was the killing of that man that had alerted him."

"Another noise?" Park-Coombs considered. "Like someone leaving in a hurry and being careless? There were metal buckets in that cloakroom, a man could trip over those in error and it would make a lot of noise."

"Exactly," Clara was growing excited. "All of which would mean Dr Browning would never see the man, never even realise where he had gone. How many of us wake from a deep sleep completely alert? It takes us all a moment to come fully to our senses. Dr Browning would have seen the body, panicked and easily missed any sounds of a person quietly slipping away in his confusion."

"It is all very plausible," Park-Coombs agreed. "I wish we could find that murder weapon. It would help a lot."

Clara was taking an interest in a row of large packing crates that had been neatly stacked at the side of the yard. They were obviously the containers for the fossils. They had been stood to one side, ready to be repacked when the exhibition moved on. Clara walked over and lifted the lid of one. It was filled with wood shavings. Another was the same, but a third had been used to stash tools. Clara noted there was a crowbar, several hammers and a hefty mallet. Carefully she pulled it from the crate.

"It looks clean," she said to the inspector as he walked up behind her.

"Always possible someone wiped it down before they left. Equally possible the murderer took the mallet he used to kill John with him," Park-Coombs leaned into the packing crate and examined the contents. "Now, that's odd."

"What is?" Clara asked.

"The mallet you pulled out is a metal one, but I was here when the exhibition arrived and was being unloaded into the town hall. I was asked to keep an eye on things, to make sure no one stole or damaged anything while everyone was busy. I could have sworn I saw a mallet with a rubber cover among the tools being used."

Clara glanced over the mallet she had lifted from the crate.

"There are different types of mallet?" She asked.

"Oh lots. You can have wooden mallets, solid metal ones, like the one you are holding, and then metal ones with a rubber cover. They are heavy enough to work, but the rubber means they don't cause so much damage to a pin or nail head as the uncovered metal ones," Park-Coombs explained. "The rubber covered one was obvious because the rubber was black. This metal one is grey."

"A rubber-coated metal mallet would certainly cause a compressive injury to the skull, but I am guessing it would leave the wound with softer edges than a solid metal one," Clara hefted the mallet in her hand, assessing its weight. "This one has obvious edges which would dig into the skull. Do you think Dr Deáth could tell us if the wound was made with a rubber-coated mallet?"

"Maybe," Park-Coombs didn't look sure. "What is really bothering me is whether I saw that rubber-covered mallet or whether I am imagining it. If I did see it, and now it is missing, then we may have our murder weapon."

"Best we check the other crates," Clara suggested.

They went through the other crates. Clara found one that contained a bucket of long nails and two more crowbars, but there was no sign of a rubber-coated mallet. Park-Coombs was still not convinced he had seen the mallet, or whether he was imagining it, but he felt it was something he needed to explore.

"Lots of mallets in Brighton," he muttered under his breath.

"Supposing a mallet was taken from this crate," Clara said. "That would imply the killer knew they were here. Someone from the exhibition for instance?"

"Maybe I need to find out if that hammer John Morley was carrying came from this crate, or whether he brought it from home as we first surmised," Park-Coombs scratched at his head.

"Either way, it is starting to look likely that someone deliberately followed Morley to kill him. It was not a chance thing. They picked up a weapon with the intention of killing him."

"No, Clara," Park-Coombs shook his head. "They still might have been carrying these tools for the purpose of breaking the glass cases. Maybe Morley decided he needed an accomplice? Maybe he wasn't brave enough to do it alone. Both men would have picked up tools suitable for smashing the cases, once inside the town hall something happened that caused the second man to strike out at Morley."

"Like what, Inspector?" Clara argued. "Are we

supposing the two men had a falling out inside without making a note of noise to disturb Dr Browning? Something sparked a man to lash out and kill John Morley. You don't hit a man with a mallet without intending to cause serious harm. I think it far more likely whoever else was in that room went with the intention of killing Morley."

Park-Coombs made a noise under his breath, but he didn't disagree.

"That still leaves us with the big question of, who?" He grumbled.

"We need to know more about Morley's associates and if he had any enemies. Quite frankly, I expect he had a few. I have seen his house, and someone battered down his door recently and broke a window."

"Then people were angry with him," Park-Coombs said. "And angry people sometimes kill."

"We mustn't rule out other possibilities, but that seems the likeliest option at the moment," Clara returned the mallet she was holding to the crate. "Unfortunately, I can think of one man who would want him dead almost at once."

"Unfortunately?" Park-Coombs asked, confused.

"The man is John Morley's brother-in-law, and a very nice fellow indeed. John Morley was cruel to his wife and that is easily reason enough for her brother to detest him. He has not been shy about stating he is glad Morley is dead."

"Then he might have followed him and killed him?" Park-Coombs mused. "Maybe John even asked for his help?"

"That's unlikely, besides, he works nights at the railway station. He would have been unable to get here," Clara was not sure why she had mentioned Harry Beasley at all. She just felt this niggle about him, and she could not hide it from Park-Coombs. It would be wrong to avoid mentioning Harry's name just because she liked the man and did not want him to be the killer. After all, she was not actually tasked with solving the murder of John Morley.

That was the inspector's job.

"At the railway station?" Park-Coombs' mind was making a similar leap to the one Clara's had. "Is he an engineer?"

"I'm not sure," Clara admitted.

"Lots of mallets around railways. You need them to hammer down those huge pins that keep the sleepers and rails in place. And for repair work on the trains," Park-Coombs' eyes were glistening. "Would be worth searching the place, just in case."

"Inspector, I feel awful now, I don't think Harry Beasley is a killer," Clara insisted. "I should not have mentioned it. I just don't like to hide things from you."

"I would have followed up on him anyway," the inspector reassured her. "You always look to family first when it comes to murder."

"Well, I really hope it was not him," Clara added. "I like him."

"I won't let your name enter the equation," Park-Coombs promised. "Now, I don't know about you, but I would like to get home to my bed."

Clara glanced one last time at the town hall, then she concurred. They walked down the alleyway, Clara noting as they left that the light still burned in the top window of the house behind.

"I'll follow that up too," Park-Coombs spotted her interest. "At least you have solved your case for Dr Browning. You know who hired John Morley and why."

"I don't feel like I have solved anything," Clara said grimly. "If anything, I feel as if I have more questions than ever before."

Chapter Fifteen

The next day Tommy beat a retreat to Captain O'Harris' home, hoping for sympathy for his plight. When he had told Clara about his problem with Miss Holbein, she had laughed so hard she couldn't speak for a minute or two. He felt her response lacked understanding. Annie was still giving him cold glances on occasion, though Clara had stepped in to defend him, at least. She had promised Annie it was all her fault for sending her assistant out to try and get information from Miss Holbein. Tommy was not sure if he should be grateful for her defence, or feel slightly insulted.

Tommy felt the only person who would really understand the inexplicable situation he found himself in was another man – thus he sought out O'Harris.

"Old boy, what a pickle!" Captain O'Harris remarked after he had finished laughing at Tommy's story.

"I thought you might be a bit more compassionate on the matter," Tommy grumbled.

"Oh, you have my compassion, don't fear," O'Harris wiped a tear from the corner of his eye. "I just can't help picturing you being fawned over by that alarmingly unpleasant woman, and your abject horror at the situation.

Then I picture you fleeing her house and I start to laugh."

"Thanks," Tommy huffed.

"What does Clara say?"

"What do you think?"

O'Harris smirked, he knew Clara well enough to know how she would have reacted.

"All right, so it's a bit of a muddle, but all you have to do is avoid the woman and everything will calm down," he said.

Tommy shook his head.

"I have this terrible feeling it won't be that simple. Miss Holbein is used to getting what she wants. Why do you think I fled here today? I feared she might actually turn up at the house and drag me from it, she has clearly discovered the address. Annie has promised to tell her I don't live there if that happens to be the case," Tommy raised his eyebrows. "I was hoping for a little sympathy too."

"And you have it," O'Harris swore. "I'll do better than sympathy even, I'll help you solve this puzzle."

"Solve it?" Tommy looked confused. "I thought I was just going to avoid Miss Holbein?"

"Well, if you are right and she is utterly determined to make you her lover, then we need to put the stoppers on her passion at once."

"How?" Tommy looked miserable. "I thought about making myself utterly repugnant to her, but she seems to like the way I repulse her."

"The complexity of the female condition, old man. They want what they can't have. Dare say we are all a bit like that, but Miss Holbein is an extreme version. What we have to do is convince her she doesn't want you, because she wants someone else more."

"Now I am baffled," Tommy slumped his shoulders, feeling a little hopeless. "You are suggesting we need to find another man for Miss Holbein?"

"There is already one available. Victor Darling."

"She says she is bored with him," Tommy said.

"She is bored with the old Victor," O'Harris clarified.

"What we need to do is convince her that Victor is something more than he appears."

"If you ask me, Victor looks keen to abandon his quest to be a kept husband and go back to tinkering with cars, and I can't blame him. Surely we are casting him into the lion's den?"

"We aren't making him marry her, just distract her until her infatuation with you wears off, and it will wear off," O'Harris grinned. "She is that sort. Always looking for the next thing, something different and novel. I doubt she'll marry Victor either. She'll get bored and he will have a lucky escape. But for the time being you and Victor have mutually compatible goals – you want to be rid of Miss Holbein and he wants her to like him."

Tommy thought about this for a while.

"Do you think Victor will play along?"

"I think if we make it plain this will keep him in Miss Holbein's favour, he will."

Tommy scrunched up his face.

"Isn't it a little deceitful? Aren't we being unfair to Miss Holbein?"

"She is toying with you both," O'Harris said bluntly. "She is surprisingly cynical for a young woman. She knows what Victor is and what he wants, which is why she is so cruel to him. She wants to see how far she can push him. It's a power game and don't think she is not enjoying every minute of it, for the second she is bored, Victor will be an outcast. Then there is you, she can't buy you with her money, which makes you incredibly enticing, yet she refuses to believe you wish to have nothing to do with her. She will do all she can to claim you, have no fear of that. I think she is callous and dangerous, that one. You don't need to feel bad for escaping her clutches."

Tommy took a deep breath. He felt a little better talking with O'Harris and having his problem analysed from a neutral perspective.

"Do we need Victor in on this?" He said.

"He has got to know the details, I think, if we want his

help," O'Harris glanced at his watch. "He said he was going to stop by Miss Holbein's in the morning and see if she wanted a day out. By now he has probably already been rejected. Miss Holbein will be confidently assuming you will respond to her summons."

Tommy cringed.

"I'll have a message sent to Victor and ask him to come over. Then we can plot together," O'Harris slapped Tommy on the back. "Just one day working for Clara and you are already in trouble. She'll never let you hear the end of this."

"Thanks very much," Tommy said without humour.

~~~*~~~

Clara decided she needed to investigate the The League for Christians Against Evolution. She had kept the leaflet she had been handed the other day by the protestors outside the town hall and after scouring its text, she had found that it was printed for the league and even sported the local address for the organisation. There was a short paragraph about supporting the campaign with financial donations and where they could be sent to, along with the location of the league's weekly meetings. Clara noted that they met every Wednesday and today was Wednesday, which meant she could invade a meeting and discover if there was any connection between the protestors and the demise of John Morley. She doubted it, somehow, she couldn't see why an Anti-Darwin protestor would attack the man, but you never knew. Besides, she was not trying to solve the murder, she was supposed to be investigating who was behind the threats on the exhibition for Dr Browning, and that had to be the league.

Only, Clara had to admit to herself that she was trying to solve the murder. She couldn't help herself. She knew that was not what Dr Browning was paying her for, but she also felt he would not want to be arrested for the murder of Morley just because no one could locate another suspect. She felt she was doing him an extra service by finding the real killer and, besides, she could not let such a thing alone. Someone had died. Maybe he was not a very nice man, and few would miss him, but that was not the point. Someone had murdered a person and that was a crime. You could not start letting people off the hook for killing people because the man they slaughtered was not very nice. Justice was blind, as they said, to such nuances.

Clara was just really hoping Harry Beasley was not responsible.

It took a little walking about to locate the correct building with the potential witness upstairs. The properties looked different from the front, then the back. When Clara was satisfied she had the right building, she entered the shop that filled its bottom floor. This was a ladies' outfitters, one of the better-quality stores in the town. Clara had bought a couple of dresses from the place in the past, but the prices made her think twice before shopping there regularly. As she arrived, she spotted a pale green number in the window, with a pattern of sequins running up the side, and it almost distracted her from her mission.

"May I help?"

Clara glanced up at the woman stood behind the shop counter. Miss Clarence was worryingly thin and extremely carefully turned out. Her jewellery was not elaborate, but it perfectly complimented her dress, and her hair was pristinely swept up into a bun, with so many pins and hair lacquer that not a strand dared fall out of place. She was almost like one of the mannequins she used in her shop to display her wares. Clara always felt hopelessly plump and unfashionable near Miss Clarence, and she had to admit that was another reason she did not come to this shop very often.

"Good morning, I have an odd question, but I am wondering who resides in the flat in the top storey of this building?" Clara came to the counter.

"Are you buying a dress?" Miss Clarence asked coldly,

her head tilting up a fraction so she looked down her nose at Clara.

Clara licked her lips.

"I like the green one," she said, deciding not to test Miss Clarence's patience. The woman was single-minded when it came to sales, nothing else interested her. "I suppose, after I have dealt with my investigations, I might try it on?"

Miss Clarence did not look impressed.

"Oh yes, you are that detective. Didn't I sell you a dress just before New Year's?"

"You did," Clara said. "It was very nice."

"I wouldn't have let you leave if it was not. I only sell people clothes that suit them and that they look good in. That green dress, for instance, will not suit you at all. It is cut far too straight."

Clara was not sure whether to be hurt as well as disappointed.

"However, there is a lovely peacock blue dress that is ideal for your shape. It will be extremely flattering on you."

"Does it have sequins?" Clara asked.

"It does," Miss Clarence managed a slight smile. "And, once you have decided upon it, we can have my niece make any necessary adjustments. She lives in the flat on the top floor."

Clara saw the way things were going and decided not to fight Miss Clarence. She wasn't getting past her without buying a dress, that was for sure.

Miss Clarence produced the peacock blue dress, which Clara had to admit was rather lovely. It had a cinched waist which Miss Clarence insisted would suit Clara far more than the straight lines of the green gown. After trying it on, Clara found she was agreeing with the keen eye of the woman. The dress did accentuate her curves, without exaggerating them. Clara was impressed, though less so when she saw the price. She found her breath catching at the back of her throat.

"It will include any alterations," Miss Clarence said

quickly. "Also, there is this rather nice necklace that will go with it perfectly, and I shall include that in the price too."

The necklace consisted of blue cut glass meant to look like sapphires on a silver chain. Costume jewellery and not worth a great deal, though it would look nice with the dress. Clara started to work out the cost of it all in her head, asking herself how badly she wanted to speak with Miss Clarence's niece upstairs. She knew she was going to buy it. She had to.

"Very well," she said at last, and then produced her cheque book and tried not to grimace as she wrote out the figure. She hoped Dr Browning was generous with her fee once she had solved the case for him.

"I shall fetch my niece," Miss Clarence said. "That hem needs a slight adjustment. I shall ask her to come down."

"I would rather go up to her," Clara quickly said, thinking she would like to see for herself the sort of view Miss Clarence's niece had of the back of the town hall.

Miss Clarence looked put out, but Clara had just spent a large sum of money, so she did not argue.

"You just have to go straight up the stairs and knock on the first door at the very top landing," Miss Clarence said, a small frown creeping onto her face and causing her to purse her lips. "My niece is always very busy during the day working on alterations, but she will answer the door."

Miss Clarence opened the hatch in her shop counter to let Clara through. She watched the detective with clear unease. Clara felt that she had crossed a divide, stepping onto hallowed ground that was the preserve of the shopkeeper and thus should not be soiled by the feet of an ordinary shopper. It was trespass, even if she had been invited (albeit grudgingly) to enter. Clara gave Miss Clarence a polite smile and then headed for a doorway that led to a corridor and a steep staircase. She could feel Miss Clarence's eyes on her until she was out of sight of the shop floor. It made the skin between her shoulder blades tingle.

Chapter Sixteen

The stairs wound their way up to the third floor. The first floor was used for storing bolts of cloth, more versions of the dresses below in different sizes and a range of accessories that could not fit into the cabinets and shelves in the main shop. Clara noted there was a range of winter coats leftover from earlier in the year carefully stored in one corner, as she glanced through an open door. The doors on the second floor were all shut, and Clara guessed Miss Clarence lived in these apartments. The stairs narrowed as they headed to the top floor and the ceiling seemed to drop by a good few inches. This was the garret space, the smallest area of what was not a vast building to begin with. Clara spotted a door, which was the only one leading off the landing and knocked.

She could hear someone moving about in the room beyond. The floor creaked extremely loudly at the slightest movement. Eventually the door was opened by a young woman wearing a pair of very thick spectacles. She lifted these to get a better look at Clara.

"Oh!" She said in surprise.

"Your aunt allowed me up," Clara explained hastily, shuffling the dress in her arms. "The hem needs altering, but I would also like to ask you a question or two about your view of the town hall."

The woman looked perplexed, but she let Clara into her small living space. The garret consisted of a neat living room, including the miniature bay window, with a stove in one corner for warmth and making tea. Through a door at the back of the room Clara could just glimpse a bed and the edge of a washstand. The two-room attic served as workspace and home for the young woman who now uneasily took the dress from Clara.

"Er, you can sit?" She motioned to an armchair squashed into the bay window. It had been turned so it mostly faced the outside world.

"The best light," Clara said as she sat, understanding why the chair had been placed so awkwardly. The unusual bay allowed a large amount of light into this section of the room.

"Yes, erm…" the woman looked undecided as to how to proceed.

"Clara Fitzgerald," Clara introduced herself. "And you are?"

"Maud Hickson," the woman said. "Miss Clarence is my mother's sister."

Maud pressed her finger onto one of the sequins on the dress, her eyes focusing on the fabric.

"I do all the alterations for my aunt's customers."

"And you live up here?"

"For the time being," Maud narrowed her eyes and blinked a little as she looked at her surroundings. "Until I get married, or something."

Maud unfurled the gown and took a good look at it.

"What was it? The hem?"

"Just needed lifting by an inch or so," Clara agreed.

Maud laid the dress over a small table and then fetched

her sewing kit. She produced a pair of scissors with a fine point and began unplucking the hem of the dress. She was endeavouring to ignore Clara.

"My real reason for intruding on you," Clara spoke, "was because I am curious about the view you have of the town hall. I was at the town hall last night and I saw the light on in this room."

"I work late a lot," Maud said without looking up. "Some of the alterations are extensive and I also make custom hats. I spend a lot of time sitting by that window."

"And looking out?"

Maud glanced up, adjusting her glasses on her nose as she did so.

"What is your point?"

"A terrible thing happened at the town hall two nights' ago. A man died. No one knows what really occurred. I was hoping you might have seen something."

Maud gave a snort.

"You bought this dress and made it past my aunt just to ask me that?" She said, amazed. "Well, I am most sorry, but I saw nothing."

Clara was disappointed, especially as she had just spent a lot of money to get that answer.

"You have a very good view of the yard of the town hall," she sighed, looking out of the window again. "I really hoped you saw something."

"Most of the time I am leaning over my work, stitching this or that," Maud shrugged.

"You must look up occasionally?"

"Of course!" Maud paused with her scissors. "But that does not mean…"

She stopped herself and a look of sudden insight crept onto her face.

"Two nights' ago," she said almost to herself. "That was a full moon, wasn't it?"

Clara tried to remember.

"It might have been."

Maud walked to the window and looked out at the

world below her.

"I didn't think I had seen anything, because I barely registered what I was looking at, at the time. I am usually so caught up in my work," Maud leaned into the bay. "But now you mention it, I do recall looking up and seeing two men in the yard of the town hall."

"This was late in the evening?" Clara confirmed.

"It was dark," Maud nodded. "I had just put on my light. I was sorting a hat for a wedding. The customer wanted these tiny beads sewn onto it, they were giving me a headache. I glanced up to stretch my neck and saw the two men in the yard. I didn't think about it much. I assumed they were meant to be there."

"What were they doing?" Clara asked.

"Standing at the back of the hall, I think," Maud hefted her shoulders again. "I really was not paying attention. I glanced up, saw them and went back to my work."

Maud stopped and a thoughtful look crossed her face.

"That was the night the police were all around the town hall, wasn't it?"

"Yes," Clara said.

"Nothing more had been said about it, I assumed it was a false alarm. I did wonder afterwards if those men were thieves."

"You didn't follow up on that thought?" Clara asked, surprised someone would be so lacking in curiosity.

Maud took a last look out her window and then walked back to the dress she had partially unplucked.

"I am usually too busy to worry about such things. I have so much to do. Honestly, I didn't see how it concerned me, so I brushed it aside as one of those things," Maud unfurled the hem of the dress and then started searching through her sewing box for just the right colour thread.

"Between seeing the two men and the police arriving, did you see anything else?" Clara asked.

Maud had decided on a dark blue thread and bit off a

long strand.

"What like?"

"A man leaving the yard, maybe?"

Maud closed one eye as she threaded a needle.

"No, I didn't see that. I was so absorbed in that hat."

"Is there anything more you can remember about those men?" Clara felt she was scraping the bottom of the barrel now.

"One was taller than the other. And one was wearing a bowler hat," Maud said.

Clara felt the statement was hopelessly unhelpful, but at least she now had a witness to confirm that John Morley knew the person who had killed him, they had gone to the town hall together. They had stood outside briefly, and Maud had looked up and spotted them.

Through the window Clara watched as Wallace Sunderland emerged from the back of the town hall and walked to one of the crates in the yard. He lifted a couple of lids and then pulled out something – Clara could not determine what it was at this distance – and walked back inside.

"You are disappointed?" Maud asked quietly.

Clara turned to her and saw the woman looked despondent at her failure to remember more.

"It's not your fault," Clara assured her. "You were not to know that those two men were up to no good."

Maud put her scissors down and stared at the undone hem of the dress. She had come to a standstill in her work, unable to focus to the task. She rubbed at her eyes, shuffling her glasses down her nose.

"So many hours I sit by that window and see nothing," she said. "There is nothing much to look at, just the backs of houses and that yard. The one time something important was going on, I missed it."

"Honestly, don't berate yourself," Clara rose from the chair and walked to Maud. "Why would you have looked, anyway?"

Maud did not seem convinced, she thumbed the edge of

the dress hem.

"Do you want to wait for me to do this?"

"I won't distract you any longer," Clara said, feeling her presence would be an anxiety to Maud. "I shall arrange have it delivered."

Clara headed for the door, as she was just leaving Maud called out behind her;

"I'll try to remember something else."

The woman looked so acutely upset at disappointing Clara that she felt bad.

"Thank you," Clara said politely. "You have been helpful, I know one thing more than I did earlier."

"What is that?" Maud asked, puzzled.

"Why, I now know that John Morley knew his killer, and that is very important."

Clara headed down the stairs, thinking that while it would have been good to have a clearer description of the man who had accompanied John to his death, she had not been lying when she told Maud she had gained some knowledge. After all, until that point, they had toyed with the idea that Morley had been slain because he was attempting to break the case of the Archaeopteryx – that was the only motive Dr Browning could have, anyway – now it appeared there was another, much more personal motive. That was something Clara could get her teeth into.

Even if she was not meant to be investigating Morley's murder. Oh well...

~~~*~~~

Victor Darling looked quite morose when he arrived at O'Harris'. The cheerful fellow of the day before had disappeared.

"What's wrong, old son?" Tommy asked him, as if he did not know.

"Ah, Miss Holbein gave me the cold shoulder this morning," Victor said. "Caught me off guard. She says she has a new suitor and I am old news. Old news."

Victor looked as broken-hearted as any man who was watching a fortune evaporate before his eyes could. Tommy was starting to think Victor and Nellie deserved each other.

"What you are saying, is you need to spark Miss Holbein's interest again, and get her mind off this new gentleman in her life?" Tommy said, acting as though he had just come up with the scheme.

"That's it exactly!" Victor declared. "But I don't know how."

They were in the front hall of the great house. Captain O'Harris now appeared from the library. He had been listening to the conversation, allowing Tommy to sow the first seeds of their plan into Victor's mind. However, he pretended to have not heard anything as he walked up to Victor.

"Good morning Victor! Glad you could come! As I said in my message, I have a couple of chaps here who would be very interested to learn more about the way car engines are tested, as you were explaining to Tommy yesterday, but…" O'Harris paused as if he had just noticed Victor's glum mood. "Whatever is the matter?"

"Miss Holbein has sent him packing," Tommy patted Victor on the shoulder in commiseration. "She has her eyes set on someone else."

"Disgraceful!" O'Harris acted appalled. "You can do better, old man."

"I don't want to do better," Victor almost wailed.

Tommy had not realised the extent of the man's feelings. Could this all be about Miss Holbein's wealth or was it just possible Victor really did care for her? Tommy found that thought slightly incredible, but stranger things did happen. The most unpleasant of people could have extremely devoted and loving spouses.

"I've told Victor we'll help him," Tommy hastened to add. "We are going to think of a way to convince Miss

Holbein that he is the only man for her."

"Quite a scheme," O'Harris said. "Have you come up with an idea?"

"Well…" Tommy looked to be thinking, "what we need to do is grab Miss Holbein's attention. She needs to see that Victor will fight for her, that he is not giving up easily."

"I'm not," Victor agreed.

"And you need to show her that you won't be pushed around," O'Harris added. "She can't control you, you mustn't allow that. Stand up to her a little."

"Oh, I don't know…" Victor cowered a fraction at the thought.

"You keep acting like that then Miss Holbein will have no respect for you, worse, she shall start to treat you with disregard. You have to make it plain you are your own man," Tommy insisted. "So far, all the men in that girl's life have fawned over her and she has told them what to do. Eventually, that gets boring and she loses interest. What she needs is a man who will sometimes defy her and not concede to her every whim."

"But, she might not like that," Victor said anxiously.

"Victor, you are her suitor, not her servant. Act like it. We are not saying you have to be a bully, far from it. What we are saying is that if Miss Holbein tells you to jump, instead of asking 'how high?' you turn around and say no," O'Harris interjected.

Victor's shoulders slumped, as if he had been asked to do the impossible, such as fly to the moon. Tommy couldn't help him with that, it would be Victor's choice whether he continued to be Miss Holbein's lapdog or something more. But he could get the man back into Nellie's affections in the first place.

"Worry about the rest later," he told Victor. "Let's start by reigniting her interest in you."

"How do we do that?" Victor asked.

"As I said, you have to prove you won't be rejected without a fight. You have to take on this new lover of hers, show him you won't be usurped so easily," Tommy explained.

"Do you mean fight him?" Victor looked uneasy.

"It's the only way, Victor," Tommy patted him again. "You need to show Miss Holbein what sort of a man you are."

"I've never fought anyone in my life," Victor said hopelessly. "I don't think this will work."

"Here's a thought," O'Harris suddenly brightened up, as if he had just had an idea. "What if we stage it completely by putting a fake suitor in Miss Holbein's path? Then you won't have to fight this stranger, but someone who is in on the plan."

"But…" Victor started.

"That's perfect! After the fight, Miss Holbein will forget all about this new suitor. She will have eyes only for you!" Tommy nudged Victor.

"But who?" Victor looked between them.

"I shall step into the breach, old boy," Tommy said with a tone of self-sacrifice. "I'll help out a fellow in trouble."

"Would you?" Victor looked at Tommy in amazement, then he let out a long breath. "I would be in your debt."

"Don't even think about it. I will be satisfied to know I have helped a man secure the woman he desires, that is all," Tommy added mentally that the relief it would bring to him would be equally satisfying. "All we need do now is arrange everything. Leave it to me and O'Harris."

"Why, you are such good sports!" Victor's face brightened. "What luck I met you two that day on the beach, else, what would I do now?"

Tommy glanced at O'Harris, catching his eye and exchanging a look that implied they both knew Victor would not be in this position had they not stuck their noses into his business in the first place.

"We chaps have to look out for each other," O'Harris told Victor warmly. "The world is changing. Women are changing. It can be tough for a man in love."

"It is most certainly that," Victor nodded. "I really can't explain how much I appreciate this all. If there is anything

I can do in return…?"

O'Harris smiled.

"Why now, if you wouldn't mind talking to those men I mentioned?"

"Of course!" Victor said at once.

"Excellent. And while you are doing that, Tommy and I shall sort out the details of our little ploy," O'Harris winked at Tommy. "Oh, and you will stay for lunch, Victor?"

"I would be delighted," Victor agreed.

"Then we shall have everything in place by teatime," O'Harris grinned. "Won't we Tommy?"

Chapter Seventeen

Clara returned home to waste a few hours before the time of The League for Christians Against Evolution meeting. Annie looked moody as she walked into the kitchen.

"Has something happened?" Clara asked her.

Annie dipped into the pocket of her apron and produced four slips of paper which she handed to Clara.

"All from Miss Holbein," Annie stated. "Wanting to know where Tommy is."

"He scuttled off to O'Harris' this morning, didn't he?" Clara asked.

"Men always go into hiding when there is trouble," Annie snorted. "How they ever won the last war I do not know."

"Don't be too harsh on him, he feels awful," Clara said lightly. "He never meant for this to happen. He was only supposed to be talking to that woman about Victor. I thought she would talk to him better than me, as she appeared to have only disdain for women."

"I'll show her disdain," Annie squeezed her hands into fists. "I have half a mind to go over to her house and tell her where she can shove her little notes. I'll slap her one, Clara, I know I will!"

"All right, calm down," Clara placed her hand on Annie's arm. She had never seen her friend so upset and angry. "Look, don't spend the afternoon in the kitchen brooding on all this. Come out with me."

"What are you up to?" Annie asked, though she was not yet prepared to let go of her anger and stormed about the kitchen glowering at the pots and pans.

"I am going to a meeting of the League for Christians Against Evolution. I expect it shall be entertaining," Clara smirked. "I think they may be behind the threats to the exhibition. Dr Browning asked me to look into the problem."

"But you know who hired Morley," Annie said. "Surely that is the matter resolved?"

"The man who hired John Morley was only trying to highlight the danger to the exhibition. He was not the threat itself. No, Dr Browning asked me to discover who was behind the threats and to discover if there was any real danger. I intend to do just that."

Annie understood.

"Wouldn't I just get in the way?" She asked sheepishly. "I'm not really all that knowledgeable on Darwin or why anyone would be against him."

"You sell yourself far too short," Clara told her gently. "I would be delighted to have your company. You can poke me when it looks like I am about to say something awful or laugh aloud."

Annie's eyes had their sparkle back as she looked at Clara.

"Are you out to cause mischief?"

"I am investigating. I shall be very neutral," Clara promised. "Well, probably I shall be very neutral. If it starts to get too absurd, I may struggle."

Annie shook her head.

"There is no hope!"

They ate a light lunch and were ready to leave the house by the early afternoon. As Clara fetched her coat, she noticed that another note had been slipped under the door while they were in the kitchen. She picked it up hastily and shoved it in her coat pocket. Annie would only begin to fume again if she saw it.

They headed off to catch the bus and travel to the far side of town. Clara had handed Annie the leaflet she had been given by the protestors, to give her an idea of what they were facing.

"I might not know a lot about science," Annie said as she read it. "But I do know that if you are going to argue against something you do actually have to state your case. As far as I can tell, this leaflet just quotes random bible passages at you."

"I believe the main crux of the Anti-Darwin argument is that evolution denies God. God created the earth and all the people and creatures upon it, according to the Bible. To imply those creatures then evolved, is to suggest that God did not create everything perfectly to begin with. It is to suggest God is fallible. Which he can't be, as he is an omnipotent being," Clara elaborated. "The reason Darwin is hated by these folks, is that his theory of evolution goes hand-in-hand with the discovery of a prehistoric world filled with creatures that are not described in the Bible, such as dinosaurs and dinosaurs turning into birds. A couple of centuries ago, someone devised the age of the earth by working out the timeline of the Bible. However, this age was much younger than what we now know to be the case based on fossils and geology. Therefore, science is claiming the Bible is wrong, and for fundamental Christians that is a very scary thing."

Annie scratched at her ear and contemplated the leaflet again.

"You know, I might not agree with them, but I do understand these people," she said thoughtfully. "If the Bible, if God, is the thing that roots you to this world, gives you security and comfort, then to have it whipped away from you must be horrible. I have always perceived the Bible as allegorical, but not everyone thinks like that. Some people prefer things to be literal, it is the only way they can cope with life. The Bible becomes their rulebook, as long as they follow it, they are ok, and then someone says the

Bible is mistaken and they are thrown into chaos. People don't like chaos and they certainly do not like change."

"Some people need God to get them through daily existence, to face the hard realities of life," Clara concurred. "They need to believe that God can never be wrong, else their fragile trust is shattered. And here you have notable scientists attacking God. It must be upsetting."

"What you really have to say is that so much of this is not about God at all, but about the way people have interpreted his words. Darwin's theory does not mean God is wrong, it just means the people who have been spreading his religion were a little out with their dating. But, then again, if you only have people to rely on for your understanding of God, that still makes things scary."

"If you cling to a thought of a soul and an afterlife to help you get through the daily grind of existence, then to suddenly question that must be terrifying. It could lead to all sorts of dilemmas about your own path in life and what the meaning of it all is," Clara paused as she considered this. "I don't really believe, but Tommy does. It got him through the war. What if he had not had that? Would he have given up when he lay in that mud wounded?"

"These people are not bad folk, as such," Annie folded up the leaflet. "They are just very worried. Not all scientists appreciate that."

"Very true Annie. There are just as many dogmatic and single-minded scientists out there as there are these protestors. But, if they have been making threats against the exhibition, that is very serious. You can't do that."

"No," Annie nodded her head. "That isn't good."

They arrived at the address which had been given for the league meeting. It was an older style Victorian semi close to the outskirts of Brighton. It was possible to walk just a little further up the road and look across a vast expanse of fields. The day was warm and the sun mellow, there was something very peaceful about the property, rather like it was the house equivalent of an old, well-to-do lady who has just sat down in a comfortable chair to relax in the sun. Clara almost felt the windows of the house smiled. She felt welcome even before they had knocked on the door.

They were greeted by a bright-eyed older woman, wearing a blouse and dress that would have been fashionable before the war, but was now rather dated. She studied them keenly, before noting the leaflet in Annie's hand.

"Ah, you have come for the meeting!" She said with glee. "I do love new faces! Reverend Parker, we have two new members!"

An older gentleman emerged from a doorway into the hall of the house and looked at Clara and Annie. He was dressed in a black suit with a grey waistcoat and his dog collar was about his neck. Clara recognised him as one of the protestors outside the hall. He had long, frizzy hair, that he swept back from his forehead and the sharpest eyes Clara had seen in a while. He recognised her too.

"You, young lady, went into that infernal exhibition," he declared in a light voice.

Clara felt uneasy and then he laughed.

"Why, we welcome all!" He said. "Don't look so startled, I have a brilliant memory for faces. You took one of my leaflets, while your male companions barged past with such distaste on their faces."

He had remembered them well. Clara was a little stunned.

"What a remarkable gift," she said. "I truly wish I had something similar. I confess I am curious about your league, but I am not convinced that Darwin was wrong."

"My dear, many like you come here. We only ask that you listen. Some will see the light, some won't," the bright-eyed woman stood back and ushered them through the door. "We allow God to decide who is ready to accept our cause and who must, for the moment, be rejected. My name is Wilhelmina Frost. This is my house and Reverend Parker is one of my oldest friends. You must come through to the morning room, that is where everyone is gathered."

"Except for me," Reverend Parker chuckled. "I was taking a moment to smoke, and Wilhelmina won't allow it in the morning room."

Wilhelmina gave Clara a look which implied they must suffer the foibles of men from time-to-time.

"Come through ladies, there is tea or lemonade, and fresh scones."

The morning room looked out onto a large garden at the back of the house. There were a dozen individuals in the room, nearly all were women. Clara was not entirely surprised. The timing of the meeting meant that most men who worked would not be around, also she suspected Reverend Parker's slightly eccentric character was more attractive to women than men. She did note a couple of older gentlemen at the edges of the room.

Wilhelmina settled Clara and Annie into chairs and then fetched them refreshments. The room was large and well-appointed. The sun flowed across a large Persian carpet and glinted on the glass front of a ticking grandfather clock. A chair had been placed alone near the windows, facing the others, and Clara guessed this would be Reverend Parker's seat.

"I suddenly feel nervous," Annie confided. "I feel out of place."

"Far from it, Annie," Clara told her softly. "This is where we are meant to be at this moment in time."

"That sounds almost spiritual!" Annie said in mild amusement.

Clara rolled her eyes.

"As part of my investigation, I mean."

Reverend Parker entered the room and accepted a glass of lemonade from Wilhelmina, before settling down on the solitary chair before the windows.

"I am delighted to see so many of you here this afternoon," he said warmly, smiling on all those present. "And some new faces too, always a pleasure."

Reverend Parker took a sip of lemonade.

"I believe a half dozen of our members are stood outside

the town hall as we speak continuing the good fight. I know some of you have felt we are achieving little, but let me point out that these two young ladies have come here today as a result of our protest. That is no small thing," Reverend Parker pointed to Annie and Clara. Clara felt a fraud in that instant, but said nothing. "We cannot expect to change the world in a day, in a month or even in a lifetime, but we sow the seeds that will continue to grow after we have left this mortal coil and have been greeted by our Saviour. On the day we say goodbye to this harsh world, then we shall be welcomed into Heaven knowing we did all we could in this life to stop the spread of lies and secularism."

Parker's eyes sparkled intensely as he looked upon his little flock. He clasped his hands before him.

"There is so much work to do as yet, of course, we are not about to consider our task complete. It shall never be complete as long as there are those who can look upon these abominations and call them science. I see the lies of the Devil at work in these men of learning, who are so blinded by their supposed education, that they are ignorant to the truth. We must not be cowed by their fancy words, their spouted facts. We are the truth, we know where the Anti-Christ works his wickedness, how he twists the minds of weak men, making them think they see evidence, proof, when all they see is another hoax. A lump of stone that is meaningless in the face of the Bible's teachings," Parker had become rather breathless in his rant, now he paused to catch his breath and calm himself. "But, my friends, we must never condemn those who have been tricked, for we are all weak, we are all fallible. The Devil could work his falsehoods upon you at any moment, let us not forget that! We are here to help those who have been fooled, not to decry them. We do so with our steadiness, with our firm hearts and beliefs. We stand before them unbreakable, so that they can see how they have been misguided. I know, my friends, that it will not be so very long before we are heard, before we are understood. People will begin to listen."

Parker stopped and the people in the room politely clapped his speech. Annie nervously put her own hands together, looking about her as if at any moment someone might pounce on her and declare she was not fit to be there. Clara clapped too, but without Annie's apprehension. She had heard such speeches before, for many different causes. Politicians made an art of such waffle that said nothing but did rally the troops. If Reverend Parker really intended to change the academic world, he was going to have to do a lot more than just remain steadfast to his beliefs.

Maybe he had already considered that, which was why he had started sending threats – if it was the League for Christians Against Evolution behind those threats.

Reverend Parker basked in the glow of his followers' applause, then he held his hands up to quiet them.

"Now my friends, let us pray."

Chapter Eighteen

Wilhelmina offered around the scones after Reverend Parker had given a second lengthy speech, detailing the plans he had for the league and how they would conquer the Archaeopteryx threat. As far as Clara could tell, these plans mainly involved further protests outside the town hall, a greater distribution of leaflets (all of which the good reverend wrote) and writing letters to the local press. Reverend Parker looked exhausted from his ranting, there was a film of sweat upon his forehead. He was most certainly a passionate preacher – how far would that passion take him?

After the speech Parker mingled with his flock. Clara hoped to speak to him, but for the moment he had been ensnared by a couple of elderly ladies intently discussing the contents of the letters they meant to write to the papers. Clara would prefer to catch the reverend when he was not so surrounded by his supporters. Some of her questions were unlikely to go down well.

Wilhelmina passed her with a plate of scones.

"Oh, have you had one, my dear?"

Clara accepted the offering with a smile, though she had already eaten one. It provided her with the opportunity to speak to her hostess.

"Is the Reverend Parker a local preacher?" Clara asked.

"I don't recall him."

"Oh no, the reverend does not have a parish. He founded the League for Christians Against Evolution and he travels wherever the cause takes him. Currently he is following the fossil exhibition and in each place it stops, so he calls together the local members of the league."

"Then this is a countrywide cause?" Clara asked, surprised as she had never heard of it before.

"It is. We all subscribe to become full members and the reverend writes a regular newsletter to inform us of what is going on, what we must be aware of and how we can assist the good fight."

"That must consume a great deal of his time, not to mention the financial burden of such travelling," Clara said, aiming for a sympathetic tone, though she was really rather cynical about it all and wondered how much Reverend Parker was pocketing from his loyal supporters.

"We are always fundraising for the league," Wilhelmina smiled proudly. "And the reverend never wants for a place to rest his head on his travels. There is always a league member ready to give him a bed."

Clara nodded as if she fully understood and was not wondering how big a scam this all was. She didn't doubt Reverend Parker's belief that he was right in his cause, but she could not help but wonder that he was making a living deluding these people into some great agenda to deny the truth that science had made plain. Clara did admit to herself, that her own lack of religious feeling probably made her harsher on the good reverend. She could not fathom how he could be so blind to reality.

"Then, once the exhibition moves on, so will Reverend Parker?" Clara asked Wilhelmina.

"Yes," Wilhelmina gave a sad sigh. "It shall be most awful when he leaves. He has stirred up such a determination in us all, I fear without him that will be lost. But he is needed elsewhere, and we cannot deny others the benefit of his presence."

"And, aside from inspiring you all, he helps with the

protests? Standing outside the town hall? Distributing leaflets?"

"Reverend Parker does attend many of the protests, yes. But he must be careful. The police might arrest him."

"Whatever for?" Clara said, feigning astonishment.

"There has been malicious talk. The police say the reverend has been making threats against the exhibition, they say he is causing a public nuisance. I think there is pressure being placed upon them by those behind the exhibition," Wilhelmina's eyes narrowed. "There is money at the heart of this exhibition and money is the root of all evil."

"I thought the exhibition was a public-spirited act?" Clara said. "To enable the wider world to see these finds."

"I'm afraid that is the lie that is being spread, but if you really looked into things you would know that a lot of money has been made already from this 'tour', with a lot more to come," Wilhelmina snorted derisively. "You ask the reverend about it all. Don't think this is about bringing science to the people, or some such rot. This is about people making a lot of money."

Wilhelmina was distracted by a woman waving at her and she excused herself from Clara's presence. Clara felt confused. She had thought that the exhibition was, if anything, a means to lose money rather than make it. The sponsors and the Natural History Museum had put up the money for the venture and, as far as she had been aware, they were not expecting to recoup even half their costs. Could it be she was wrong?

Clara glanced about for the Reverend Parker. He was talking to an elderly gentleman and they had moved to the edge of the room, a little way from the rest. It was the perfect time for Clara to strike.

"Reverend Parker?" Clara politely interrupted the man. "Might I have a word?"

"Ah, our newest initiate!" Reverend Parker flashed a smile at her. "Will you excuse us, Mr Bunn?"

Mr Bunn removed himself and Clara was alone with the

reverend.

"How may I help you?" Reverend Parker asked her.

"I have a lot of questions," Clara said plainly.

"No doubt, I shall endeavour to answer them all," Parker was beaming with confidence, as if there was not a question in this world Clara could ask that would trouble him.

"I understand the purposes of your cause," Clara began, trying to be diplomatic. "I have read your leaflet."

"I am glad to hear it," Parker sounded delighted.

"I have no issue with public protest, as a means of having your voice heard," Clara added. "However, I have heard disturbing rumours that vicious threats have been made against the exhibition in town and that troubles me."

"My dear, that is understandable. Let me assure you that none of those threats have come from the League for Christians Against Evolution, and certainly not from me. It would be against everything I stand for to take aggressive action and would harm us rather than aid us."

"But I hear the police believe you, or some of your supporters, are responsible?"

Parker seemed a little put out by Clara's question, she guessed it was not often he was interrogated. Mostly people fawned over him.

"The police have been misled, that is all," Parker shrugged. "I have explained to them that we protest in a perfectly legal fashion. I do not promote violence in any form. May I ask who has been saying such things about me?"

Clara saw no reason to hide her source for the information.

"The gentleman who spoke to me gave his name as Sam Gutenberg."

"Oh, the Golden Archaeopteryx Society," Reverend Parker rolled his eyes. "They are almost as bad as those pushing this exhibition. Their argument hinges on the Archaeopteryx being an early bird. They still believe in evolution and thus are anathema to us."

"Mr Gutenberg takes the threats against the exhibition very seriously."

"As he should, as we all should. Anyone prepared to write about such violence cannot be ignored. Maybe it is just a malicious writer, or maybe it is someone who would do something if an opportunity presented. It is not any of my people, however," Parker was beginning to look annoyed by this line of questioning and Clara knew she would get no more from him on the subject, so she changed direction.

"Wilhelmina said something to me that I found most curious, she said I should ask you more about it."

Parker's frown eased a fraction.

"And what is that?"

"She told me that the exhibition is a scheme to make money. I thought it was a philanthropic endeavour to bring exhibits at the Natural History Museum to a wider audience?"

Parker chuckled.

"That is what they want you to think!" He declared. "There is nothing philanthropic about all this. Do you know who the main sponsor for the exhibition is?"

Clara admitted she did not.

"The Earl of Rendham. He has his own private collection of fossils he wants to sell, including an Archaeopteryx. This exhibition is stirring up interest for him. As soon as it is over, he shall put his collection up for sale and the extra publicity will see the price soar. Not to mention the money he is making in the sales of tickets and booklets. There have been fancy dinners held among the exhibits with the Archaeopteryx as the guest of honour, the cost of attending those was extortionate. Private viewings have been arranged for foreign royalty and other notables, all with suitable fees. The Earl has already recouped his costs and is now looking at making a tidy sum for his efforts," Reverend Parker snorted with indignation. "The Devil strikes a man who is a fool to money easily. He plays on his greed and therefore the fellow is lost."

"Then, the Earl would be extremely upset if something were to happen to prevent the exhibition continuing?" Clara observed.

"I imagine he would not be pleased if he had to lose the ticket sales, but then again the publicity this threat business is providing him with is all to the good of his main scheme," Reverend Parker tilted his head to one side. "Why all this curiosity?"

"I am merely getting my head around this all," Clara explained. "I like to have all the information at my fingertips before I commit myself to anything. It is upsetting to hear that what I thought was a charitable endeavour is really a money-making ploy."

"You shouldn't be surprised. There is very little real charity in the world."

"Surely that is a rather cynical statement from a man of God?" Clara replied, genuinely surprised.

Reverend Parker's eyes had taken on that familiar sparkle once again.

"I see the world as it is, I am not blind. Man is hard and cruel, he must rise above his natural instincts to be anything better."

"I don't suppose you ever heard of a man named John Morley?" Clara asked him.

"The name doesn't ring a bell," Parker seemed to be telling the truth. "Who is he?"

"A man hired to smash the glass display case containing the Archaeopteryx."

"Ah, so whoever has been making those threats has decided to act."

Clara did not disabuse the reverend of this idea.

"John Morley was murdered in the course of his crime," she said instead. "His killer is unknown."

Reverend Parker looked at her curiously.

"You do have a remarkable knowledge of the exhibition," he said, "and of all the people involved in it."

"I keep my ears open," Clara smiled. "I like to know

what is going on. Honestly, I have a cynical heart too."

Reverend Parker's smile slowly returned.

"I hope you have found our meeting enlightening."

Clara could not say she had, but she did not speak that aloud.

"Thank you for your time Reverend Parker, I am glad to hear your cause is devoted to peaceful protest. I feared it might be otherwise."

"Violence begets violence," Reverend Parker said solemnly. "If we want to be heard and taken seriously, we cannot go about causing harm. No one listens to people who punctuate their words with acts of rash violence."

"That is certainly wise," Clara agreed.

Clara wandered across the room and found Annie who had become embroiled in a deep conversation about lace-making. Clara gently tapped her shoulder and motioned they were leaving. Annie made her excuses and followed.

"Well?" She asked as they headed towards the front door.

"Reverend Parker is a very clever man. I don't think he is stupid enough to make threats against the exhibition. They would achieve little."

Annie was confused.

"But I thought that foreign fellow said he had made the threats?"

"Sam Gutenberg and his society suspected the threats came from the League for Christians Against Evolution, which would be easily done. After all, why look further than the organisation that is protesting against the exhibition for potential suspects?" Clara opened the front door and let Annie through first. "The obvious assumption was that the group who has been calling the exhibition the work of the Devil would be behind any threats."

"You know, I found some of their talk very…" Annie gave herself a moment to think of the right word, "persuasive."

"Annie," Clara groaned.

"Well, no, Clara, I mean why would God make animals

that are not perfect from the start?"

"Why do we plant seeds and watch them grow?" Clara replied. "The keen gardener takes pleasure not just from his fully-grown shrubs and flowers, but from the growing of them from scratch. He takes delight in the first sprout and every inch of growth. Perhaps God takes such delight in watching creatures develop and change? Look at humanity. We have changed dramatically from our earliest ancestors. We have learned so much, invented so many things, from trains to cars. We may not have evolved in a physical sense, but we have mentally evolved and adapted our world. We created vehicles so we could travel longer distances faster. Reverend Parker, himself, takes advantage of such transport to get across the country. Yet, those trains, those cars, even the carriages our grandparents rode in, were not the work of God. Should we deny them too because God did not create them at the dawn of time?"

Annie was frowning and looking perplexed.

"You know I am not religious, Annie," Clara told her. "But it seems to me that if there is a God, he likes to see his creations grow and develop, just like a keen gardener, or a devoted father watching his children mature. Evolution is a part of that growth. I honestly do not believe God and evolution need to be viewed as exclusive of one another. I think evolution is all part of God's plan."

Annie was silent a while, considering all this.

"Then you think Reverend Parker is wrong?"

"I think he is the one the Devil is pushing, if there is such a thing, which I am not convinced there is," Clara replied. "I think he has found a cause to keep him going and that is that. Remember, it was a man who worked out the age of the earth based on the Bible, and who is to say he got it right?"

Annie still looked uncertain.

"I'm starting to think I should have stayed at home."

"What did you make of the scones?" Clara changed the subject onto one she knew would distract Annie.

"Call those scones!" Annie declared in a sharp voice.

"I've made rock cakes lighter than those!"

Annie spent the rest of the journey dismantling Wilhelmina's refreshment choices. All concerns about God and evolution were forgotten. Clara secretly smiled to herself.

Chapter Nineteen

They were stood outside Miss Holbein's house.

"You understand the plan?" Tommy asked Victor for the fifth time. He was more agitated than anyone over this plot working.

"Leave him alone," Captain O'Harris said languidly. "He knows what to do."

Tommy stared across at the house, bracing himself.

"All right then, Victor, I'm going in," Tommy glanced at his two comrades, still hesitating. "This feels like crossing No-Man's Land."

"Without the shellfire," O'Harris dismissed his concerns.

Tommy grumbled and marched across the road. He was bracing himself for all sorts of trouble. Miss Holbein had to be one of the most obnoxious women he had come across in a long time. He really didn't want to be at her front door again, but there was no choice. He had to resolve this matter once and for all, or she would not leave him be.

He stood on the front step and knocked. A few moments passed and he almost retreated, but then the maid opened the door.

"Thomas Fitzgerald calling to see if Miss Holbein cares for a walk?"

The maid looked at him with a strange expression, he

wondered what was going through her mind. Then she disappeared, shutting the door on him. Tommy counted slowly in his head to pass the time, he figured if he reached one hundred before Miss Holbein appeared it was fair enough for him to retreat. He promised himself he would not have to endure longer. Unfortunately, Miss Holbein appeared at the door before he had reached sixty-three.

"Oh Tommy, you scoundrel!" Miss Holbein snapped at him, hands on hips, dark eyes glaring. "You ignored my notes!"

"I had things to do," Tommy shrugged at her. "I am not at your beck and call."

Miss Holbein gasped and then her face broadened into a smile. Tommy felt ghastly that the woman was actually enjoying his defiance and disregard.

"I'm here now, if you want to go for a stroll," Tommy acted as if he really didn't care one way or the other. Actually, he would rather like it if Miss Holbein refused.

"I shall just grab my hat!" Miss Holbein declared in excitement, much to his disappointment.

Tommy glanced over his shoulder to where he had left the others, while Miss Holbein was busy. He couldn't see them at all, which was good, because they were hiding. He just hoped they had not abandoned him. He really felt he was being quite the hero in helping out poor Victor, who seemed truly smitten with this appalling woman. It was quite remarkable.

Miss Holbein returned, wearing the most enormous sun hat and with a parasol on her arm for good measure.

"You know, I was beginning to think I was going to have to come and fetch you!" She said as she stepped outside.

Reluctantly, Tommy offered her his arm.

"How did you find out my address?" Tommy asked her casually.

Miss Holbein laughed.

"Mrs Wilton spilled it out when I mentioned your name to her. She almost jumped at the idea of you replacing

Victor Darling in my affections. Apparently, you are wholly respectable compared to him," Miss Holbein chortled, it was a rather vulgar sound. "That woman is so obsessed with my life! I really want to scream sometimes."

"She cares what will become of you," Tommy defended poor Mrs Wilton, though he was close to adding that he couldn't see why she cared so much.

Miss Holbein simply laughed again.

"She cares more about my late mother's reputation and what people might say," she snorted. "Mrs Wilton does not really care who I marry, as long as they are from the right social echelon. She doesn't worry about how they might treat me, only if they will try to steal my money. Honestly, I would rather marry a poor man who understands he must be kind to me to earn my money, than marry a rich man who can do as he pleases."

"Surely it would be better to simply marry a man who loves you?" Tommy frowned, feeling that Miss Holbein had missed the point.

"You really think love makes for a good marriage?" Miss Holbein raised an eyebrow at him. "How many relationships that start with love end in misery and hardship? The beaten wife who loves her abuser. The cuckolded husband who adores his philandering spouse. The starving couple with too many children and only 'love' to console them. I am not so dim. I see the world for what it is, and I use that to my full advantage. How many women marry a man simply because he is wealthy? It is the backbone of the upper- and middle-class marriage market, and don't think otherwise. The first thing a girl asks her friends when she looks upon an eligible bachelor at a party is how much is he worth? She does not contemplate his looks, his temperament or even his age, she judges him by the money he has in the bank.

"No one questions that. It is accepted as part of life. So why should I be any different just because I am a wealthy woman rather than a wealthy man? People assume that I am vulnerable because of my money, but no one thinks that of a man with money. These days, a girl can tie up her money so her husband can't touch it. It's not like in the past where a woman's property became that of her husband the second they married. No, I am in full control of my fortune. Better still, I understand what motivates these men to court me and that is a power I have over them."

"I don't like how cynical that all sounds," Tommy said.

"Because you are a gentleman," Miss Holbein laughed. "But you can't deny that this is the way the world works. I don't expect a man to love me, I expect him to love my money."

Miss Holbein paused.

"That is, until you came along."

Tommy suddenly felt uneasy, remembering why he was there and why he had to extract himself from the situation as fast as possible. They were now walking together along the road and Tommy surreptitiously glanced about for any signs of Victor making his move. He was starting to sweat under the anxiety.

"Miss Holbein, you have misunderstood my intentions. I am not here to court you."

"What? Is this about friendship? You came today, did you not?"

"I only returned your handkerchief," Tommy pointed out. "I was being courteous."

"Give it time," Miss Holbein smirked. "You'll come to like me, and if you don't, well, there is always my money."

Tommy could not get his head around how crass and blunt the girl was, how she considered her fortune her only asset and somehow perceived that as a good thing. Talking was not going to change her mind, probably nothing would except the cruel passage of time and the hard knocks of life that shake the most firmly held beliefs.

"I can only hope…" Tommy started.

He was interrupted by the sudden appearance of Victor Darling, who darted across the road, narrowly missing a passing milk cart. He stood breathlessly before the pair as if he had been running for some time.

"Aha! So, this is the man who you have allowed to usurp my place in your affections!" Victor declared as he stood before them.

"Victor!" Miss Holbein said in astonishment. "I thought I told you to stay away?"

"You! You have stolen the affections of my dearest!" Victor pointed his finger at Tommy. "I shall not have it!"

"Oh, do go away Victor," Miss Holbein groaned. "You are making an exhibition of yourself."

"Good!" Victor stated, his voice rising up an octave. "I won't let you slip away so easily, my love. If I must prove myself to you, so be it."

Tommy would have loved to have stepped aside at that instant and said that Victor could have Miss Holbein with his thanks, but he knew he could not. Instead he held his place.

"What is this all about?" He said, acting as if he had no clue who Victor was, even though he had spoken to him at length on the beach in Miss Holbein's presence.

"Victor was my former..." Miss Holbein waved a hand in the air, the word not forthcoming. "He was walking out with me before you showed up. Don't you remember him on the beach?"

Tommy pretended he did not.

"Oh, so this is Victor? I do recall him vaguely."

"You will unhand my dearest, sir!" Victor stood just inches away from Tommy. "You will step back and never return."

"Victor, don't be so idiotic," Miss Holbein snapped. "I really think you should leave."

"You think I am a fool, Nellie," Victor said grimly. "You think I will just walk away. I will not. You are my love, my only one and I shall fight for you! Do you hear that, sir? I will fight you for her!"

Tommy disengaged his arm from Miss Holbein's.

"Is that necessary, old boy," he raised up his hands. "I am really not serious about her."

"Thomas!" Miss Holbein looked appalled. "Stand up for

154

yourself!"

"To be frank, I am not about to fight over a woman," Tommy told her coldly. "I don't need the hassle."

"Why, you cowardly, dastardly…" Miss Holbein kicked Tommy squarely in the shin.

Tommy stumbled into the road with a gasp. The blow had been surprisingly painful. He went to place his hand on his leg as Miss Holbein marched towards him to continue the assault. She smacked him hard around the head and tried to kick him again before Victor bravely swept her up into his arms.

"My darling, you need not waste your time on him, I am here!" Victor opined, like some star-crossed lover in a silent movie.

Tommy had hopped further into the road to avoid being attacked again by the irate woman. She was scowling at him like some sort of banshee, her fury rather terrifying.

"I have never been so ashamed to walk with a man!" Miss Holbein spat at Tommy. "What a disgrace you are!"

Tommy almost went to defend himself, then recalled this was exactly what he had wanted. He managed to stand up straight and put his sore leg to the ground.

"My dear, there are times in this life when a man must fight and times when it is best he withdraw," Tommy said with as much dignity as he could muster.

"I think you should leave now," Victor told him with a surprisingly fierce twist to his voice.

Tommy was relieved to escape. He turned and, with a slight limp, walked across the road and around a corner. It did not take him long to locate Captain O'Harris; the laughter led him to his friend. Tommy scowled at him.

"You think that was funny?"

"Old boy, I have not seen anything that entertaining in weeks!" Captain O'Harris had to wipe tears of mirth from his eyes. "But cheer up, you achieved what you set out to do. Miss Holbein is back in the arms of Victor and you are well and truly off her Valentine's list."

Tommy rubbed at his head where Miss Holbein had

slapped him.

"She has a vicious hand."

"Be relieved you are out of her clutches," O'Harris clapped him on the shoulder. "Your bravery in the face of the enemy was most extraordinary. Your sacrifice shall not be in vain."

"Oh, shut up," Tommy shoved him, though not without a smile on his face. "Do you really think this is a happy ever after for Victor?"

"At least until next week," O'Harris grinned. "That harpy has no intention of settling down anytime soon, but we did our part and you are free of Miss Holbein."

"Is it a charitable act when both parties are only out for either power or money?" Tommy mused.

"I've lost my ability to understand all this," O'Harris shrugged. "Somewhere along the line I became completely baffled by it all. Still, you are now a free man and Victor has a temporary reprieve in the eyes of Miss Holbein. As good deeds go, it might not be the best, but it is at least a triumph."

"She gave me a headache," Tommy pressed a hand to his temple. "She actually made my ears ring with that blow."

"I think she would have done more than just that if Victor hadn't stepped in."

"I supposed I owe him my thanks."

"Don't worry about it," O'Harris said. "After all, the whole point was so he could inspire Miss Holbein's affections once again."

"Which would not have been a problem if I had not interfered in the first place," Tommy pointed out.

O'Harris was blithe about the whole thing.

"She would have found someone else if you had not come along, she'll probably find someone else as it is," O'Harris kicked at a stone on the pavement. "She is that sort of woman. Victor is blissfully unaware of the fact that she will cast him aside, eventually."

"Or maybe he is the one she will keep coming back to.

She'll dally with others, but Victor will be the man who is always steadfast and there for her."

"You think that is a good thing?" O'Harris looked surprised. "Poor fellow always playing second fiddle to some novelty lover?"

Tommy had to admit he had not thought that one through.

"You know, as remarkable as it seems, I actually think Victor is fond of Miss Holbein," O'Harris said thoughtfully. "I think he started out by being interested in her money, but then he got to know her and, as challenging for us as it may be to understand, he actually appears to have affection for her. There is clearly a part of her less than charming personality we have failed to see."

"Love is blind," Tommy grimaced. "Now I feel we should have Victor confined for his own good."

"Don't worry about him, we all make our own beds to lie in. Probably they'll be happy in their own way."

"Do you really believe the nonsense you spout sometimes?" Tommy taunted the captain.

O'Harris laughed.

"I think life has a way of working out, sooner or later," he said, trying to ignore Tommy's smile. "Now, what do you say to a pint before we tell Clara what we have done?"

Tommy came to a sudden halt. O'Harris walked on a pace before he too stopped, so suddenly had his companion become motionless.

"I forgot about Clara," Tommy said. "I forgot what this was really about."

O'Harris patted his shoulder sympathetically.

"I think you are going to need that pint."

Chapter Twenty

"You did what?"

Clara flopped into an armchair, aghast at what Tommy and Captain O'Harris had just told her. Annie was stood to one side, a strange look on her face.

"It was the only way Clara, I appreciate it was not what the case was about…"

"All you were meant to be doing was learning who Victor Darling really was," Clara groaned, rubbing wearily at her eyes. "Not encouraging the romance between the two of them!"

"On that front we do have good news," O'Harris quickly interjected. "We are confident that Victor Darling is really a test engineer in a plant that specialises in putting mechanical components through their paces. We don't know much more than that, as he is being very cagey, but he seems a decent fellow."

"We are both agreed that he seems devoted to Miss Holbein too," Tommy added. "We think it is about more than her money."

Clara sighed.

"Well, what is done, is done," she pulled a face as she thought about telling all this to Mrs Wilton. "Dare I leave you in charge of finding out more about this man for the sake of the case?"

"Clara, I made one error…"

Clara glared at her brother. Annie folded her arms across her chest and scowled.

"All right, it was a big error," Tommy admitted to them both, hoping to dissipate their bad humour. "But I'll make it right. I'll find out everything there is to know about Victor Darling and then you will have done your duty to Mrs Wilton."

Clara shook her head.

"I really don't know what to say about all this."

"How is your other case going?" O'Harris tactfully changed the subject.

"Well, so far I have no suspect for the murder of John Morley, though I am convinced he was accompanied by someone to the town hall. As it stands, I am not supposed to be investigating his death, only who might be behind the threats levelled at the exhibition and, on that count, I have come to a dead end."

"I thought you were going to talk to the League for Christians Against Evolution," Tommy said.

"I did, their leader, Reverend Parker, denies that the league is behind the threats. Though who else might have sent them I can't say. I am going to go back to the Inspector and ask to see the letters. Maybe that will provide some insight."

"I am very sorry, Clara," Tommy said apologetically. "I never meant to make life difficult for you."

Clara waved away his apology.

"Oh, it doesn't really matter, as long as you and Annie are friends again."

Tommy glanced at Annie. She scowled for a moment longer, then broke into a smile.

"Only a true gentleman would take a beating for a girl, from another girl," she said.

"And that is that," Clara smiled. "Right, I am going to go and…"

They all came to a halt as the doorbell was rung vigorously. Captain O'Harris was stood just inside the bay window of the front parlour and could see who was at the door.

"It looks to be a police constable," he said.

Clara jumped up and hurried to answer the door. The arrival of a constable could only mean that Inspector Park-Coombs had made progress in John Morley's murder. She opened the door and almost surprised the constable with her sudden appearance.

"Excuse me, miss, but the Inspector wanted me to bring you a message."

"Go ahead," Clara said, desperate to know what had happened.

"The Inspector has made an arrest in the murder of John Morley," the constable continued.

"Oh no, Dr Browning?" Clara asked, fearing that Park-Coombs had been pressured by his superiors into arresting the unfortunate, heavy-sleeping academic.

"No, miss. He has arrested a Mr Harry Beasley. He thought you would want to know."

Clara's stomach sank. From the moment she had spoken to Harry Beasley and learned of his dislike for his brother-in-law, which was bordering on hatred, she had been concerned about him being a suspect. You rarely had to look far to find a person's killer, it was usually someone they knew very well, often a member of their family.

"I think I best come at once," Clara stepped back into the hallway and collected her handbag and hat. "I can't think how Mrs Beasley is taking all this."

"Not well," the constable confided.

"Clara?" Annie called from the hall.

"I'll be back later, the Inspector has made an arrest," Clara answered, then she slipped out the front door and followed the constable back to the station.

It was now late in the afternoon and the station was proving busy. There were a couple of vagrants sitting in the front lobby, complaining about kids throwing stones at them and trying to convince the Desk Sergeant to put them in a cell for the night, so they might at least have somewhere peaceful to sleep. A fraught woman was reporting that her pet tortoise was missing from her garden and wanting a full police search for him, while a couple of girls were puttering in a corner, having been brought to the station for pilfering stockings from the local Woolworths. The constable helped squeeze Clara through the crowd and to the back rooms of the station. Inspector Park-Coombs spotted her as he emerged from one of the offices.

"Sorry affair, Clara," he said glumly.

"What has happened?" Clara asked him.

"My men have been searching everywhere for the weapon that killed John Morley. They went to the train station and inspected all the mallets used by the workers, they found one with a suspicious substance on the end. It looks like dried blood and hair. Anyway, the handle has the letters H.B. carved into it."

"Inspector, surely this cannot be accurate?" Clara was amazed. "If Harry Beasley killed his brother-in-law two days ago, why on earth would he not have cleaned the mallet?"

"People act rashly," Inspector Park-Coombs shrugged. "Anyway, Harry has not been at work these past few days due to taking care of his very ill sister. It looks likely she will be dead before the week is out. The way I see it, Harry Beasley goes with his brother-in-law to smash the display case. John thinks Harry is helping him, but really Harry sees this as a way of killing the man he hates and casting the blame onto someone else, namely Dr Browning. Harry slips away from his work and brings along the mallet he uses at the train station, just as John brings along his own hammer. Once they are inside and John is distracted, Harry clobbers him. He goes down quickly and almost in silence, so Harry can leave without being seen.

"When Dr Browning does wake and finds John Morley's corpse, he raises the alarm, but there is no sign of the killer and considering the circumstances, suspicion naturally falls on the academic. Meanwhile, Harry heads back to the station and acts as if he was never gone. He doesn't have time to clean the mallet, so leaves it in his locker, meaning to sort it out later. But then his sister becomes seriously ill and he does not have a chance to retrieve the mallet. He hopes that no one will go there and look at it, but unfortunately he is wrong."

Inspector Park-Coombs laid the story out so matter-of-factly that it was very convincing, but Clara could see many holes in the scenario.

"Why would John ask Harry to help him? They hated each other. He would not want to split the money with Harry."

"We only have Beasley's word that they detested each other," Park-Coombs pointed out.

"Your arrest relies on the fact Harry would want John dead," Clara countered. "Therefore, he detested him, and he could not have hidden that from John."

"Well, maybe John Morley was trying to make amends for all the trouble he had caused him in the past," Park-Coombs replied. "Really, Clara, the evidence speaks for itself."

"What does Harry Beasley say about all this?" Clara asked.

"He denies it all, says he was never at the town hall or with John that night."

"And the mallet?"

"He says he used it to smack a big rat that was down by the train tracks. It was at the end of his shift and he was too tired to clean the mallet before he went home."

"Can Dr Deáth find out if the blood came from a rat?" Clara asked.

"I've sent him the mallet, we shall soon find out," Park-Coombs answered. "Honestly, Clara, sometimes people are just careless. They don't think things through."

Clara still could not quite believe it, even though she too had pondered on how Harry had access to a mallet, it seemed uneasily convenient to find it covered with blood and hair. Maybe, she said to herself, she also did not want the murderer to be Harry Beasley. It broke her heart a little to imagine him murdering his brother-in-law, even thought she could understand why he might want to.

"Can I speak to him?" Clara asked.

Park-Coombs looked at her with a serious frown.

"I didn't think this was your case," he pointed out.

Clara sighed. No, it was not her case. She was stepping on the inspector's toes for no reason other than her own curiosity.

"I suppose I have become rather caught up in this all," she said to him. "I keep forgetting that John Morley is not my concern. I am supposed to be hunting down whoever is behind those threats to the exhibition."

"Any success on that front?" Park-Coombs asked, his expression lightening.

"Not really," Clara laughed. "I visited the League for Christians Against Evolution and spoke to their leader, Reverend Parker."

"I've heard of him," Park-Coombs grumbled. "He was one of the names I was given to look out for in Brighton. Full of himself, that one. Had a chat with him, told him the protests were one thing, but if he started to disrupt the exhibition or stopped people entering, he was in trouble."

"He denies making threats against the exhibition."

"He would," Park-Coombs snorted. "That sort of fellow lies through his teeth. He'll be behind it, no doubt."

"And what if he isn't?" Clara pointed out. "What if the real culprit is banking on us assuming the League for Christians Against Evolution is behind it all?"

"Come on Clara, who else would be behind this?" Park-Coombs shook his head. "Sometimes it really is the obvious blighters. Not everything has to be a double-bluff."

"I would be happier reporting back to Dr Browning with solid evidence that it is the Reverend Parker he has to concern himself with," Clara said, feeling slightly affronted by Park-Coombs dismissal of her doubts. Maybe she was being too generous to Reverend Parker, but he did not strike her as a man who would sink to petty letters, it would be against his calling as a man of God.

"You can look at the letters received in Brighton, if you like," Park-Coombs shrugged, clearly thinking it was a waste of time. "We kept them for the purposes of thoroughness. Truth is, there's not much we can do with them. Now, if something actually happened at the exhibition, we might start considering them evidence. So far, the letters are just a nuisance."

Park-Coombs walked her to a desk where a constable was filling out reports on dangerous cycling incidents. The inspector leaned down and pulled out a drawer.

"We put them here," he said, producing a bundle of five letters.

He set them on the desk before Clara. She thumbed through them, noting first the thickness of the paper they had been written on. It was very heavy paper and not the sort people typically used for stationary. Secondly, she saw that each of them had been written in large capital letters, to disguise the writer's hand. The first one read – THE HAND OF GOD DESCEND ON YE! WICKED SINNERS THAT DENY OUR LORD! Clara placed the paper to one side and read the next.

BEHOLD, HE SHALL STRIKE DOWN THOSE WHO SPREAD WICKED LIES AND DETEST HIS NAME!

"I'm detecting a pattern," Clara said sarcastically to Park-Coombs.

He grinned.

"The writer is not afraid to stick to his theme and milk it for all its worth," he chuckled.

The third letter read –

JUST AS THE WALLS OF JERICHO FELL, SO SHALL FALL ALL FOLLIES OF MAN THAT DENY THE CREATOR AND MASTER! BE AFRAID, FOR HE IS COMING!

"Slightly more threatening, that one," Clara nodded. "The others were rather vague."

"They do become less subtle over the course of time.

I've seen some of the ones sent to the exhibition at the very start of the tour, and they are quite bland in comparison."

The fourth letter was where things started to get nasty –

AND THE BLOOD OF THE WICKED SHALL POUR FORTH. YOU SHALL BE CURSED AND YOUR CHILDREN CURSED, AND YOUR CHILDREN'S CHILDREN CURSED. AND ALL SHALL CRUMBLE AS THE REDEEMER STRIKES YOU DOWN!

"Sounds like Reverend Parker, doesn't it?" Park-Coombs nudged Clara. "It's the sort of evangelical stuff he spouts."

"He did not strike me as a man who would express his views so violently," Clara replied. "I attended one of his meetings and the theme was understanding and not judging those who supported Darwin. He described them as misguided rather than wicked."

"Easier to get vicious on paper," Park-Coombs winked. "Read the fifth letter, it came the day before John Morley entered the exhibition."

HE WILL COME WIELDING A HAMMER OF JUSTICE. HE WILL CRACK THE SKULLS OF THE IGNORANT AND BLASPHEMOUS AND REDUCE TO ASHES THEIR SIGNS AND SIGILS. BEWARE, FOR THE END COMES TO THE WICKED!

"If that does not describe John Morley entering the town hall to smash the Archaeopteryx case, I don't know what does," Park-Coombs said triumphantly.

"But, Inspector," Clara placed the fifth letter with the others, "we know that John Morley was hired by Sam Gutenberg, not by Reverend Parker. And, as far as I am aware, Mr Gutenberg had not seen these letters. Therefore, the appearance of John Morley with a hammer has to be pure coincidence."

Park-Coombs froze as this realisation struck him. He had obviously allowed the connection between Sam Gutenberg and John Morley to slip his mind.

"That complicates things," Park-Coombs scratched his

moustache, a sure-sign he was worried. "But, no, that does not stop these letters from being written by Reverend Parker."

"It does not stop them being written by someone else either," Clara observed. "In fact, we could argue that they might have been written by the Golden Archaeopteryx Society, since Sam Gutenberg hired John Morley to do exactly what this last letter states."

"That would be nonsensical," Park-Coombs huffed. "At least we can agree on why Dr Browning was so worried about the exhibition and why seeing John Morley with a hammer would have scared the living daylights out of him. If I did not have good evidence against Harry Beasley, Dr Browning would still be the most likely culprit for the crime."

"About Harry Beasley…" Clara started.

"He is not your case. Usually I would allow you some leeway, but there are a lot of eyes watching me. I have my superiors breathing down my neck," Park-Coombs looked genuinely sorry. "This time Clara, I have to say no. I'm sorry about it, but there is nothing I can do."

Chapter Twenty-one

The next morning, Tommy received a message from Captain O'Harris stating that Victor wanted to express his thanks to them and was going to come to the Home to speak with them in person. Tommy felt relieved as he looked at the note. At least now he might be able to solve the problem he had first been charged with and Clara may not be so disappointed with him. Annie came into the hallway as he was picking up his umbrella; rain was threatening in the deep purple sky.

"Not going to get yourself into trouble again?" She teased.

Tommy blushed just a little.

"I'm going to find out once and for all who this Victor Darling is and prove to Clara I can make a worthwhile accomplice in her detective business," Tommy answered.

Annie crossed her arms and smiled.

"Why not be blunt with the fellow, instead of pussy-footing around? Ask him straight out, who are you really Mr Darling and should Miss Holbein's friends be concerned?"

"If you had met Miss Holbein, you would know that it is Victor's friends who should be worried," Tommy paused just before opening the front door. "You know, I think he genuinely loves her. Isn't that remarkable?"

"It takes all sorts," Annie said wisely. "Be home for lunch, I bought some pressed ox tongue."

Tommy promised he would be, then hastened outdoors.

He had to catch a couple of buses to get to O'Harris' house on the outskirts of Brighton. By the time he descended from the second bus the heavens had opened and heavy rain splattered down on his black umbrella. Tommy hurried along, avoiding the great puddles rapidly forming on the dry ground. The tall gates of the convalescence home were open, as always, and he dashed inside thinking what a marked change it was from the other day when he, Victor and the captain had strolled in the gardens in the sunshine, feeling rather hot and remarking on the dryness of the grass. Tommy had said then that they were due some rain.

He made it to the front steps of the house with only getting a little damp and let himself in.

"Hello?"

A young man appeared from the library, holding a book in his hand. He had a grey, sombre face and Tommy recognised him as Private Peterson, the one guest who was causing O'Harris sleepless nights. He had a morose expression at the best of times, and it was hard to know what would raise the young man's spirits sufficiently to get him to smile.

"If you are looking for the Captain, he is out at the old orangery. We now know where that stray cricket ball went last week. Smashed a pane of the glass roof and there is water flooding in," Peterson explained.

"Oh no, on the parquet flooring?" Tommy grimaced. "That will take some clearing up."

"Lucky one of the gardeners went past and saw there was water pouring out from under the doors," Peterson nodded.

Tommy picked up his umbrella, having just put it into a nearby holder.

"Any sign of Victor Darling?" He asked Peterson.

"No, you are the only person to have walked in this

morning," the private answered. "The fellow is some sort of genius with car engines, I understand?"

"Something like that," Tommy agreed, not really sure how to otherwise describe Victor. The man was too cagey about who he really was. "If you see him, tell him where we are."

"Will do," Peterson wandered back into the library, hunched up like an old man.

Tommy wondered what the future held for the lad and shuddered a little to think that he had not been so far removed from ending up the same way. The depression that hung over Peterson, along with his far more alarming symptoms, echoed with Tommy. It was not something he cared to dwell on.

He headed outside and found O'Harris with his shirtsleeves rolled up, hammering a piece of wood over the broken pane in the orangery roof. It was remarkable how much water had tumbled in, in such a short space of time. A gardener with a broom was trying to sweep out the worst, but the floor was probably ruined, along with a cushioned sofa that had been directly under the leak.

"It never rains but it pours!" O'Harris grinned at him. "Any sign of Victor?"

"Not yet," Tommy answered. "Need a hand?"

"Nope, nearly done," O'Harris hammered in a last nail and then stepped off the ladder he had been using to see if there were any further leaks. "I think we have stopped it for the moment."

He accompanied Tommy back to the house, unrolling his shirtsleeves as they walked.

"We need to find out the truth from Victor today," Tommy said as they walked. "No more beating about the bush. We need answers."

"Who he really is, you mean?"

"Exactly," Tommy said.

"On that I do have a little news," O'Harris looked pleased with himself. "I rang up Red Lion Engineering, spun them a line about testing an engine I was working on.

Said I had heard of an engineer by the name of Victor Darling and that he was supposed to be one of the best for testing engines."

Tommy was impressed by his duplicity.

"What did they say?"

"They said, 'yes, Victor worked for them but was currently on his annual leave. If I wanted to make an appointment for when he was back they would ensure he was involved in the tests on my engine.' I said I would get back to them."

"He is using his real name," Tommy said in amazement. "I thought he would be using a pseudonym."

"Well, that would complicate things, wouldn't it?" O'Harris pointed out. "How much more do you need to know?"

"I suppose what his intentions are," Tommy shrugged his shoulders. "I doubt Mrs Wilton will be much impressed that a car engineer is courting Miss Holbein, but if his intentions are genuine, maybe we shouldn't judge."

"You mean if he loves her?"

"I mean he is a braver man than I to dive into that lion's den. Whether it's for the money or real feelings…" Tommy tailed off, because the man in question had just appeared.

Victor waved to them. He had no umbrella and was getting wet as he hurried towards them.

"I am glad to catch you both," he smiled at them, his eyes alive. "I wanted to say thank you in person, and to give you a gift each."

He handed them both small green boxes, they were oblong in shape and roughly the span of a hand.

"You might want to open them indoors," Victor seemed to have finally noticed the rain.

They entered the house through the garden room and Tommy propped his umbrella in the fireplace, where it could drip without harming anything. He opened the box in his hands and whistled in delight as he found it contained a miniature car, perfect in every detail. It was a Rolls Royce, with a shiny green enamel body and white-walled tyres.

"You can open the bonnet to view a perfect replica of a Rolls' engine," Victor informed him proudly.

O'Harris had opened his box to reveal a matching model.

"These are beautiful Victor, but you really didn't need to," O'Harris' eyes twinkled as he examined the car.

"I wanted to, you stood up for me and you helped me out when many would not have bothered," Victor shoved his hands in his pockets and looked awkward. "People don't think I should be with Miss Holbein, I know how it is. They think I am out for her money."

Tommy had not expected such candidness from Victor, he decided he ought to be candid in return.

"Are you, Victor? I'm not judging, just curious."

Victor traced a rose in the carpet with the toe of his shoe.

"At first I was, I have to be honest with you two because of how kind you have been," he said. "I read about the death of Miss Holbein's mother in a newspaper, and it said how the daughter was now a wealthy heiress. The newspaper forecast that the girl would draw the attention of money hunters. It made me stop and think, why should some other fellow marry her for her money when it could be me?"

Victor did not look ashamed at this comment. Tommy decided they would have all acted more shocked, had they not met the abominable Miss Holbein. His ears still rang when he thought about her.

"I was cynical, that's the truth of it. I was looking for a way to pursue my dreams, but I didn't have the money."

"What are your dreams, Victor?" O'Harris asked.

Victor gave a long sigh.

"I want to break the world land speed record in a car," he said. "It's all I have ever wanted to do. But only rich men can afford such dreams and I am not rich."

Victor looked between the two of them.

"I think you had already guessed that."

"We had," Tommy nodded. "We know you work for the

Red Lion Engineering company."

"It's a reliable job, and not badly paid," Victor said. "But not enough to make a man rich. I was feeling pretty rough when I read that piece in the newspaper. Something inside me said, 'why shouldn't I marry a rich girl?' I'm a nice fellow, I have manners, I would look after her. I would make a jolly good husband, and I didn't have any attachments to worry about."

"And you came to Brighton to find Miss Holbein?" O'Harris elaborated.

"Yes, and I saw some of the men hovering around her and they made me shudder. Real sharks, they were. It would be a terrible thing if they got their claws into her," Victor shrugged his shoulders. "I guess I convinced myself it was my duty to rescue her from them. That made it simpler. Of course, I hadn't actually met Miss Holbein then."

Victor smiled at them shyly, knowing what they must think of Nellie Holbein.

"She is a difficult woman."

"You can say that again, Victor," Tommy shook his head.

"She's challenging, but there are other qualities to her," Victor could see they did not believe him, and laughed a little. "I know, they are hard to see, but she does have some nicer qualities. I believe, with a little work, she could blossom into a lovely…"

Victor caught himself.

"Into a reasonable human being," he corrected. "I suppose, in a funny sort of way, I've taken to her. I don't know if I can call it love, but certainly a deep affection. Maybe it's foolish, but I can't deny the way I feel. I hope she can learn to feel affection for me too."

Victor glanced at Tommy, then at O'Harris.

"You think I am kidding myself?"

"No," Tommy lied. "I'm just worried she will disappoint you."

"I'm prepared to take the chance," Victor said. "Anyway,

I may get my dream of taking on the land speed record through her, so there is always that. And that is why I am grateful to you both for getting me back in her good graces, but not just that. I took your advice that I should not let her push me around. I'm being firmer now. I think it is making her respect me a little more."

Victor looked pleased with himself and Tommy felt he could not take what little hope the man had away from him. If he wanted to believe he could turn the fearsome Miss Holbein into a loving wife, so be it, after all, he might be right. Stranger things happened. At least now he had answers for Clara.

"What about Red Lion Engineering?" O'Harris asked Victor.

"I'll have to hand in my notice. I thought to hang onto the job a while, but I am worried about Miss Holbein finding someone else if I have to be away in London working."

Tommy wasn't convinced that Victor should burn his bridges so swiftly, but he kept his mouth shut. It was not his decision.

"If it all goes pear-shaped, Victor, pop over here. I am sure I can make use of a good car engineer for teaching the lads mechanical skills," O'Harris offered generously.

"That's very kind," Victor smiled. "I hope you won't think me being rude if I say I am sure I will not need to take you up on the offer."

"Not at all," O'Harris assured him. "But the offer stands, nonetheless."

"Thank you, but now I must go. I have arranged a lunch date with Miss Holbein."

They escorted Victor to the front door and watched him walk down the path to the gates. Tommy wondered if they would ever see him again, or whether his plans with Miss Holbein would work out.

"You are right, Mrs Wilton will not be pleased," O'Harris remarked, closing the front door on the rain. "Weren't you supposed to find out who Victor was so she could get rid of him?"

"She wanted him discredited, revealed to be a money hunter. Well, we have discovered that he planned on taking Miss Holbein's money to begin with and then he got swept up in this romantic image of himself as some sort of knight in white armour, saving the woman's wicked soul," Tommy chuckled. "People are remarkable how they twist around reality to make it fit their own fantasies."

"Hmm," O'Harris was staring into the middle distance, his mind elsewhere.

"I suppose that's that," Tommy tried to attract his attention. "Anyway, I promised Annie I would be home for lunch."

"Oh, thank you for coming by," O'Harris remembered himself. "Give Annie my best."

Tommy retrieved his umbrella yet again and prepared to set out into the rain. The temperature had dropped too, and he shivered, wishing he had brought a coat. It was the first sign that the long summer was drawing to a close. He was about to step outside when O'Harris paused him.

"About twisting ideas to suit our fantasies," he said, "would you say that… erm…"

O'Harris frowned.

"I mean, there seems this spark between me and Clara, but maybe… maybe…"

"She is head-over-heels for you, old man," Tommy smirked at him. "Sooner you realise that the better. You two are both so damn independent."

O'Harris looked relieved.

"And what about you and Annie?" He said, returning Tommy's grin.

"What about us?" Tommy asked in surprise.

Chapter Twenty-two

Clara was on her third cup of tea as she tried to make a decision on what she was going to tell Dr Browning about the threatening letters. There was only a circumstantial link between Reverend Parker and the messages, she was just not convinced they were his style. She had asked to borrow one of the letters and the inspector was happy to give her one. He had five, after all, and there were many more in the drawers of police stations across the country. Clara had taken the most recent one and had compared the text to that found in the pamphlet from the League for Christians Against Evolution. Aside from them both being of a religious bent, there was no similarity that she could see.

For instance, Reverend Parker was fond of heavily quoting Bible passages to make his point. Most of his pamphlet was made up of these quotes, with very little in the way of actual explanation of his dislike for Darwin. There was nothing to say why he felt Darwin was wrong, no carefully worded argument to counter the Theory of Evolution. In short, it was a waste of paper.

On the other hand, the threatening letters did not quote scripture, though they cast their threats in seemingly Biblical language and mentioned God regularly.

Reverend Parker's pamphlet did not make threats. It

did not call Darwin or those who believed in his theory wicked. It did not suggest that the wrath of God would come down upon them. There was none of the violence or aggression seen in the threatening notes. While it was not impossible that both the letters and the pamphlet were written by Reverend Parker, they were of such a different style and attitude that it seemed unlikely. Clara believed Reverend Parker when he had said such threats would be against the purpose of his campaign. All they would do was alienate and frighten people, make them angry at the League for Christians Against Evolution; they would not change minds.

That being said, there was nothing to suggest the letters could not have been written by one of Reverend Parker's followers without his knowledge.

Clara felt she had nothing of use for Dr Browning as yet. She could not justify telling him that the League for Christians Against Evolution were behind the threats, just because the police and Sam Gutenberg thought so. For that matter, she ought to talk to Sam again…

There was a ring on the doorbell. Clara was in the front parlour and was sooner at the door than Annie who appeared from the kitchen at the back of the house. Emma Beasley was on the doorstep, looking extremely distressed. She had her hands clasped together and her eyes were red from crying.

"S…sorry to bother you," she mumbled.

Clara invited her in at once and took her through to the parlour. Annie went on immediate tea duty and appeared within a minute with a cup. Knowing Annie, it would be heavily laced with sugar. Emma Beasley was so racked with emotion that she could hardly catch her breath. She looked fit to collapse as Clara helped her into a chair.

"Sorry… so sorry…" Emma repeated, rocking forward as she clenched her hands into her lap.

"Don't apologise," Clara told her firmly. "Take a sip of tea and try to calm down."

Emma obeyed, though her hands shook, and Annie

hovered in anxiety over the china teacup being dropped and smashed.

"This is about Harry," Clara said to Emma, trying to help her.

Emma nodded her head hard.

"They've… a…arrested him…"

"Yes, I know. I tried to speak to him at the police station, but I was not allowed since I had not been specifically asked by anyone to investigate the death of John Morley."

Emma gulped.

"If I ask you… c…can you speak to him?"

"That would be different," Clara confirmed. "If I was privately employed to investigate the matter, then the Inspector should grant me leeway to speak with Harry."

"I would l…like you to," Emma continued. "I don't have much m…money, but…"

She started to fumbled in the pocket of her skirt. Clara pressed her hand over Emma's and stopped her.

"Do not worry about that," Clara told her. "I would be glad to help you."

Emma looked surprised. Clara just smiled.

"I have been trying to investigate the death of John Morley off my own back, I simply can't ignore a crime, I suppose. Now, at least, I can be justified in what I am doing and should be allowed to speak to your husband. But, first Emma, I must ask you, is there any possibility of Harry being angry enough with John to kill him?"

Emma shook her head at once.

"You must be honest with me, if I am to help you," Clara persisted. "Your husband seemed to hate his brother-in-law."

"He did," Emma admitted, her voice firmer. "There was no love-loss between them. Harry hated how John treated Ruby, but he is not a murderer."

"The theory the police are pursuing is that John asked Harry to help him break into the town hall, presumably offering a share of the money he was getting for the job.

Harry took the opportunity to kill him," Clara said.

"If you knew those two, you would know that John would never ask Harry for help!" Emma scoffed at the idea, her tone bitter. "Harry would go over to his sister's house and see if she was all right, maybe he would mend something that John's bad temper or the people he upset had broken. If John caught him at the house, he would kick him out, and he would hammer on our door and yell at Harry for fixing things. That man would never have asked Harry for help, if he was the last man on earth."

Emma had calmed, her voice was steady as she defended her husband.

"And Harry would never take part in breaking and entering into the town hall. He is a law-abiding man, and he would never have participated in trying to smash the cases of those rocks. He was going to go look at them, he was enchanted by the idea of that bird thing."

Clara recalled her conversation with Harry about Darwin and the exhibition. He had seemed genuinely interested in the exhibits. There was too much of the police's theory that failed to add up.

"If only we knew who John did ask to help him that night," Clara said. "You don't know a person he was likely to have involved?"

Emma shook her head.

"I rarely saw John, other than when he was angry at Harry. I only called on Ruby when he was out, or too drunk in his bed to come downstairs. I avoided him and he certainly would not speak to me."

"Someone must know," Clara sighed. "How is Ruby?"

Emma pulled a face, it did not suggest she was hopeful for her sister-in-law.

"She wakes from time-to-time, enough to have a little to eat and drink. I'm not sure she knows where she is, or that John is dead. Maybe that is just as well," Emma dipped her head. "I asked my neighbour to watch over her while I came here. It was why I could not come sooner. I was so torn between finding help for Harry and watching over

Ruby. You must help my husband, Miss Fitzgerald! He does not deserve to hang for this."

"I will do everything in my power," Clara promised her. "I believe in your husband's innocence."

Tears of relief sparkled in Emma's eyes, she clutched at Clara's hand.

"I was so scared you would tell me there was nothing you could do."

"There is always something," Clara smiled. "Now, if you think of anything that could be of use, let me know. What time did Harry go to work the night John died?"

"He works from eight in the evening until eight in the morning," Emma said. "He left the house around half seven, just after his supper."

"And he arrived home as usual?"

"Yes," Emma said.

"Thank you," Clara squeezed her hand.

Emma finished her tea, thanked Annie and Clara profusely and then headed for home. She had Ruby to think of and could not impose on her neighbour for too long. Once she was gone, Clara grabbed her hat and her handbag. Annie watched her.

"What if he did do it?" She asked solemnly. "What if Emma is wrong?"

"I don't think she is," Clara told her friend. "I think there was someone else behind this murder. I just haven't discovered them yet."

Clara left the house and hurried to the police station. She arrived late in the morning, a little out-of-breath as she had run from the bus stop. She felt a sense of urgency she could not quite explain. As she entered the police station, she saw Inspector Park-Coombs escorting a man towards the front door. The man was well-dressed in a smart suit and his bearing suggested someone of authority. There was an arrogance to his swagger as he walked out of the station. The inspector held the door open for him and as it closed, he turned and met Clara's eyes with a look of slight despair.

"That was the Earl of Rendham," he said. "Come down to Brighton to see that this mess is straightened out speedily."

Clara glanced at the door, as if she would see the earl disappearing down the road.

"I have it on good authority that the earl hopes to make a small fortune selling his own collection of fossils, including an Archaeopteryx, with all the publicity generated by the exhibition he has sponsored," she said.

Park-Coombs raised an eyebrow.

"Which good authority?" He asked.

"Reverend Parker," Clara gave a shy smile, appreciating that others would not consider him a reliable source. "I have no reason to doubt the statement."

"No reason to trust it, either," Park-Coombs snorted. "The earl is the enemy of Reverend Parker."

"I don't think the man sees things quite like that, he is not looking at those hosting the exhibition as the enemy."

"Don't be naïve, Clara, they are his nemesis. A useful nemesis, of course, as they sustain his desire for glory and adoration. Reverend Parker travels the country, enjoying the hospitality of people with more money than sense and being fawned over by his followers," Park-Coombs laughed coldly. "That man has an enormous ego. His little league is a way of feeding it."

"You are such a cynic," Clara grinned at the inspector.

"I believe that is why we get on so well," Park-Coombs chuckled. "But I imagine you are not here to talk about Reverend Parker and the Earl of Rendham?"

"No," Clara said, becoming serious. "I've just had a visit from Emma Beasley, she has asked me to look into the situation regarding her husband."

"Mrs Beasley?" Park-Coombs was surprised. "I would not have thought her able to afford a private detective."

"She can't," Clara shrugged her shoulders. "I said I would help her for free. She is in a terrible state."

"Well, of course! Her husband just turned out to be a

murderer!"

"Inspector," Clara regarded him with a reproving look, "I am sure you have realised the flaws in that assumption. The case against Harry Beasley is very poor."

"We have a bloody mallet," Park-Coombs pointed out.

"Has Dr Deáth proved that the hair and blood on the mallet is that of John Morley?"

"Not as yet," Park-Coombs admitted. "But Harry has a motive."

"As do a number of people in town. John Morley made enemies better than he made friends. Besides, whoever killed him went with him to break into the town hall. He had to have asked that person to accompany him, perhaps offering a split of the money. He would never have asked Harry Beasley for assistance," Clara said. "Whoever killed John was a friend, or at least someone John thought was a friend. That is not Harry."

The inspector looked grim. He had not missed the holes in his case and as Clara repeated them it was plain that the odds of Harry being the killer were slim. The bloody mallet was the only real evidence they had. That and Harry's dislike for his brother-in-law.

"The earl is breathing down my neck," Inspector Park-Coombs dropped his voice and whispered to Clara. "He wants the man responsible found. The exhibition can't leave town until we have the killer under arrest."

"Arresting the wrong man won't help with that," Clara replied. "You are better than that, Inspector."

Park-Coombs lowered his head, abashed that he had been harangued into making a rash decision.

"There was a valid reason for arresting Harry Beasley," Park-Coombs defended himself. "A bloody mallet was found in his locker and his brother-in-law was killed with a mallet."

"Fair point, but beyond that?" Clara asked.

The inspector gave a small groan.

"If that mallet turns out to have human blood and hair

on it, you know what that means?"

"It means it is probably the murder weapon," Clara nodded. "Still does not conclusively prove Harry Beasley killed his brother-in-law. Are the lockers at the station kept locked?"

"No," Park-Coombs winced. "Only the door to the room they are in, and that is often left unlocked as people have to come and go."

"Hmm," Clara said, deciding not to push the point. Park-Coombs already knew his case against Harry was unreliable without her rubbing it in. "Inspector, I do not mean to cause you bother, I never do. I would like to help you resolve this matter and get the Earl of Rendham off your back."

"You want to talk to Harry," Park-Coombs scratched his chin. "Now you are technically hired by the family, it would be petty of me to deny you the chance."

"I want this killer found as much as you do, Inspector," Clara agreed. "John Morley might not have been a very nice man, but no one deserves to be clobbered over the head with a mallet."

"Oh, I don't know about that…" Park-Coombs glanced in the direction of the vanished earl. "You know, I might be sceptical about old Reverend Parker, but it would explain the earl's heightened interest in this matter if he had more than just the sponsorship of the exhibition at stake. He did seem more alarmed than you would really expect about all this."

"I shall be investigating that too," Clara assured him. "But first things first."

"Of course, "Park-Coombs escorted her towards the back of the station. "Harry is in a cell. I'll bring him to the archive office for you to speak to him."

"Thank you, Inspector," Clara said.

"If you can get that earl off my back, I'll be thanking you," Park-Coombs huffed. "Make yourself at home and I shall fetch Harry."

Chapter Twenty-three

Harry Beasley was relieved to see Clara when he was shown into the archive room by the inspector.

"Call for a constable when you are done," the inspector said to Clara and then he vanished.

Clara was sitting at one of the tables in the room and motion for Harry to take the spare chair. He sat down as if he might fall down at any moment. There was a definite tremble to his hands. All the fight had gone from Harry Beasley in the face of the police's accusations.

"Your wife came to see me," Clara explained to him. "She has asked for my help."

"Miss Fitzgerald, please don't think me rude, but my wife is not thinking straight. We don't have the money to afford a private detective…"

Clara interrupted him.

"I have already told your wife I am happy to investigate your case without charge."

"That is good of you, Miss Fitzgerald," Harry said. "But I could not possibly ask you to do that."

"You don't have to ask me," Clara grinned at him. "I am

already doing it. I want to help."

Harry seemed a little startled by her generosity, Clara didn't give him the chance to think about it too hard.

"I don't like to see innocent people accused of crimes they have not committed. I can't ignore that."

"You believe I am innocent, Miss Fitzgerald?" Harry said, looking so astounded by her declaration that it tore at Clara's heart a little.

"I do, Harry," she said, "and please, call me Clara. Miss Fitzgerald is too formal for my liking."

Harry looked truly stunned by all this and had to take a moment to regroup.

"Everything has happened so fast," he said. "I barely understand it all."

"The police found a mallet in your locker at the train station with blood and hair on the head. A mallet was used to kill your brother-in-law."

"I already told them, I used the mallet to strike a big rat that was roaming about the station yard. We have a terrible time with rats, and we all try to kill 'em if we see any," Harry explained.

"You didn't bother to clean the mallet?" Clara observed.

"It was the last few minutes of my shift," Harry sighed. "By then I am so exhausted I can barely think to find my way home. You work all night repairing anything that needs repairing. The tracks, mainly, but sometimes the signal boxes or general maintenance. Its heavy work, hammering sleepers back into place, keeping the tracks in good nick. Not so bad this time of year, but in the winter it takes the life out of you. Honestly, I could not be bothered to clean that mallet there and then. I was planning on sorting it when I went back to work the following night. But then Ruby came to ours and I had to look after her. The foreman has been very kind and let me have the time off to sort things out. And then this…"

Harry waved vaguely at the walls, implying the whole affair of being arrested and incarcerated.

"I'm scared I'll lose my job and then what will become

of Emma and Ruby?"

"Don't worry about that," Clara reassured him. "It is my intention to prevent anything like that from happening."

Harry gave a small moan and hung his head.

"I cannot express how glad I am you have come to assist me," he said. "I thought I was doomed."

"The case against you is poor," Clara told him. "The tests on the mallet should prove the blood and hair is not human and you will be a free man. In the meantime, why don't you explain to me what happened that night at the station? Did John Morley come there?"

"John never came to the train station," Harry laughed in bleak amusement. "Why would he?"

"You never saw him that night?"

Harry shook his head.

"I didn't know he was dead until you told me."

"John died around midnight, do you recall what you were doing at that time?"

Harry had to pause to think.

"There is so much to do, and I don't often check the time," he scratched at an eyebrow. "We had a problem with a buckled track. It had been getting worse for weeks and needed replacing. Could have caused an accident," Harry confided. "Trouble was, we needed a new piece of track and the trains had to be re-routed to enable us to work. It was that night the new track finally arrived, and we fitted it. I'm sure we were still working on it at midnight. It was a long job. Nothing wanted to fit right. My foreman was there supervising, because it was such an important thing."

"What is your foreman's name?"

"Bill Turnbull," Harry said. "He does carry a watch. Maybe he checked the time? All I know is that when we were done with that piece of track it was getting light and we all needed a cup of tea. They like us doing jobs like that overnight as there are fewer trains running, less disruption, but it's hard on us as we have to work by lamplight."

Harry shook his head.

"My word, was I exhausted. I remember I wanted to lie down and kip there and then. But there was no rest, we had some fencing to fix next."

"Thank you, Harry, with any luck Mr Turnbull will supply you with an alibi for the time John Morley was killed."

"Ali… aliby?" Harry had never heard the word.

"He'll be able to confirm to the police you were working on the track when the crime occurred," Clara explained. "You'll be out of here before you know it."

Harry slumped in his chair at the news, the tension dropping from his shoulders.

"You don't know how good it is to hear that."

"Give me time to work on this and I am sure I shall have you home before you know it," Clara smiled, her optimism was not just wishful thinking, she felt that there was a great deal of evidence to support Harry's innocence.

~~~*~~~

Mr Turnbull would not be available to speak to Clara for several hours, so she headed to the town hall, hoping to get some insight into the murder of John Morley. The League for Christians Against Evolution was outside as before, handing out pamphlets and trying to buttonhole people so they could speak to them. Clara glanced among the faces to see if there was anyone who might recognise her. She spied Wilhelmina in the group and her heart sank a little. She did not want anyone in the League for Christians Against Evolution to see her there, if she could help it. She might have to speak to the Reverend Parker again and he would be reluctant to talk to her if he was aware of her links to the exhibition.

Unfortunately, Wilhelmina caught sight of her.

"Ah, my dear, are you here to join us?" She cried in

delight and hurried forward to clasp Clara's hand.

"Not at this moment," Clara apologised hastily. "I was actually trying to get into the town hall yard."

Clara tried to extract her hand from Wilhelmina's grasp, the woman was not so easy to escape.

"Whatever for?"

Clara opted to provide her with a modicum the truth.

"A gentleman died here the other night. I have been asked by his family to find out what happened," she said as vaguely as she could.

"Died here?" Wilhelmina hissed. "Well, I knew science was godless, but…"

"This is about money rather than science or God," Clara quickly interjected. "I am also very concerned that threats have been made against the exhibition and the staff, and that the police believe the League is behind them."

"Reverend Parker has warned us about these accusations," Wilhelmina nodded keenly. "He has stated that threats of violence are not a way to make people sympathetic to our cause. We may find our work frustrating, we may feel we are ignored and ridiculed, but that does not mean we should lower our standards. Just one convert makes all the work worthwhile."

"I agree with Reverend Parker," Clara said. "And I have told the police I don't believe he is behind these threats, but they are hard to persuade. I thought by looking around the town hall I might get some answers to both problems."

"That is most valiant of you, what an asset you are to the League!"

Clara wished Wilhelmina would lower her voice a touch, she was trying to avoid associating herself with the League, especially in public.

"I need to get on," Clara pulled her hands from Wilhelmina's. "There is so much to do."

"Yes, I must not delay you further. I hope you can find the answers you seek," Wilhelmina moved back to the group of protestors and Clara slipped away.

She headed down the side of the town hall and into the

yard. She paused for a moment to look up at the window of Maud Hickson, but she could not see the woman sitting in her chair. What a shame she had not caught a better glimpse of the second man in the yard with John Morley, it could have made such a difference.

Clara wasn't entirely sure what she was looking for in the yard, other than inspiration. She walked about the packing crates and thought about all the tools they contained. There were plenty of mallets and hammers that could have cracked John Morley's skull. They could then have been washed clean and replaced. She opened a couple of lids and examined the contents. There had to be a dozen potential murder weapons inside the crates.

Clara dropped the crate lids and looked at some of the smaller boxes near the back door of the town hall. She lifted the hinged lid of one robust wooden case and found it contained a pair of scissors, balls of string and several large sheets of paper. The paper intrigued her, and she plucked a piece out. It was very thick and sturdy and looked remarkably similar to the paper the threatening letters had been written.

"Can I help?"

Clara jumped at the voice, she had been so absorbed in her search she had not realised someone else had arrived. She saw Wallace Sunderland standing beside her.

"Just continuing my investigations," she told him lightly.

"I've come to fetch a screwdriver. One of the legs has come loose on a display case," Wallace shrugged his shoulders. "You ask me, it's all those people crowding around and leaning on it. And think how many times we have unscrewed and screwed back on those legs these last months? I reckon the screw holes have worn."

Wallace glanced at her hands.

"You've been in the fossil rodent case," he said.

"Is that what it is?" Clara said. "I wondered why it contained paper?"

"That's for wrapping up the more delicate fossils before

they are packed. That thick paper folds into a sheath for the fossil, just in case any small bones or bits get knocked loose during transport. You shouldn't lose anything that way."

"You must go through a lot of paper," Clara noted.

"We have reams of it," Wallace shrugged again. "If you'll excuse me."

He reached past Clara for a metal toolbox she had not noticed by the wall and rummaged around for a screwdriver. He stood up and adjusted his cap.

"Have you travelled all the time with this exhibition, Wallace?" Clara asked him.

"Since it left London," Wallace replied. "I'll be travelling a few months as yet, but its good money and the work is not that hard."

"Where is home for you?" Clara persisted.

Wallace grinned.

"Funnily enough, here in Brighton. Well, I grew up here, my parents lived here until they passed away. My wife lives in Hove."

"Then you are getting to spend plenty of time with her?" Clara smiled back.

"It's rather nice," Wallace beamed. "I go home every night, sleep in my own bed instead of a boarding house bunk. Right nice. To be honest with you, I don't mind the police threatening to keep us here until they figure out who done in that fellow Morley. Means more time at home."

"Sounds very pleasant," Clara agreed with him.

"Not that I'm complaining about the work, mind," Wallace added swiftly.

Then he touched the brim of his cap and disappeared through the back door of the town hall. Clara thought about following, to have another look around, but she was not sure what she would achieve and, with the place packed with people looking at the fossils, it would be difficult to see anything. She also was trying to avoid Dr Browning until she could offer him some answers.

She rubbed her thumb over the paper in her hand. She

was no expert, but this thick stock seemed exactly like the type used by the threatening letter writer, which implied they had taken it from this case where, as Wallace had said, there was reams of it. The paper in the crate was much bigger than the letter, but Clara could see how you could cut it into four smaller sheets for the purpose of writing threats. All of which raised one alarming point – if the letter writer was using the packing paper for their messages, then they were somehow connected to the exhibition. They had access to the crate and the paper at all times as they travelled with the fossils across the country.

But why would they do it? Why work for such an exhibition if you believed it was godless and wrote angry threats to express your distaste? It was hypocritical at best, downright deceitful and nasty at worst. Clara decided she was going to take the piece of paper she had found and compare it to the letters. Maybe that would offer her an explanation.

She took a final look around the yard and glanced once more at Maud Hickson's tiny flat high in the eaves of her aunt's shop. Maud was in her chair now, Clara could just make out her shape. She waved, but didn't think she was seen. No matter. She would have to solve this case the hard way. Clara left everything as she had found it and headed back out into the road. The League for Christians Against Evolution were in a heated conversation with two police constables and Clara slipped away before Wilhelmina saw her. She didn't want to become involved. She might not think the League was responsible for the threats against the exhibition, but that did not mean she approved of their behaviour. They were deluded, especially Reverend Parker, but that was not her problem. She had a murder to solve, a threatening letter writer to uncover and an innocent man to save. She didn't need any moral campaign to add to her burden.

Chapter Twenty-four

Clara returned to the police station and sought out Inspector Park-Coombs. He happened to be in his office with Dr Deáth.

"Grand timing Clara," Park-Coombs said as she appeared, though there was something slightly sarcastic about his tone.

Clara looked between him and the police coroner, who gave an apologetic smile.

"Good news for Harry Beasley?" She surmised.

"We analysed the blood and hair on the mallet, I have just finished my report," Dr Deáth said.

"And the blood is not human?" Clara guessed.

"We can't determine that," Dr Deáth looked mildly ashamed at his failure in this department. "However, I can say with a high degree of certainty that the hair was not human. It is from a small animal, probably a rodent of some sort."

"Which fits with Harry's story that he hit a rat," Clara declared.

Park-Coombs did not look impressed.

"He isn't ruled out. He is the only person I know of, at

the moment, with motive to kill his brother-in-law and that blood on the mallet could be human."

"Clutching at straws, springs to mind," Clara said, folding her arms.

"You find me another suspect," Park-Coombs responded. "Or prove conclusively that Harry was not there at the time of the murder."

"I'm working on it," Clara swore. "Now, I have come across something of interest and it is fortuitous that Dr Deáth is here, as an expert opinion could be needed."

"That does sound intriguing!" Dr Deáth brightened up, he had obviously felt bad to have had to admit to Park-Coombs he could not definitively state the mallet they had found in the locker was the murder weapon.

"What do you have, Clara," the inspector said in a dull tone that suggested he didn't really care.

Clara placed the piece of paper she had taken from the crate at the town hall on the inspector's desk.

"I am fairly confident, Inspector, that this is the paper used to write those threatening notes. What struck me about those letters was the unusual quality of the stock, it is thicker than standard writing paper."

Park-Coombs picked up the sheet and rubbed it between his fingers.

"I suppose you want to compare it to the letters?" He reached down and opened a drawer in his desk. "After we last spoke, I thought it might be a good idea to store the letters in my office. I had the feeling they might prove important."

He took out one of the letters and set it on top of the paper stock Clara had brought with her. He examined them together.

"They do appear similar, what are your thoughts Dr Deáth?"

Deáth picked up the two pieces of paper and held them to the window to examine them in the same light.

"There is a watermark," he said. "Very faint, could be in the shape of a rose. It is on this large sheet, in the centre.

What of this letter?"

He turned the letter in the light.

"It seems to me there is something in the corner of the paper, maybe a rough shape. Could be a rose petal. What if I do this?"

He overlaid the letter on the large sheet of paper and held them both to the window so the light could shine through. Clara came and stood by his shoulder, trying to see what he was doing. The paper was so thick the light barely crept through the two layers, but it did seem as if there was an impression that matched on both pieces. Dr Deáth turned the letter over and placed it on a different area of the large sheet. He did this a couple of times before he appeared satisfied.

"Here we are. If I was in the morgue, I would get a very powerful light and could see better, but I do believe that there is a fragment of a watermark at the corner of this letter which matches with the watermark in the centre of the large sheet. What do you think Clara?"

Clara peered as hard as she could. If she was honest, she struggled to make out the watermark on the big sheet, let alone trying to glimpse the edge of the mark on the letter. She thought there was something there, but nothing she would stake her life on.

"I'll take your word for it," she had to admit.

Dr Deáth grinned.

"That alone is hardly conclusive," he agreed. "Now, the paper stock is of a similar thickness and notice the lines through the paper of the mesh frame these sheets were made on. It matches. They have the same lines in the same place. There are other tests I could run and if I spoke to the manufacturer of this paper they could probably offer me a way to say for certain they were the same. But even without that, I am fairly confident this letter came from the same source as this large sheet."

Inspector Park-Coombs was looking brighter.

"Where did you come across this paper, Clara?"

"Behind the town hall," Clara explained. "There was a

hinged crate containing sheets of it. They use the paper for wrapping up the smaller fossils before they pack them."

"My word," Park-Coombs gasped. "But that means…"

"Hmm, someone from the exhibition is behind the threats," Dr Deáth finished his sentence. "Or at least someone who has access to the same paper."

"Which is not going to be Reverend Parker," Clara remarked. "He would not buy the same paper as the exhibition. This is not stationary paper. I think, whoever is writing the threats, is taking advantage of the ready supply of paper stock travelling with the exhibition."

Park-Coombs gave a whistle of surprise.

"That opens a whole new can of worms," he shook his head as if trying to shake out the thought. "The Earl of Rendham will be furious."

"I do not believe the earl employs you," Dr Deáth told Park-Coombs with a slight hint of reprove.

"No, but he makes a fuss to the men who do employ me," Park-Coombs looked bleak. "Thanks for bringing this to my attention Clara, even if it only muddies the water further."

"Sorry about that," Clara said and meant it. "I'll keep digging about, I'm sure to unearth something good soon."

Dr Deáth grinned at her.

"I say a similar thing when going about my work," he said.

Clara was not sure if that was meant as a joke or a serious statement. A quick glance at the inspector told her that he was not sure either. She gave a polite laugh to be safe and then excused herself.

Clara was on a roll now. She was one step closer to knowing who was writing those letters, and to clearing Harry's name. What she really needed was insight into the politics behind the exhibition. How did all these people click together? Who had organised the thing in the first place? Was it true that the Earl of Rendham was fronting the money for his own benefit? These were the sort of questions that could take weeks of digging to unravel, time she did not have. But Clara knew of someone who was used to rooting out such secrets and who might be able to offer her help. After all, there were not many people in Brighton more tenacious and nosier than Clara Fitzgerald, but she did know of one.

The Brighton Gazette was situated in an unusually shaped building, with a narrow frontage and a double-height downstairs and a solitary office for the editor on a mezzanine level above. No one could quite remember what the building had been originally constructed for. Some said it had been a chapel, others that it was a storehouse, there was even a theory it had been built for net-making, the long floor space being ideal. But it was in the wrong place and far too ornate for such a mundane purpose. In any case, for as long as post people could recall, it had been the home of The Brighton Gazette.

Clara walked into the reception, which was partitioned off from the main floor by a light wooden wall with a door in the middle. The partition did not go above eight foot, and so it did not reach the ceiling and you could hear all the noise from the room beyond; the clank of the presses, the furious typing of writers and proof-readers. The noise was somewhat over-powering. Clara paused near the girl who manned the front door and supposedly stopped people from just entering. She was a different girl from the one who had been working there on a previous visit.

"I want to see Gilbert McMillan," Clara told her.

"We have a procedure for making complaints," the girl said with a weariness to her tone that suggested she heard a similar thing day-in and day-out.

"I'm not here to complain," Clara laughed. "I want to talk to him."

The girl eyed her suspiciously, maybe others had tried to get past her that way.

"If you like, go see him and say that Clara Fitzgerald wants a word. I have some questions I hope he can help me with."

The girl still looked uncertain, but she did finally rise

from her chair and head to the main floor. Clara waited patiently, tapping her food and listening to the rumble of the heavy presses being prepared for yet another edition.

Behind her a man rushed in. He was stout and red in the face, whether from anger or having hurried to the office she could not tell. He looked at her, then at the empty desk.

"I want to see Gilbert McMillan!" He informed Clara, seeming to assume she could somehow help him.

"That's nice," Clara said, slightly affronted. "He seems popular."

"Stupid oaf wrote a ghastly report about the Brighton Town Flower Committee meeting the other night!" The man puffed up his chest and waved his hands about. "Said we were floundering in our own sea of ignorance and indecision! And they printed that! Printed that in the paper!"

Clara rarely had time to read the newspapers, but she was aware that Gilbert's shrewd, but rather cutting, writing style had a tendency to offend nearly everyone he wrote about. It also sold the papers, which was why the editor did not deter him. Gilbert McMillan could turn the dull meeting of the local parish board into a dramatic episode full of intrigue and biting remarks. You read those pieces just to see what Gilbert was going to say next. Of course, it did also generate complaints.

"The man can't say those sort of things," the gentleman next to Clara continued to protest. "I have rights!"

"We all do," Clara observed, trying not to get involved.

The man, however, was determined to air out his grievances on her.

"We are all volunteers and we don't take any cut of the money, as Mr McMillan implied. We are allowed to claim expenses, naturally, but nothing excessive. I think it was all very rude, very rude indeed!"

The man suddenly threw himself down onto a chair near the door and flapped a hand in front of his face.

"Bloomin' hot today," he moaned. "None of this is good for my heart. My doctor tells me to take things easy. You would think being on a flower committee would be exactly that, but no, you have all these problems and people like McMillan stirring up trouble where there is none."

The reception girl reappeared. She caught a glimpse of the man who had entered, and her face told Clara she recognised him and was not pleased to see him. No wonder the last girl had left, if every day was about confronting those people Gilbert McMillan had made furious.

"He said to come through, Miss Fitzgerald," the girl told Clara.

"Hey, hey! If you are letting her through, I can go through!" The man had jumped up from his seat again.

"We have already had this discussion Mr Brown," the girl responded firmly.

Clara disappeared through the door as Mr Brown worked himself up into a temper again. She could hear his voice rising as she escaped into the din of the newspaper office.

There was nothing orderly or tidy about the ground floor of The Brighton Gazette, desks were roughly arranged in two rows down the centre of the room and provided working space for the various journalists, typesetters and proof-readers who kept the paper running. Each desk was a swamp of paper, pencils and pens, along with the more complicated tools of the typesetter as they laid out the latest edition. Paper flopped onto the floor, some in sheets, some in crumpled balls of disgust, none appeared to make it to the wastepaper baskets provided beside each desk. Hats and coats were flung on the backs of chairs or teetered on the very corner of a desk; bags and briefcases caused trip hazards in the aisles between them, and there was all manner of random items strewn about. Clara kicked a half-eaten apple to one side with the toe of her shoe as she headed for Gilbert's desk.

Gilbert was waiting for her and smiled broadly. He was a shabbily dressed young man who looked like someone had thrown clothes at him and hoped for the best. His hair was a little too long for the current fashion and his fingers bore the stains of leaking pens and nicotine from endless cigarettes. He had the worst teeth Clara had seen in a long time, they seemed to be crowding each other and arguing over space, they were also stained brown by his intensive smoking habit. If his appearance was not precisely charming, he was at least amiable and a good source of gossip when Clara needed it. He also had the good grace to welcome Clara with a handshake – most men would not.

"You want to talk to me?" He said.

"I want to pick your brains over something. You've been writing all the material on the recent fossil exhibition at the town hall?"

"I have," Gilbert said proudly. "Have you read my articles?"

"For once I managed to find the time and yes I believe I have read most of them," Clara said, knowing how to butter up Gilbert. "They were most insightful and intelligently written. Not just a rehash of the usual stuff. That is why I hope you can help me."

In the office foyer, Mr Brown's voice had risen to a pitch where it could be heard over the rattle of typewriters and rollers. Gilbert ducked his head involuntarily at the sound.

"Let's talk somewhere quieter," he suggested. "We'll slip out the back door, if you don't mind?"

Clara was merely amused.

"Lead the way Mr McMillan," she told him.

Gilbert grabbed his hat and pointed to the back of the building. They just managed to exit, before Mr Brown barged his way into the newspaper office.

Chapter Twenty-five

Gilbert knew of a little café in a back street close to the newspaper office. It was cheap and it was quiet, the haunt of most of the journalists when they wanted strong tea, greasy bacon rolls and a bit of peace. Gilbert opened the door to the place which did not appear to have a name, at least there was no signage at the front to suggest this was a café, just a notice on the door that stated the business was open. Clara walked into a wall of smoke as she entered, and discreetly coughed. There were four men already inside, dotted about the handful of tables, and each of them was smoking for Britain. The café owner was stood behind a narrow wooden counter and he too was smoking, the ash tray next to his hand revealing he was a chain smoker much like his patrons. Clara hoped he put his cigarette to one side when he actually cooked.

Gilbert ordered them two teas, which came in thick white ceramic mugs, that looked like they might bounce if you dropped them on the floor. Then he ushered Clara to a table by the window at the front of the café. They were screened from the outside world by a net curtain that blocked the lower portion of the glass. Gilbert sat down and instantly started to roll a new cigarette. His fingers worked speedily and with practiced dexterity, the roll-up was soon lit and in his mouth. He winked at Clara.

"Can't think without it."

"I've never been a smoker," Clara shrugged.

"It's good for you," Gilbert gave a hearty cough. "Clears the lungs. Now, what can I help you with?"

"I know what you are like Gilbert and I am sure you dug up a lot more information about the exhibition than the editor would allow to be printed in the paper."

Gilbert grinned, pleased with himself and that someone else recognised his abilities.

"I have heard rumours, but I am curious to know if there is any truth to them," Clara continued. "In particular, I am wondering about the Earl of Rendham's involvement in this whole affair."

Gilbert's eyes lit up.

"What have you heard?" He asked eagerly.

"That the earl is hoping to make a lot of money off the back of this exhibition and that is why he is its main sponsor. He is also very agitated about the murder that occurred at the town hall the other night. He is in town trying to hurry the police into making an arrest."

"Now I didn't know that," Gilbert was gleeful for this nugget of information. "I can answer a number of your questions, I can probably give you more information than you want to be truthful. The earl has invested in several quarries across the country, and from them have come a few fossils over the years. Nothing hugely spectacular, until last year the skeleton of an Archaeopteryx was found."

Clara pricked her ears.

"I heard he has his own Archaeopteryx," she said.

"It's a good specimen too, pretty complete from what I have heard. More importantly, it is the first of its kind found in Britain. Most of the other specimens have come from quarries in Germany. The earl is a smart businessman, he knows the value of his find to museums and the like, but he also knew the real money is with private collectors," Gilbert tapped cigarette ash into the ashtray on the table. "This exhibition is all about drumming up interest. Let people have a real good look at an Archaeopteryx, be dazzled by its rarity and uniqueness, then, bam, as soon as the exhibition is over, put the only British specimen on the market."

"We are talking a lot of money," Clara surmised.

"With all the attention this exhibition has aroused, I think you could be looking at a small fortune. And the earl would appreciate that. His father died a couple of years ago, leaving him the title and a lot of debt. The late earl did not have a head for business and wasted money on surplus servants, decorating the family home and landscaping the estate. He was one of those Victorian gentlemen who couldn't resist building extravagant follies and redecorating the house every six months," Gilbert chuckled to himself. "From what I have heard, the estate is close to ruin and the earl either marries someone with a lot of money or sells up. He hasn't had much luck with the former and he doesn't want to resort to the latter."

"The discovery of a British Archaeopteryx was rather lucky for him," Clara observed.

Gilbert's grin became wicked.

"Some might argue the earl makes his own luck."

Clara did not have to say anything to indicate her curiosity at that statement, nor did Gilbert need any encouragement to carry on.

"I can't verify the details, but I heard it from someone who should know, that this new Archaeopteryx may not have come from the quarry, it may, in fact, have been cooked up in some sculptor's studio."

Clara's eyes widened.

"They are suggesting it is fake?" She dropped her voice, feeling this was too great a thing to speak loudly. "But how could he possibly get away with that?"

"If it is a good enough fake it would fool a lot of people. All the more reason to sell it to a private collector too. In a museum there would be a lot of experts taking a look at it and potentially spotting that it was a fraud. Private collectors are unlikely to have that sort of expertise."

"Yet someone must have authenticated it?" Clara said. "The earl would need the word of a trusted scientific establishment to get the price he hopes for."

"The earl only needs the word of a reliable expert in the field," Gilbert explained. "And he has one, in the form of the current director of the fossil department at The Natural History Museum. The same gentleman behind this exhibition. This man has authenticated the earl's Archaeopteryx, even wrote a paper on it for a scientific journal. That's how you get these fossils recognised, you know, have an expert write a paper on it and have it published in one of the leading journals on the subject."

"The director has put his reputation on the line," Clara said, thinking of the potential consequences the man could face. "If it is discovered he deemed a fake the real thing, the backlash could be terrible."

"That is a risk," Gilbert nodded. "But I expect the man is going to be well-compensated for taking a chance. He'll get a cut of the sales and the more that fossil sells for the greater his portion. So, you see why the earl would be so concerned about the exhibition getting stuck here?"

"I do," Clara agreed. "I also feel alarmed at it all. Such underhand behaviour from men you would expect better from. And, should this prove true and it all be revealed, can you imagine the pleasure it will give to organisations such as the League for Christians Against Evolution?"

"They will use it to bolster their case that the Archaeopteryx is some sort of scientific fraud, designed by atheists to attack the Church," Gilbert suggested.

"Exactly," Clara sighed. "And that would be truly awful."

"But not our problem, well, maybe my problem, but not yours," Gilbert tried to cheer her up. "I'm going to try to get better proof so I can print this story and nip the whole thing in the bud. I could really make a name for myself if I reveal this scandal. My editor won't print anything without sound evidence, however."

"At least now I know why the earl is in town and breathing down Inspector Park-Coombs' neck. If the earl had his way, poor Harry Beasley would be charged with murder."

"Who?" Gilbert frowned.

"The dead man, John Morley's, brother-in-law," Clara explained.

"He is a suspect?" Gilbert asked with interest.

"Only because he disliked his brother-in-law, there is no real evidence against him. I am hoping to prove he was at work at the time John Morley died."

"Then, who did kill him?" Gilbert asked. "I've started an article on the crime, but it is really rather boring at the moment."

"I don't know who killed John Morley," Clara admitted. "He went to the town hall with someone else, someone who was supposed to help him. That man is the killer, but I don't know who he might be. Hence why Harry Beasley has come under suspicion."

"I've been trying to get an angle on this case and have so far failed," Gilbert said, for the first time looking a little crestfallen. "No one seems to have an idea why John Morley would suddenly break into the town hall and try to destroy a prized fossil."

"He was paid by the Golden Archaeopteryx Society," Clara explained. "But you can't repeat that, I don't want to alienate them when I might still need their help."

"Wait, wait, why would they hire him?"

"I am told they were worried about the security of the Archaeopteryx fossil, due to threatening letters sent to the exhibition. They wanted to shake the exhibition staff by demonstrating how easy it would be for the fossil to be destroyed. John Morley was never supposed to harm the fossil."

"And you believe that?" Gilbert said with a snort of

203

disbelief. "Sounds like a cock and bull story to me."

"It has its logic," Clara replied, feeling stung by his derision.

Gilbert shook his head.

"I wouldn't take that at face value at all. For that matter, what do you really know about this 'Society' because it is the first I have heard of them, and I have been rummaging about in this business for weeks."

Clara was beginning to feel uneasy, wondering if she had been spun a line by Sam Gutenberg and accepted it without question. Had she been tricked?

"I met the man who admitted to hiring John Morley. His name is Sam Gutenberg, he claims to be part of this Society. He is from South Africa."

"Never heard of him," Gilbert replied. "I'm intrigued though, just who is this fellow and what is he really up to?"

"You have me wondering that too," Clara felt foolish. "I have his address. I shall pay him another call and see what he has to say."

"I wouldn't mind tagging along," Gilbert said. "I like to know all the angles on this matter."

Clara was reluctant to agree, seeing as she already felt stupid for being so quick to accept Sam Gutenberg's statement. She should have looked into the Golden Archaeopteryx Society and confirmed for herself that it existed. She didn't like to think she had been gullible.

"As for those threatening letters..." Gilbert hinted, wanting to hear what she knew about them.

"I suspect they have been written by someone involved in the exhibition," Clara said. "I found the same paper used for the threats at the town hall. It is unusual quality and very distinctive."

"An inside job? This little business gets more and more devious by the minute. You know, if I discover that anyone genuinely wanted to let the public see the Archaeopteryx fossil for purely educational purposes, I think I might be somewhat shocked!" Gilbert laughed.

"Do you know anything about Dr Browning?" Clara

said, beginning to wonder if he had been spinning her a story too when he hired her to investigate the threats. "Is he a party to all this mischief?"

"As far as I am aware Dr Browning is just what he says he is," Gilbert smiled. "So, there you have it, I just contradicted myself! Dr Browning has worked at the Natural History Museum since 1904, he is a world-renowned expert on the Archaeopteryx, having worked for a number of years at a Berlin Museum, where one of the best specimens found in the country was kept. Of course, that was long before the war."

Clara paused him.

"Wait, if Dr Browning is the top expert on this and is travelling with the exhibition, must we assume he too is in on the scheme to sell a fake Archaeopteryx?"

"I think it more likely he knows nothing about that," Gilbert said. "I found Dr Browning rather innocent in his outlook on life. I interviewed him for that piece on the newspaper. I can't imagine him being a good liar or someone prepared to stake their academic reputation for money. He was proposed for this job by the director of the fossil department. I would guess to get him out of the way while his superior worked on turning a fake into a fortune."

"You mean Dr Browning might be so damn honest, that he would reveal the fraud if he learned about it?" Clara nodded. "I could see that as a possibility. Instead, he gets sent across the country, completely distracted by all that is going on, and unable to interfere with the plans of the director and the earl."

"It's only a guess," Gilbert answered. "I think poor Dr Browning is finding this whole experience exhausting. I went over and spoke to him after the break in and murder at the town hall. He was pale as a man on his death bed and looked fit to give up the ghost."

"I hope I can resolve this matter for him swiftly," Clara said. "I have this other nagging worry. What if I prove Harry Beasley is innocent and then the earl needs a new scapegoat and the only one to hand is Dr Browning? There is no real evidence against him, but the circumstances could be enough to convict him. I have heard of people being hanged for a lot less."

Gilbert became serious.

"It would get a potential problem out of the way for both the earl and the director too. But would they be that callous?"

"Now you are being naïve, Gilbert," Clara smiled at him. "Money makes men do the cruellest of things. Not that I am saying the earl orchestrated this crime, but it would make life simpler for them if Dr Browning took the blame. It would mean the exhibition could move on and there would be no 'world-expert' to decry the first British Archaeopteryx. It's the sort of opportunity wicked men take advantage of."

"And I thought I was cynical," Gilbert shifted in his seat.

"Well, if I can find the real killer, none of that will happen," Clara said. "Ready to go meet with Sam Gutenberg?"

Gilbert stubbed out his cigarette.

"Ready!"

Chapter Twenty-six

Sam Gutenberg was staying in a luxury hotel overlooking the beach and the sea. Clara and Gilbert located him in the hotel lounge after having one of the porters look for him. Sam was enjoying a cup of black tea and crumpets. He greeted Clara warmly, but eyed Gilbert with suspicion.

"I thought I might see you again," he said to Clara, motioning for his visitors to take seats. "You have more questions?"

"I do," Clara said. "For a start, I am curious about the Golden Archaeopteryx Society."

"What about it?" Sam asked innocently.

Gilbert grinned, he was itching to speak. Clara responded first.

"I am having trouble finding information about it," she said.

Sam looked surprised, then he caught the expression on Gilbert's face, and he became angry.

"You think I am lying? That there is no Society?" He demanded.

"Hey, I said nothing," Gilbert replied, the question having been clearly directed at him. "I just haven't come across the name before."

"That's because we are largely based in South Africa and Europe," Sam said coldly. "We only have a handful of members in Britain. You see, in England there is the Association for the Greater Understanding of Prehistoric Birds and their Fossils. They deal with the Archaeopteryx."

Sam looked deeply offended.

"If you want, I can give you names of people you can contact within the Society," he grumbled.

"That won't be necessary," Clara told him gently. "The question had to be asked. A man is, after all, dead."

Sam Gutenberg became sombre and some of his ire diminished.

"That is awful," he agreed. "I never meant for that to happen. I explained my intentions. I wanted the organisers of the exhibition to take better precautions over the display of the Archaeopteryx. I wanted to get them to see how reckless they were being."

"You must be one of the few people involved in this whole affair that actually cared about that fossil for its sake alone," Gilbert said, though some of his antagonism had disappeared.

"How do you mean?" Sam Gutenberg looked puzzled.

"Have you heard about the Archaeopteryx that has been found in a British quarry?" Clara changed the subject.

"Yes," Sam nodded. "I had heard a rumour. No one has come forward and said for certain it is a new discovery."

"I think there will be a lot more talk after the exhibition has finished," Gilbert said drily. "But that is only my opinion."

"The Society would be interested in something like that?" Clara persisted.

"Of course," Sam almost laughed. "Is it not in a museum already?"

"It belongs to the Earl of Rendham, he found it in one of his quarries," Gilbert explained.

Sam took a moment to let this sink in.

"Really?" He said. "But he is the main sponsor of the exhibition, why has he not come forward to discuss this new find with the Archaeopteryx touring the country?"

"It's all rather complicated," Clara said. "Sam, is there anything more you can tell me about your arrangement with John Morley? Anything, even a minor thing, might reveal who went with him and killed him."

Sam pulled a face as he thought hard.

"When we first spoke, John was very keen, he liked the sound of the money, I knew that," Sam said thoughtfully. "But, when we met in the pub and I handed over the first half, he seemed less sure of himself. I had the impression he had never done anything quite like this before and there had been a lot of police attention around the exhibition. He seemed nervous.

"He started to talk about involving a second person, someone to accompany him. I was not terribly happy about that. He said he had a friend who was reliable and was already linked to the exhibition. He said he could get him into the town hall. Then he started asking for a bit more money to pay this friend of his. I almost walked away at that point. He changed his tune quickly, said the original money was fine, but that he was going to ask this friend to help him. I didn't protest further."

"He said the friend was connected with the exhibition?" Clara found this interesting. "Mr Gutenberg, I now suspect that the person sending the threats to the exhibition is connected to it. In fact, I am certain of that. The threats are being sent by someone who works with the fossils."

Sam Gutenberg looked genuinely surprised.

"What? But…" he frowned. "That makes no sense. Why would someone work for the exhibition and send threatening letters?"

"I'm still investigating that," Clara said. "But you have now told me about a second connection between someone at the exhibition and a crime committed there. Did John tell you anything more about this friend who was going to help him?"

"No," Sam shrugged. "He just said he was an old friend and reliable. I was annoyed with him and didn't pry further."

Sam clasped his hands together uneasily.

"Had I known John was going to end up dead, had I thought something like that could happen, I would never have even suggested the plan. Had I known Dr Browning capable of killing a man…"

"You think Dr Browning did this?" Clara interrupted him.

Sam looked at her in astonishment.

"I can't fathom why the police have not already arrested him. He is surely responsible?"

"Why would you say that?" Gilbert leaned forward, excited by this new gossip.

"Do you not know?" Sam shook his head. "It was well hushed up at the time and no charges were ever pressed, but Dr Browning was suspected of having murdered one of his colleagues when he worked at a museum in Germany. They were alone in one of the exhibit halls, preparing a display for the public. Dr Browning always claimed that an intruder had snuck in to try and steal a fossil to sell on, and that this mystery man had killed his colleague. Dr Browning said he was in his office at the time, getting some display tags. He heard a commotion, rushed back to the hall and found his colleague groaning on the floor tiles. A man was just disappearing through a door.

"He chased the man, but lost him, and then summoned the local police and a doctor. His colleague died before the doctor arrived. He had been smacked on the back of a head with a hammer."

Sam Gutenberg looked triumphant. Gilbert whistled through his teeth.

"That is quite a coincidence," he said.

Clara had to agree. She suddenly felt foolish; could it be, after all, that Dr Browning was their man? Had his appearance of being an anxious, overworked, but innocuous academic, been just a façade? Had she been gulled by him?

Clara was starting to wonder if she was going soft,

losing her cynical edge.

"Dr Browning was never arrested for that crime?" She asked Sam.

"Never, as I say, it was hushed up. I know about it because one of the members of the Society used to work at the same museum. He always said there was something a little sinister about Dr Browning. Something he did a good job hiding from the world," Sam gave a derisive snort. "Guess he couldn't hide it anymore."

~~~*~~~

Clara walked with Gilbert back to the newspaper office.

"Have I got this all backwards? Did I ignore the obvious?" She said.

"You tell me," Gilbert said, though he smiled with it. "You have more information on this affair than I do. I've met Dr Browning briefly. He didn't strike me as a man with blood on his hands."

"Exactly," Clara replied with satisfaction. "Have we both been blind?"

They had reached the back door of the newspaper office. Gilbert paused with a hand on the door handle.

"Are you starting to doubt yourself Clara Fitzgerald?" He asked, a mischievous look in his eye. "If you were one of my colleagues, I would tell you to get out there and stop being so self-absorbed. Go find the man responsible and leave behind the self-pity. We all make mistakes, that's a certainty. It's what we do about those mistakes after we make 'em that matters."

Clara gave a short laugh.

"All right, Gilbert, I am duly chastened. I shall go solve my case."

"Excellent, and if you need anything more, you know where to find me. I am going to dig about in the Earl of Rendham's past and see what I can drag out. Not that I think he is a killer, but I can smell a story in this mess."

"Glad I could help," Clara laughed.

She headed off in the direction of the town hall. She wanted another chat with Dr Browning and as the exhibition would be closing shortly, it was a good time to catch him.

Dr Browning was sitting on his chair near the Archaeopteryx case. He looked ill, like he was coming down with a cold. He seemed on the verge of falling asleep, his head tipping forward every now and again as he nearly nodded off. As Clara approached him, he roused himself.

"Do you have news?" He asked hopefully.

"I have questions," Clara said in an apologetic tone. "I have discovered that the paper used to write the threatening letters is the same as you use to wrap up the more delicate exhibition specimens. The obvious conclusion is that someone with access to that paper has been writing those notes."

What little colour had been in Dr Browning's face now drained away.

"Someone working at the exhibition?" He said with horror. "Oh no."

"You did not have any suspicions?"

Dr Browning slumped his shoulders as he replied in a weary voice.

"No. None."

"You never noticed the paper for the threats was the same as the packing paper?"

"I don't pack the fossils," Dr Browning replied. "Wallace and Percy are responsible for that. They unpack them when we arrive and pack them when we leave. The only time I would interfere is if there was a problem, and so far there have been none."

"Wallace is from Brighton?" Clara asked.

"Yes, I believe so," Dr Browning nodded. "He has been staying at his own home while we are here."

"Are any of the other members of the exhibition crew local?"

"To Brighton?" Dr Browning wrinkled his forehead.

"No, only Wallace."

Clara filed away that piece of information for later. She took a look around the room and noted that the only other person present was an older gentleman studying the cases near the main doors. There was no one to overhear her next words to the academic.

"Dr Browning, I have been made aware of an incident that happened to you in Germany many years ago. It seems that incident was almost identical to what happened here the other night."

Dr Browning looked startled, he had to grab a handkerchief from his pocket and wipe his forehead where a cold sweat had formed.

"Oh," he groaned and held the handkerchief to his mouth as if he felt unwell. "I hoped to never hear about that terrible night again."

"I am curious that the police do not appear to be aware of it," Clara pointed out.

"It happened in Germany in 1901," Dr Browning said solemnly. "No charges were pressed against me, nothing was ever mentioned in the British press. No one knows about it, I thought it was all forgotten."

Dr Browning hung his head forward. He looked worn out, a tired old soul who could go on no longer.

"Clearly someone has not forgotten," he said in a voice that was barely above a whisper. "I've never told anyone. Even my superiors at the Natural History Museum are unaware. I do not have a criminal past, if someone has implied that…"

"Dr Browning, the events that happened here the other night are startlingly similar to the events that occurred in Germany in 1901. You can't be blind to that?"

Dr Browning clutched the handkerchief in his hands and let out a little sob.

"Miss Fitzgerald, I feel very unwell," he said weakly. "Would you kindly help me onto my camp bed?"

Clara wondered if the man was trying to play the poor academic, a martyr to his nerves, yet again. However, she could not deny that he looked quite sick and seemed fit to fall from his chair. She glanced around and spotted the camp bed tucked up a corner. She fetched it and unfolded it before the Archaeopteryx display case. The town hall was now empty and the porter at the door was beginning to rattle his keys and contemplate locking the doors for the day.

Clara helped Dr Browning to lay down on the camp bed. There was no pillow that she could see, but he didn't complain. He just looked relieved to be resting at last. Clara pressed a hand to his forehead and discovered he was feverish. She felt for his pulse and it was racing. Even the most creative of actors could not fake those symptoms. Dr Browning was genuinely sick.

Clara stood up and found the porter in the little foyer outside the main room. He went to hold the front door open for her and she raised her hand to pause him.

"I think Dr Browning needs a doctor. He seems very unwell."

The porter looked surprised. He stepped to the doors of the main room and it took him a moment to spot Dr Browning laid out on the camp bed. The man had shut his eyes and seemed to have fallen into a deep sleep. The porter glanced back at Clara, clearly baffled by the turn of events.

"Sooner rather than later, might be good," Clara prodded him. "I'll keep an eye on him while you fetch help."

"Miss, I can't leave you here alone."

Clara rolled her eyes.

"Fine, I shall fetch help, but you need to watch him closely, make sure he keeps breathing. Do you know what to do if he stops?"

The porter looked panicked.

"Well, you have a choice," Clara said. "Either fetch a doctor or play nurse to Dr Browning. Personally, I have nursing experience and know what I am doing around a man in a fever. I think Dr Browning's condition is quite serious and he needs to be monitored until the doctor arrives. Else, he may very well slip away. Do you understand?"

The porter had his mouth hanging open, as if he had just been told the king had popped by to say hello. He had to shake off his confusion and make a decision.

"I'll fetch a doctor," he told Clara. "You stay here, but don't touch anything."

Clara was offended, but the porter was already disappearing out the front doors. She went back to Dr Browning and sat by his side. He was taking shallow breaths and his cheeks had taken on an unhealthy flush.

"Oh dear, Dr Browning," Clara picked up his hand and continued to feel for his pulse. "What a mess this all is."

Chapter Twenty-seven

Dr Browning was taken to hospital. Clara had suspected that would be the case; the doctor who had been fetched feared the fever was a sign of a serious underlying illness. For the time being, Clara could not interrogate the academic further about the incident in Germany. She went home and had tea with Annie and Tommy, before turning out again to find Harry's foreman and at least resolving one aspect of this case.

It was just after eight when she arrived at the train station and she was in time to see the 8.05 leave the platform. Clara had always had a fondness for trains; the big engines seemed to have a personality that belied the fact they were merely machines of steel and steam. It did not take her long to find Mr Turnbull. He was dealing with a problematic drain that led off the platform. It had become clogged and was producing a foul smell. Several of his workmen were stood around it, poking and prodding into the gloom of the drain with iron rods. Mr Turnbull stood back a pace watching, a handkerchief pressed to his nose to try and eliminate the smell.

Clara was just about to speak to him when the odour from the blocked drain struck her and she gagged. Coughing hard into her hand she found her eyes streaming and her voice gone. Mr Turnbull glanced in her direction and hastily ushered her away.

"Sorry miss, should have put a board up to stop the public coming that way," he apologised, though he looked annoyed.

"Actually…" Clara coughed, and the words slowly came back. "Actually, I was hoping to speak to you, Mr Turnbull."

Mr Turnbull was surprised. He was a short man in his fifties, with wiry grey hair and the lean, but powerful physique of a man who has done manual labour all his life. He was wearing a pair of brown overalls over his shirt and trousers. They were clean and had been recently ironed, marking him out from the other men in his charge, whose overalls were dirty and crumpled.

"Why would you want to talk to me?" Mr Turnbull asked.

"It's about Harry Beasley," Clara explained, wiping tears from her eyes. "I hoped you could help me."

Mr Turnbull glanced over at his workers, plodding on with the drain blockage.

"I'll be back shortly lads!" He called to them, before turning back to Clara. "Let's talk somewhere quiet."

Mr Turnbull showed her into the workers' locker room, where Harry's locker stood with its door ajar. So much woe had been caused because of the contents of that locker.

"I was shocked when Harry was arrested," Mr Turnbull said, his own eyes wandering to the locker. "And when they found that mallet…"

He was too appalled by it all to finish the statement.

"Harry says the blood and hair on the mallet was from a rat he struck," Clara told Mr Turnbull. "The police surgeon has confirmed the hair on it is from a rodent. He can't, unfortunately, say if the blood is human or animal."

"We do have a rat problem," Mr Turnbull shrugged his shoulders. "There are always food scraps about the line. People drop half-eaten sandwiches and apples, or stuff rolls out of crates when the goods trains are being loaded. It's a paradise for rats. We tried keeping a cat or two, but they were prone to crossing the train tracks at inopportune moments."

Clara winced at the thought.

"The lads will take a swing at a rat if they see one. We all do it. They are such a pain and they can spread nasty diseases. A couple of years ago one of the workmen became really sick, nearly died, and the hospital said it was something he caught from a rat. The stationmaster told us to deal with the problem, clear them out, but he didn't actually give us anything to sort them with," Mr Turnbull snorted at the idiocy of his employers. "We've tried all the usual poisons, but the rats get clever and seem to know which is the poisoned bait. In any case, there are just so many of them."

"Then, what Harry says is completely feasible? That he was nearly due to go home, saw a rat and took a swing at it, then left his mallet to clean up the next day?"

"Crikey, I think if you looked at every fellow's mallet you would find the same!" Mr Turnbull replied. "It is completely feasible. I would be surprised if you found a mallet here that did not have a bit of rat blood on it. I started to give the chaps a shilling every time they smacked a rat and brought me the body, but it was getting too expensive!"

"Harry says he was working on repairing a piece of track that had buckled when his brother-in-law was murdered."

Mr Turnbull nodded.

"We had quite an issue with that section of track. Had to have a whole new length made, then closed off that portion overnight and replaced it. What a nightmare," Mr Turnbull whistled at the memory. "We were told we had to have the track repaired by morning, as they wanted to reopen the line. It was all hands to the deck to deal with it. Only just had it done when dawn came up. I do wonder at the people who come up with these ideas, they seem to think it is so easy to do these things."

"Then Harry was working on that track all night?"

"Harry and all the men," Mr Turnbull agreed, then he looked abashed. "Should I have told the police that? I didn't think. I only heard about Harry being arrested when I came to work last night, and I didn't give it a lot of thought. I was surprised, mind, never considered Harry the sort to get in trouble with the police."

"And you are certain that around midnight on Monday night Harry was working on that piece of track?"

"Oh yes," Mr Turnbull insisted. "I was there. He never left until we were done."

"Mr Turnbull, I need you to come with me to the police station at once to tell them this."

Mr Turnbull looked alarmed.

"I can't just leave work! I'll be in trouble for that!"

"Not as much trouble as Harry Beasley is in right now," Clara persisted. "I shall speak to the stationmaster on your behalf."

Mr Turnbull was grim-faced, but he did agree to go with Clara. They found the stationmaster and Clara made it plain that she was the one insisting that Mr Turnbull go with her to speak to the police and help poor Harry Beasley. Clara could be very persuasive when she needed to be, and the stationmaster did not make a fuss. She wasted no time in escorting Mr Turnbull to Inspector Park-Coombs. The Inspector was putting in a lot of late nights working on the case, and he was not entirely delighted to see his only suspect walk free from his cells, but once he had listened to Mr Turnbull, he could not keep Harry any longer. It was obvious the man was innocent and the Earl of Rendham would have to lump it.

Mr Turnbull returned to work, though not before telling Harry he would be delighted to see him back at the station the following night. Clara walked with Harry back to his house. He could not stop thanking her for helping him and he was almost overcome by emotion. He had started to envision a noose about his neck.

Emma Beasley was elated to see her husband, and insisted Clara come in and at least have a cup of tea for all she had done. Emma ended up cooking tiny thick pancakes, which she served to Clara with homemade jam, all the time having to dab her eyes to keep tears of delight from falling down her cheeks.

"I think you saved my life Miss Fitzgerald," Harry Beasley said, enjoying the pancakes his wife had made. He ate like a man who has been starved for days. "I really thought I was doomed."

"But you did not kill John," Clara reminded him. "Truth always comes out in the end."

"Are you any closer to knowing who did kill him?" Emma asked, her voice tight with emotion. "Ruby woke up this afternoon and asked for him. I didn't know what to say. I said he was not here."

Emma trembled with the sadness of it all. Harry reached out and clasped her hand. Clara was so glad she had reunited the pair; they clearly meant all the world to each other. She wanted to smile at seeing them together but realised it would be inappropriate.

"I am slowly unravelling this mystery," Clara told them, and then she recalled something she had been meaning to ask them for a while. "I was wondering if you ever heard of a man called Wallace Sunderland?"

Emma shook her head, it was not a name she knew. Harry was frowning.

"There was a Wallace in our school," he said. "I went to the same school as John, but I was two years above him. I'm pretty certain there was a boy named Wallace, can't recall his surname. You don't really pay attention to those things as a kid."

"I went to a different school," Emma shrugged. "I'm sorry I can't help you. But maybe Ruby would remember something?"

Harry looked sceptical.

"I don't think we should disturb her," he said.

"I think she would like to help, if she could. We might have had little time for John, but she adored him," Emma sighed. "I don't understand it myself. He was a brute, but

Ruby would have died for him. I think she is strong enough to talk for just a little while."

"I wouldn't want to do anything that might upset her or make her unwell," Clara insisted, feeling anxious any questions might make Ruby's already fragile health worse. If Ruby had forgotten her husband had died, Clara was not sure she wanted to disabuse her of that fiction, not when her own time on this earth was likely short.

"She doesn't need to know that Harry is dead," Emma said. "You think this man Wallace was involved in John's death?"

Clara picked her words carefully.

"I think there is a fair chance, only, I can't see a motive for him killing John just yet."

"John made enemies like other men make friends," Harry snorted. "You never knew him alive. He borrowed money and favours, then pretended he knew nothing about either. He had men hammering on his door demanding he repay his debts. He was a lousy drunk, who picked fights and had a nasty tongue. If he didn't use you, or punch you, he certainly insulted you. I can't fathom how anyone can be sorry he is gone."

Clara thought of the three men they had met in the pub, who had seemed genuinely saddened by the news John had been killed. Friendship was a complicated business, she concluded.

"John asked someone to assist him to break into the town hall the night he died, someone who was an old friend and who was connected with the exhibition. Wallace Sunderland fits part of that description, but I don't know as yet whether he was friends with John. If he was not, then maybe there is someone else I have not even heard the name of yet."

"You must speak to Ruby," Emma replied. "She is the only person who might know."

"Ruby was in the same class as John," Harry said, looking as though that was the worst thing possible. "If the boy called Wallace is the same as this man you are investigating, Ruby should know. I guess you best speak to her."

Emma reached out and clasped his hand, giving him a gentle smile.

"She would want to help," she said softly.

Harry just dropped his head and gave a deep sigh.

Emma took Clara upstairs to the bedroom where Ruby was resting. There was a bit more colour to Ruby's face, but she still looked gaunt. Her hands rested on top of the blanket, the bones of her knuckles and finger joints prominent.

"Ruby?" Emma went to her sister-in-law's side and gently touch her cheek. "Ruby, are you awake?"

Ruby's eyelids fluttered, she took a deep breath which ended in a rattle, and then looked up at Emma.

"I'm awake," she said weakly.

"This is Clara," Emma motioned to Clara and Ruby tilted her head a fraction. "She has a question for you. It might help John."

"John," the words were almost silent as they slipped from Ruby's mouth, it was more the motion of her lips that told the women what she had said. "Is he all right?"

"He's in a bit of bother," Emma said lightly. "That's why Clara needs to ask you a question."

Ruby's head rolled back on the pillow and she slowly licked her dry lips and gave a slight cough.

"What's the question?" She asked.

"Have you ever heard John mention the name Wallace Sunderland?" Clara asked her.

Ruby's lips curled into a smile, she gave a hoarse laugh.

"Wallace..." she let the name slip away. "Wallace and John were thick as thieves, before he left to serve in the war."

"Have you seen him with John recently? Has he mentioned him?" Clara tried not to press the woman too hard, but she was suddenly excited, seeing a possible solution to the case coming into focus.

"He... came over the other day... had fish and chips

with… us," Ruby took a shuddering breath. "Little Wally. Done all right for himself. Got a job. Got a wife."

Emma glanced at Clara, the look in her eyes hopeful. Clara nodded to her, she had what she needed.

"Thank you, Ruby, for answering my questions," Clara said softly.

Ruby mumbled something inaudible and then slipped off to sleep. Emma and Clara left the room and headed back downstairs.

"What does this mean?" Emma asked Clara as they paused in the tiny hallway that divided the front and back of the house.

"I think there is a strong possibility that Wallace Sunderland murdered John. I can't say why, but the evidence all points in that direction," Clara paused. "He also was very close to the town hall when John died, which he shouldn't have been. He should have been at his home."

Emma gave a small gasp. It seemed odd to have a name for the murderer of John Morley, it suddenly made everything feel more real.

"What will you do now?" Emma asked.

Clara glanced out the window, at the darkening night. It was late, too late to chase down Wallace Sunderland.

"I'm going home," Clara said. "Then, tomorrow, I am going to track down the man I think killed John Morley."

Chapter Twenty-eight

The rain clouds had appeared the next day, which rather summed up Clara's mood. She felt unsettled, and gloomy, a sense of foreboding hanging over her. Tommy accompanied her to the town hall, having been restored as her budding assistant in the detective business. He had been forgiven for his mishap with Miss Holbein, especially after he had told Clara all he had learned from Victor and that the man genuinely seemed to care about Nellie. Clara thought it was remarkable, in a way, but everyone deserves a little love in their life, and maybe Victor would bring out the best in Nellie, after all. She was not looking forward to explaining all this to Mrs Wilton, but that was a problem for another day.

"Wallace Sunderland," Tommy had been musing on what Clara had told him about the man as they had walked. "Would he really murder an old friend?"

"I don't know, Tommy, but he fits all the facts I have so far learned. The only other solution is that Dr Browning is really a murderer."

"And that poor fellow does not look likely to live long enough to confess, if that's the case."

Clara had rung the hospital before they had left the house and asked after Dr Browning. It had taken some persuasion to get the information she was after, but she had finally spoken to a nurse attending the academic. It seemed his fever was affecting his heart, and there were grave concerns as to whether he would survive.

"The nurse said that they would know more by tonight if he was likely to recover," Clara replied. "If he did kill John Morley, the toll it has taken on him is worse than any prison sentence and will likely cost him his life."

"And if he is innocent in all this, the strain of events might have killed him. Tragic."

They mounted the steps to the town hall and the porter automatically asked for their tickets. Clara was slightly annoyed that Dr Browning had failed to explain adequately that she was allowed access to the exhibition any time she wished. She had lost count how many times she had told the porter about her reason for being there, and each time he had insisted on speaking to Dr Browning first before he would let her in. Only, today, there was no Dr Browning present.

"I'm looking for Wallace Sunderland," Clara told him.

The porter looked at her snootily, he really had a chip on his shoulder.

"He went to the yard, last I saw him. You can go around the back."

Clara wanted to give the man a piece of her mind, but she held her tongue and obediently walked down the alley to the back of the town hall. Tommy was humming to himself and Clara thought he was amused by events. She tried to shake the tension from herself as they entered the yard. Wallace was stood at a bench, fitting a pane of glass into a wooden frame. He looked up as they appeared.

"Would you believe an elderly gentleman managed to put the end of his walking stick through one of the display cases?" He grumbled in exasperation. "Why do old people wave their sticks about like that? He was pointing out a fossil to his wife and he smashed the glass to shards. What a mess."

Wallace carefully rested the glass in the frame and started to fix it in place with putty.

"Wallace, why did you tell no one that you knew John Morley?" Clara asked him quietly.

Wallace froze, the putty slopping off the tiny palette knife he was using.

"What did you say?"

"You went to school with John Morley," Clara persisted. "You could have identified him for the police, but you didn't. You acted as if you did not know him."

"It was a long time ago," Wallace said. "I went to the war. I forgot about John."

"Really?" Clara said, her tone sharp. "Because I know that John asked a friend to help him break into the town hall the night he died. A friend who had a connection to the exhibition and could get him in."

"Oh no!" Wallace dropped the putty knife and stood up straight. "No! You are not blaming his death on me! I was not here that night!"

"I think you were," Clara continued calmly. "You fetched me from my house only a short time after the murder. You had to be nearby, not at home as you were meant to be. What other reason could there be for you being here than that you had helped John break in?"

"That's not it!" Wallace shook his head furiously. "I was never inside the town hall that night, I swear!"

"Then why were you here?" Clara demanded. "If you were not helping John Morley, why were you not at home?"

"You've got this all wrong!" Wallace was clenching his teeth as he spoke. "I would never kill John!"

"Are you saying he did not ask you for help to get into the town hall?" Clara pushed him.

"No!" Wallace clutched his head in his hands.

"Quite frankly, I'm not convinced," Clara folded her arms and glared at him. "So far I have heard no reason why you were here and not at home, which makes me suspect you are lying."

"No!" Wallace dug his fingers into his hair, looking

distraught. "I'm not going to be hanged for that man."

"Which man?" Tommy asked.

Wallace was muttering under his breath, arguing with himself. He finally rounded on them.

"I never killed John, but I was here that night," he said, breathless at the confession. "It was a coincidence, that's all."

"I am finding that very hard to believe," Clara gave a bitter laugh at the nonsense he was spouting.

"Look, I came to the town hall to…" Wallace bit on his lip, the words not wanting to be spoken. "I can't believe this is happening. You have to understand, I did not know that John intended to break in that night. I wasn't with him, I never knew anything until Dr Browning came rushing out and was calling for the police. He was in such a state, I didn't give it a thought, I just ran over to see what the matter was."

"Then why were you here?" Clara demanded in exasperation.

Wallace didn't want to explain himself, but the only other option was to face arrest for the murder of a friend – and there was a death penalty for murder. He bit so hard on his lip it went white.

"Look, you mustn't tell the police or anything," he said.

"I am making no promises," Clara told him coldly. "As far as I am concerned, you are a murderer unless you can give me a good reason as to why you were here and not helping John Morley."

"I have a reason," Wallace groaned. "But it will cause me so much trouble if it gets back to Dr Browning."

"More trouble than a noose about your neck?" Tommy asked.

Wallace sagged, he saw the hole he was in and that there was no real way out without explaining himself to Clara.

"I was only doing as I was asked," he said. "I want you to understand that, you don't say no to a man like that."

"Who are you talking about?" Clara asked in annoyance,

wanting to shake the information from Wallace.

"The Earl," Wallace slowly admitted. "He has been paying me since the exhibition began to write and deliver threatening letters to Dr Browning."

Clara did not react with the surprise he was expecting.

"I saw that the packing paper you use for the smaller exhibits was the same as that used to write the letters," she said. "I knew someone from the exhibition was writing the notes."

"It was me," Wallace threw up his hands as he exclaimed this. "The Earl told me what to write at first, but I got the hang of it all and started making my own up. The night John died, I was coming here to slip another note under the door. I always deliver the notes by hand, so there is no postal mark. The Earl told me to do that. You can ask him."

Clara believed Wallace could be the note writer, she just wasn't so sure that excluded him from also killing John Morley.

"That is the truth!" Wallace insisted when he saw the look on her face.

"I believe you wrote the threats," Clara told him. "I just don't see how that prevents you from murdering John Morley."

"I'm explaining why I was here!" Wallace shouted at her. "You have to believe me!"

"I think you are going to have to speak to the police, old boy," Tommy said quietly.

"I didn't kill him," Wallace was almost tearful as he pleaded with them. "I should never have agreed to have supper with him. He always was getting me into trouble, even as boys. My father said the war did me a favour, breaking my ties with him, and now I am accused of his murder."

Wallace grimaced and then hid his face with a hand.

"I was as shocked as everyone else when I saw his body."

"Come on Wallace," Tommy took him by the arm. "The

Inspector will want to know all this."

Wallace started to follow Tommy from the yard, defeated, when Clara put out a hand and stopped them both.

"Not yet. Something isn't quite right," Clara glanced between them. "Why would Wallace kill John?"

Tommy paused. It was the one question none of them had been able to answer – why had John been killed?

"I had no argument with John," Wallace hastily added. "I hadn't seen him in years."

Tommy looked unconvinced, but Clara would not be budged. She had this feeling, an instinct, that told her Wallace was not her man.

"You will have to tell the police about the letters," she told Wallace. "But, for the time being, I'm not accusing you of murder."

"Thank goodness!" Wallace gasped with relief. "I would never hurt John. He was a friend. I had no quarrel with him."

They allowed Wallace to go back to his work on the glass pane. He was shaking from head-to-foot and Clara thought there was a risk he might break the glass by accident, but that was not her problem. She and Tommy turned to leave the yard.

"If not Wallace, then who?" Tommy asked his sister.

Clara had come to a halt, looking up at the houses behind the town hall.

"What is it?" Tommy said.

"Maud Hickson is waving at me," Clara replied, her eyes on the top floor of one of the houses. "I think she wants to speak to me."

They headed around the roads to Miss Clarence's shop. The woman gave Clara a suspicious look as she entered.

"Was the dress not to your satisfaction?" She asked cautiously. The overpriced gown had been delivered the previous day to Clara's home address.

"It is lovely," Clara said. "But I would like to ask your

niece to make some adjustments on another item for me."

Clara lied smoothly.

"Which item?" Miss Clarence narrowed her eyes.

Clara thought quickly.

"The dress I am wearing, the bodice is just not right," Clara was wearing a coat, so Miss Clarence could not see the dress and determine for herself if it needed adjustment.

"My niece does not do odd jobs for people," she commented coolly. "She only adjusts items customers have bought here."

"Now I think about it," Clara said slyly, "I'm not so sure about that other dress. I might have to return it."

"No returns once adjustments are made," Miss Clarence said fast.

"Oh dear, then I may have to tell my friends about my dissatisfaction," Clara placed special emphasis on the last word and Miss Clarence was quick to respond.

"My niece could spare you a moment or two, but this will not become a habit. She is not your personal seamstress."

"Thank you," Clara smiled politely, heading for the doorway behind the counter.

Tommy started to follow, and Miss Clarence nearly went purple with indignation.

"I shall not have a man in my back corridor!" She told him firmly.

Tommy was so startled he took a step back from her, then he looked to Clara.

"You wait here," she told him. "You know, maybe have a look at some pieces of jewellery for Annie. She deserves a little present after the trouble you have put her through lately."

Tommy opened his mouth to protest, but Clara hurried to slip through the door. She could only imagine the glee on Miss Clarence's face as she contemplated a sale. The woman's avarice was truly remarkable, along with intimidating. Tommy would be unlikely to escape without buying something and that would give Clara plenty of time to speak to Maud.

She wondered what the girl wanted. She had been waving quite frantically to get Clara's attention from the window. It must be urgent. Clara made her way up the stairs, finding the steep flights just as exhausting as the first time she mounted them. She was out-of-breath as she knocked on the door to Maud's rooms. The girl opened the door quickly and gave a sigh of relief.

"I am so glad you came!" She said, shuffling back so Clara could enter. "I have been hoping to catch you. I couldn't leave my work to find you, my aunt would never have allowed it. I should have fallen dreadfully behind."

Clara did not voice her opinion that Maud's aunt was a slave-driver, taking advantage of her niece.

"When I saw you in the town hall yard, I so hoped you would look in my direction!" Maud clasped a hand to her chest, looking almost horrified at the thought she might have missed Clara. "I could not think what else to do!"

"Why do you want to see me?" Clara asked.

"Oh Miss Fitzgerald, since you last spoke to me, I have spent so many hours thinking over and over that night," Maud said. "I wanted to be helpful to you."

"You were," Clara soothed her.

"No, I wasn't," Maud brushed off her comment. "But that doesn't matter now. I have remembered something Miss Fitzgerald! Something very important!"

Chapter Twenty-nine

Maud had Clara sit in the armchair by the window.

"I have been sitting here and thinking ever since I last saw you," she said. "Trying so hard to remember that night and to recall anything that might be helpful. Honestly, for a long time I could not think of anything, then, last night, I was staring out of the window as the moon broke through the clouds and thinking how its light glinted on any shiny surface it hit, and then I remembered!"

Maud was almost breathless with excitement.

"When I saw the two gentlemen in the yard it was the night of the full moon. It seemed almost as bright as day as I looked out. If only I had seen those men's faces, I am sure I would have recalled every detail of them," Maud crouched down by the arm of the chair and pointed out the window. "The men were moving back and forth, I think they were looking in the crates. Anyway, they caught my attention and I glanced up; as I did, one of the men turned his shoulders towards me and I saw the moon glint off something just for a moment. I had forgotten all about it, until I sat here looking at the moonlight. That man had something on his right lapel, something that was shiny and could reflect the light of the moon just for a moment. I think that might be important, don't you?"

Clara was unsure, many people wore things on their

lapel. It could have been something in a top pocket, like a cigarette case, or it could have been a brass button that had been polished.

"Another thing," Maud persisted, "everything came back to me as I was sitting here thinking. And, maybe this is not of interest to you, but I thought to myself what a nice jacket the second man was wearing. I spend a lot of time looking at clothes and I can tell when someone has had an item made for them and when they just bought a rough fit.

"The other man, his jacket hung loose on him, it was a size too big I would say, and the shoulders were too wide. It had no shape to it and, without meaning to sound crass, you could tell it was a working man's jacket. But the second man, his jacket fitted him perfectly, it had been either made for him or adjusted to fit him. Probably no one else would have noticed such a thing by moonlight, but I did. Is it of use to you?"

Clara was thinking fast – a well-dressed man with something shiny on his right lapel – that indicated one person in particular, but why would he have killed John Morley?

"Maud, you have helped me enormously," Clara told her. "I cannot thank you enough."

Maud was delighted with herself.

"I am so glad I could be of use! I spend so much time looking out of this window," Maud sighed. "And there I thought I was a forgotten seamstress of no interest to anyone."

Clara rested a hand on her arm.

"You are of interest to me," she reassured her.

~~~*~~~

She returned to Tommy downstairs. Miss Clarence gave her a snide look and Clara guessed she would not be welcome in future unless she was buying something expensive. Tommy had a thin, square box in his hand and was looking a little dazed. Clara gave him a questioning look as they left the shop.

"Did you know jewellery cost so much?" He asked Clara.

"She sold you something then?"

"I think it was the priciest thing in the shop," Tommy shook his head, trying to refresh his senses. "I feel as though I have been at the wrong end of a terrifying interrogation."

"Miss Clarence does that to you," Clara reassured him. "It's her selling technique."

"And people come back to her?" Tommy gasped.

"It would appear so," Clara laughed. "But at least I have learned something from Maud. Although, I am not yet sure what it all means."

Clara frowned.

"Before I do anything rash, I would like to speak to Dr Browning. There is something I am missing, and that man seems to be at the centre of all this without trying. It's nearly early visiting time at the hospital, let's see if our academic is awake enough for visitors."

They caught a bus to reach the hospital. Clara had spent a lot of time within the building during the war when she had volunteered as a nurse. The place had a tendency to bring back bittersweet memories, especially as it was here that she first was reunited with Captain O'Harris after believing him lost for good.

Clara asked at the front desk if Dr Browning was allowed to receive visitors and was pleased to learn that he was doing a little better and could be seen. He might not be awake, but she was welcome to look in on him. Only one visitor at a time, however. Tommy resigned himself to waiting for her in the large foyer of the hospital.

Dr Browning was on the Men's Fever Ward, a place where people could be suffering from a range of conditions, which all had one thing in common – the symptom of a fever. Clara had spent time on this ward and knew it was a place where many died. Fever was a symptom of a great deal of illnesses, many fatal, and there was often little that could be done for the patient but to make them comfortable. Among some of the more morbid doctors, the ward had been remained the Morgue Waiting Room. It was sad to see Dr Browning in there, surrounded by so many who were slowly dying. Clara did not yet know if Dr Browning might join them.

She found his bedside and at first thought he was asleep, but as she got closer, he opened his eyes. They were brighter than she could have hoped for and he seemed remarkably alert.

"Good morning, Miss Fitzgerald," he said, his voice soft but not weak.

Clara smiled.

"How are you feeling?"

"A little better," Dr Browning replied. "The doctors think it was something to do with my heart. They say rest will help."

"You had me worried," Clara said.

"I had myself worried," Dr Browning joked. "But I think I shall be fine. There is a question mark over whether I can continue with the exhibition, unfortunately."

"You need to take things easy," Clara told him gently.

"So the doctors keep saying," Dr Browning groaned at the prognosis. "I can't think what I shall do with myself if I cannot continue my work."

"You shall read and you shall catch up with the latest papers on fossils," Clara told him. "And you shall eat well, sleep well and get quite strong again."

"Well, that does not sound the worst medicine to me," Dr Browning laughed lightly, and there was a spark in his eyes that gave Clara a lot of hope. "Did you just come to see how I was doing?"

"I confess I had an ulterior motive," Clara became serious. "I am still working on your case and trying to get to the bottom of all this business. I am sorry I gave you a shock yesterday when I brought up the incident in

Germany."

Dr Browning lifted a hand to stop her.

"It took me by surprise, that is all. I thought no one knew about it over here. I have not specifically kept it a secret, I simply do not mention it. Nothing came of the matter. Who told you about it?"

"A man who is part of the Golden Archaeopteryx Society. His name is Sam Gutenberg."

Clara was hoping the name might ring a bell with Dr Browning, but he did not react.

"I wonder how he came to know? The whole affair was little reported. It was very sad, a horrible night."

"The similarities between that incident and what happened at the town hall are striking," Clara said carefully.

Dr Browning fixed her with his eyes.

"You mean, they both link to me?"

"I do," Clara admitted. "But, I cannot say what that means just yet, only that you have been connected to two very unfortunate deaths."

"I see it as just bad luck," Dr Browning said, a hint of reproach in his tone.

"And yet, others may not. If the police were to learn of the events in Germany, which they probably will at some point – though not from me I may hasten to add – then they would likely make an unhappy link between the two crimes. More troubling is that the Earl of Rendham is pulling strings to have someone arrested for the murder and thus enable the exhibition to move on. I don't think he is entirely fussed if it is the correct arrest either, as long as it suits his purposes," Clara's tone implied everything her words had avoided – that Dr Browning could easily become a handy scapegoat.

"You think I might be arrested?" Dr Browning asked her, needing to hear her say the words.

"I think it is possible," Clara replied. "That is why I would like you to tell me about that incident in Germany.

The more I know, the better I can help you."

Dr Browning placed one hand atop the other and stared at his fingernails.

"I try not to think about that night too much," he said.

"I would not ask if it was not important."

"No," Dr Browning agreed. "I do understand that. I am just not sure what I can tell you. I was working with my colleague Frank Baumberger to set up a display of ancient gold and silver jewellery found in the region where the Gauls once lived. Everything was priceless. I had gone back to my office to collect display tags; the little printed cards that explain the exhibits. My office was a long way from the gallery where the display was. I left Frank arranging a case of glass beads.

"I don't really know what happened. I must have been gone around twenty minutes. When I came back, Frank was lying on the floor in a pool of blood. There was a hammer discarded next to him. I called his name and then I heard someone running. I glanced up in time to see the door to the gallery closing. I ran to the door and I saw someone heading down the main stairs. I followed them, but they were too fast and I lost them.

"When I returned to Frank, I knew his condition was grave. I hurried to summon the police and a doctor. They tried to save his life, but there was no hope."

Dr Browning became grave.

"Honestly, that was the worst night of my life. The police never found the culprit. There was no sign of someone breaking in, but there was a door to the basement which was unlocked. Probably an oversight by the caretaker. Someone could have come in that way. It looked like they were going to steal some of the jewellery, but Frank got in the way."

"What an awful tragedy," Clara said.

"I have thought over and over, why could it not have been me? I have no ties, no one depends on me. Had I been in that room, instead of Frank, at least only I would have suffered. Instead, Frank's wife and son found themselves in a difficult position. Mrs Baumberger opted to emigrate."

Clara felt that little click in her brain when an idea slipped into place.

"Where did she go?"

Dr Browning considered.

"South Africa, I believe. I think she had family there."

Another mental click for Clara.

"Do you recall the name of Frank's son?" She asked Dr Browning.

He frowned, trying to drag the detail up from his memory.

"It has been a very long time," he said, lifting a hand and scratching at his temple. "I did meet the boy once. He was very keen on fossils, rather like his father. Frank was just an assistant to me, not a trained academic. His family did not have the money to send him to university. If only they had! The mind on that man was fantastic!"

"You were fond of him?" Clara asked.

"He was a friend," Dr Browning nodded. "I can't tell you how often I wish I had sent him to fetch those tags, but it was such a menial task and he was so absorbed in putting together the bead display. I thought I would let him get on with his work. Oh, how I have regretted that choice! If I had been there... I told his wife that at the funeral. If I could have swapped places with him, I would have done so in an instant. But, what was the son's name?"

Dr Browning tapped at his temple with a finger.

"Frank wanted his son to have a better life than he did, he wanted him to go to university. He talked about him all the time, brought him to see the displays whenever he could. The boy was fascinated by the Archaeopteryx on display. He stared into that case for hours, ah..." light had dawned on Dr Browning's dimming memory. "Of course, Frank said his name so often. His boy was called Samson, as in the Bible. Samson Baumberger."

"And I imagine he was often called Sam," Clara felt the final click and knew what she had to do. "Thank you, Dr Browning, while I am still not sure why this is all happening, I now have a good idea of who is behind it."

Dr Browning's frown evaporated.

"That sounds hopeful!" He said.

"Nothing is for certain just yet," Clara replied. "But there is enough for me to talk to the police. Thank you, Dr Browning, I do hope you are feeling a lot better soon."

"I feel better already," Dr Browning smiled. "I feel hopeful at last."

Clara bid him farewell and then hurried downstairs to collect Tommy. Her brother looked at her keenly as she appeared.

"What now?"

"I need to find the Inspector," Clara said. "I think I know who killed John Morley. Quite why he did it eludes me, but I see the start of the solution to this riddle."

Tommy grinned.

"Right then, let's get this case solved!"

Chapter Thirty

They found Inspector Park-Coombs in his office, just about to have late morning tea and biscuits. His face fell as Clara walked in.

"Today I have good news, Inspector," Clara promised him. "I think Sam Gutenberg killed John Morley. I can't tell you quite why he did it, but I think it links back to another murder in Germany in 1901."

Inspector Park-Coombs put down his biscuit.

"I feel I have missed something."

"I shall explain while we head out to arrest Mr Gutenberg. I think we ought to hurry, he might already be thinking of leaving."

"Clara, on what evidence am I arresting this man? He hired John Morley."

"Yes, but not for the reason we all thought. Look, I have a witness who has given a good description of a man who resembled Sam Gutenberg outside the town hall with John Morley," Clara knew that was overblowing Maud's evidence, but she needed to get the inspector moving. "We know that Gutenberg has a connection to John, and I think he may have been the son of a man who was killed in Germany, under very similar circumstances to what happened here the other night."

"And just why did he kill John Morley?" Inspector

Park-Coombs flapped his hands in exasperation.

"That is something I am unsure of," Clara admitted. "But if you were to search his room at the hotel, I think you would find a jacket with blood on it. He must have been spattered when he killed John."

Park-Coombs groaned.

"I can't arrest a man on so little."

"Can you not search his room?" Clara begged.

Park-Coombs stared at his cup of tea, his brow furrowed as he regarded it with a degree of annoyance.

"You have a witness who saw him with John Morley breaking into the town hall?"

"Yes," Clara said firmly, hoping she was not barking up the wrong tree.

"Well, I can't see why he would hire a man just to kill him, but I may be able to search his room on that basis," Park-Coombs rose from his seat. "You better be right Clara."

Clara tried to appear confident, when in reality her stomach had flipped over a little.

"I am sure on this," she lied.

They went to the hotel where Gutenberg was staying. He proved to be out when they asked for him, but that was not such a bad thing. The inspector was able to use his authority to persuade the hotel manager to open Gutenberg's room for him. He went in with two constables to search it, insisting that Clara and Tommy remain outside in the corridor.

Clara was nervous; she had made a guess based on a few likely clues, she could easily be wrong. At least Sam Gutenberg was not there to see what was happening. There still that unsettling lack of motive for him killing John Morley, why would he do such a thing? Clara could not see how he could have known John before he hired him to break the glass case, and if he didn't know him, then why kill him?

Clara was beginning to have serious doubts as time ticked by without the inspector finding anything damning in the room. She was about to admit defeat and ask the inspector to call off the search when Sam Gutenberg appeared in the corridor. He glanced at Clara in surprise, and then at his open hotel room.

"Hey, what are you doing?" He cried, running to the door just as the inspector was holding up a jacket he had found in the wardrobe.

"Mr Gutenberg, just in time," Inspector Park-Coombs said drily. "Would you mind explaining how you come to have spots of blood on this nice jacket and also on a shirt my constable found a moment ago?"

Sam froze before the inspector, his eyes flicked about the room and then he bolted straight back out. Tommy had seen the move coming and as Sam tried to escape, he threw himself at him and tackled him to the ground. Sam cried out in fury and struggled, but Tommy was able to pin his arms and there was soon a police constable aiding him.

"You could have waited for the best bit, Mr Gutenberg," Inspector Park-Coombs said, stepping out of the room with a rubber-covered mallet in his hand. He had wrapped a handkerchief around the handle to prevent him putting fingerprints on it. The mallet had been crudely washed, but the red stain on the wooden handle indicated that Sam had been unable to completely remove the evidence of his crime.

"Where was it?" Clara asked.

"In the cavity between the bottom drawer of the chest of drawers and the floor. You wouldn't believe how often people hide things in that little space," Park-Coombs had not taken his eyes off Sam. "I imagine, when you could not get the mallet clean, you panicked and thought it was better to hide it than to put it back. Were you going to leave it here, or throw it into the sea when you had a chance?"

Sam refused to say anything, his face was angry and he was breathing hard into the carpet of the corridor floor as his fury bubbled up uselessly.

"I will definitely be arresting him," Park-Coombs

turned to Clara. "Thank you."

"I am very relieved Inspector," Clara remarked. "I was starting to doubt myself."

"Your instincts were right where they needed to be," the inspector smiled at her. "Now I just want to know what this fellow had against John Morley."

The inspector turned to his men.

"Come on, lads, let's get him back to the station."

~~~*~~~

Sam Gutenberg did not want to talk, but there was far too much physical evidence for him to deny what he had done. He might have tried to excuse the bloody clothing by saying he had cut himself shaving, but the mallet was conclusive.

The coldness of the crime struck everyone; there seemed no reason for it. Why had John Morley died?

After a fraught hour of getting little more than silence from Sam, the inspector decided to take a break and to communicate with his police equivalents in South Africa and see what they could tell him. He wanted to know if Clara's hunch that Sam Gutenberg and Samson Baumberger were one and the same was correct. That meant urgent telegrams to another country and then an impatient wait.

Clara decided there was little she could do for the time being, so she suggested to Tommy they head over to see Mrs Wilton and wrap up the Miss Holbein affair. Tommy looked a little reluctant, but Clara patted his arm.

"I am sure we can convince Mrs Wilton that everything has worked out for the best," she lied.

Tommy didn't believe her.

They headed to Mrs Wilton's villa with its spectacular sea views. The sea was a little rough that day and the white heads of the waves crashed on the shore below. Mrs Wilton's maid said that her mistress was feeling unwell and might not wish to receive visitors, she then disappeared to tell the woman that Clara was on the doorstep. Clara heard Mrs Wilton cry out that she was most certainly receiving those guests before the maid reappeared with a sheepish look on her face.

"Don't worry," Clara winked at her.

Mrs Wilton was in her sitting room, which had the best views of the sea. She was lying back on a couch with an ice bag on her forehead.

"Oh my dears!" She said. "I hope you have brought me good news!"

Tommy flashed a look at Clara, but she ignored him.

"Are you unwell?" Clara asked Mrs Wilton.

"A headache," Mrs Wilton sighed. "It's all this worry about Nellie. Please tell me you have news!"

"I do," Clara admitted. "But whether it is good news, or bad, I am not sure."

"You are worrying me Clara, please explain yourself!" Mrs Wilton propped herself up on the couch, still clutching the ice bag to her head.

Clara took a deep breath.

"Victor Darling is a very intelligent young man who works for an engineering company testing engines for new cars and other vehicles. He has a genuine affection for Miss Holbein, to the point he would do anything for her and probably allows himself to be used a little more than he should," Clara tried to speak fast so Mrs Wilton could not interrupt. "It is my opinion that he could be a good influence on Miss Holbein and should not be someone to be worried about."

Mrs Wilton was so stunned by this information, that for a moment she didn't speak. She cleared her throat and stiffened.

"An engineer?"

"Yes," Clara replied. "He is a very nice young man. Kind, thoughtful and though not from a monied background…"

"I thought Nellie had taken a liking to your brother?" Mrs Wilton interrupted, casting a stern glance at Tommy.

"That was an unfortunate misunderstanding," Clara

explained patiently. "Tommy was working on my behalf to gain information about Mr Darling."

"I am very alarmed by all this," Mrs Wilton looked more angry than alarmed. "It appears you are saying that you think this Victor fellow, though clearly unsuitable, should be considered a worthy suitor for Nellie?"

Clara could see that tact was not going to win the day, Mrs Wilton was not going to be convinced by gently mentioning Victor's good points. She had to be told bluntly why Clara thought Victor should remain with Nellie.

"Mrs Wilton, I have spent time with Nellie these last few days, as has Tommy, and we have come to understand the girl a great deal. For one thing, she is truly cynical about life and about her place in this world. She seems to think that money means power, and that her only worth comes from her wealth. You must appreciate that is a very sad state of affairs, even if Nellie does not yet understand that. She is young and naïve, but I think she could end up in a very bad position if she carries on with the notion that her biggest bargaining chip in her life is her inheritance. You have good cause to be concerned about the men who pursue her," Clara spoke fast, when Mrs Wilton looked about to interrupt, she quickly carried on. "We are all aware that it is not just poor men who might look at a woman for her money over who she is. This world of ours is built on an idea of marrying for money, and the higher up the social scale you climb, the more pronounced that idea becomes. There is nothing more fearful to a man who has a fortune than the thought of losing it all.

"Nellie is in a position where scoundrels will flock to her and they may not be penniless scoundrels. There are many men of a reasonable background with a similar affection for money who would see Nellie's wealth as something they could use. Nellie, herself, would become no more than a pawn in this game. Which is awful, especially as Nellie believes she cannot expect love from any marriage she makes. It all creates a very unhappy situation. Nellie's entire future could be staked on this."

"Precisely!" Mrs Wilton burst in, unable to hold back any longer. "We must keep the wolves from her door!"

"Which is exactly why I suggest you allow Victor Darling to continue his courtship. In fact, I suggest you embrace him, for that man genuinely cares about Nellie's wellbeing and that is far more important than whether he is an engineer or an earl," Clara did not add that she thought the odds of Nellie finding another man able to look past all her faults would be slim.

Mrs Wilton froze, Clara's words suddenly hitting her. She opened her mouth, but words did not come out.

"You asked me to find out all I could about Victor," Clara continued. "I found out that he is, yes, an engineer, but that he has a strong affection for Nellie and a remarkable loyalty to her. I believe he will take good care of her. Whether she will ever consent to marry him I really do not know, I think it possible she will grow tired of him and cast him aside. Which would be a shame for her, but not something I can change. Nellie is very headstrong and a touch over-confident, she does not take advice readily."

"No," Mrs Wilton said slowly. "She doesn't really listen to anyone."

She was silent a while, thinking about what Clara had said.

"You really think this Victor Darling would look after her?"

"I think his influence on her a very positive thing," Clara promised.

Mrs Wilton groaned and sank back on her couch.

"But he is an engineer! Nellie's mother would be appalled!"

"Wouldn't she want to know there was someone out there who cared for her daughter and wanted to look after her?" Clara said. "There are plenty of eligible young men who would marry Nellie for her money and then misuse her."

Mrs Wilton screwed up her face, trying to get her head

around everything she had been told.

"Oh Clara! I can't fathom this all. Surely there must be a nice young man out there who would care for Nellie and who is also of a similar social rank?" Mrs Wilton's eyes flicked back to Tommy, and he edged away a little.

"I have done my part," Clara had no more energy to argue the matter. "I think we both know that Nellie will do as she pleases, and nothing anyone says can change that. She may decide tomorrow that Victor bores her and she will be looking for someone else to keep her amused. Then this discussion will be all in vain."

Mrs Wilton seemed to resign herself. She nodded her head.

"Nellie is a complicated girl, you are very right. I am glad I asked for your help. Whatever comes of this Clara, thank you for taking the time to find out all you did about Victor Darling," Mrs Wilton sighed. "I am not blind to Nellie's nature. Maybe if I met this Victor and saw how he treated her, it would put my mind at ease?"

"I think that would be a good idea," Clara smiled, pleased to seeing Mrs Wilton was mellowing. "Now, I don't wish to disturb you any longer. I hope you feel better soon."

Clara shuffled Tommy out of the room as Mrs Wilton laid back her head and shut her eyes. They escaped the house without alerting the maid. Tommy puffed out his cheeks as they stood outside.

"Thanks Clara, for not mentioning my, ahem, interference in this matter."

Clara chuckled.

"Mrs Wilton doesn't need to know about that. And I meant every word I said, I think Victor could be very good for Nellie Holbein, if only she will let him," Clara glanced at her watch. "Now, let's see how speedily the South African authorities respond to a telegram from England."

Chapter Thirty-one

There was activity at the station when Clara arrived. A police constable was rushing into the back office and Dr Deáth was lurking on the stairs. He grinned at Clara.

"I've run a crude test to determine if that red stain on the mallet is blood. The results are positive," he told her. "Also, the stains on the shirt and jacket are blood too. I can't say for sure whose, or if it is human, but the inspector seems pleased."

"Where is he?" Clara asked.

Dr Deáth's eyes lit up.

"He just had word that a telegram had arrived for him, he seemed excited by it."

Clara felt excited too. She could only hope that telegram contained confirmation of what she suspected.

"The mallet looks like the right sort of weapon to have killed John Morley?" Clara asked Dr Deáth, with one eye looking out for the inspector.

"Oh yes, I have no concerns about that," Dr Deáth said merrily.

"Clara!"

Despite keeping her eye open for him, Inspector Park-Coombs had managed to appear without her noticing. He looked serious, but there was a liveliness to his tone that made Clara hopeful he had good news.

"Well?" She hurried over to him.

"Your suspicion was accurate," Inspector Park-Coombs smiled at her. "Turns out that the South African police had no trouble informing me of Sam Gutenberg's origins. He was not lying about his family being extremely wealthy and owning mines. His stepfather, Gustav Gutenberg, is one of the richest men in the country. Sam's mother emigrated to South Africa and met Gustav. He was considerably older than her and looking for a wife, she was looking for security for herself and her son. They married and Sam took on his stepfather's name. He has six half-brothers and sisters from his mother's second marriage.

"The police in South Africa informed me that there has been some family trouble recently. Sam is, of course, his mother's eldest, but in the eyes of his stepfather he is an interloper and he places his own children over Sam. This has caused tension, especially after the recent death of Sam's mother. There was a violent scuffle between Sam and his stepfather at the funeral and the police were summoned.

"Shortly afterwards, Sam disappeared without a word. His stepfather cared enough to report him missing and the South African police have been looking for him ever since. They never expected he would turn up in Brighton."

"That still does not explain why Sam killed John Morley," Clara pointed out.

"Why don't we ask him," the inspector said.

He headed to the cells at the back of the station where Sam Gutenberg was being held. Clara followed. Sam Gutenberg scowled at them when they first appeared, then he looked away.

"Samson Baumberger," Inspector Park-Coombs held up the telegram. "The son of a man who died in Germany in remarkably similar circumstances to John Morley. Maybe you could explain that."

Sam snorted and ignored him. Clara stepped towards

the bars of the cell.

"They never found who killed your father," she said. "All these years, that has burned you. And your mother remarried, but her new husband could never be a father to you. He was not your father. Not the man you visited in the museum and who showed you around the displays. Your father did not deserve to die, and no one ever explained why it happened."

Sam's face had become grim, he closed his eyes tight shut.

"I'm guessing you laid some blame on the shoulders of Dr Browning. Had he been in that room when it happened, your father would still be alive. It would have been Dr Browning dead on that floor instead," Clara continued.

"No!" Sam snapped, his head shooting up to her. "You are the same as them all!"

Clara was confused.

"What do you mean?"

Sam gave a bitter laugh.

"I suppose the game is up then?" He looked at the inspector. "You have all the evidence you need, you know who I am, who I really am. And you have the mallet and my clothes. You just don't know why, why it all came about. I almost feel like keeping that my secret, except by doing so I let that damn man off the hook."

"Dr Browning?" Clara asked, somewhat surprised.

"Yes! Him! If I never speak up, if I never explain, then you will go around thinking that he was some innocent academic and no one will ever know what he is really like," Sam's eyes were bright with tears, fierce grief had been buried within him too long. "You still think he is this bumbling old man who could not hurt a fly? You are wrong, and I tried so hard to make you look again, but no one would see past his façade!"

"But you killed John Morley," Clara said, trying to bring some sense to this riddle.

"Yes, I did, but only so that people would open their eyes and start to ask questions about my father's death in

Germany. The problem was, it was all so well hidden. I didn't bank on that, I had to give you so many clues before you discovered that story and, in the end, that was my undoing," Sam rubbed at his eye. "I had no argument with John Morley, he was just a convenient dupe. He was a drunk and so many people hated him. I didn't think he would be much missed and he was so keen on the money."

"You hired him to accompany you to the town hall on the pretext of smashing the cases," Clara understood. "When you told us he intended to get someone to help him it was all a lie to throw us off your scent."

"I could see that you were heading in the wrong direction," Sam shook his head. "You were supposed to assume that no one else could have committed the crime except Dr Browning. I thought I made that so obvious. And when the Earl of Rendham appeared and began fussing about the time the investigation was taking, I honestly thought I had succeeded. Sooner or later you would just accept the obvious and arrest Dr Browning. I didn't expect you to be so damn curious! You asked so many questions!"

"And then Harry Beasley got in the way," Park-Coombs mused.

"I could see it was all going wrong, so I tried to point you in the right direction again," Sam grimaced as he remembered his efforts. "Instead, you came after me. You were not meant to even consider me a suspect."

"You certainly had me fooled for a while," Clara said. "But, ultimately, you were trying too hard. John Morley died, not because you had a grudge against him, you didn't even know him, but because you wanted to see Dr Browning accused of murder."

"I wanted to see him hang," Sam growled the words. "It would have been for the wrong man's death, but he still would be dead and his name shamed forever!"

"Because your father was killed that night in Germany instead of Dr Browning?" Park-Coombs said in astonishment.

Sam leapt from the bed in the cell and slammed his hand against the bars.

"No! Because Dr Browning killed my father! It was not some fluke of fate that my father died that night, it was because Dr Browning intended it!"

"You really believe that?" Clara said in astonishment, thinking of the ailing academic in his hospital bed.

"I know it!" Sam insisted. "My father discovered that Dr Browning had miscatalogued a number of exhibits, that was when it began. My father could not fathom how an academic of Dr Browning's standing could make such simple mistakes when cataloguing finds. He started to watch his mentor more closely and he noticed other little mistakes and he started to wonder. So he contacted the university were Dr Browning was supposed to have obtained his degree and learned that Browning had never gone there.

"Dr Browning was a fraud. He had no formal qualifications, but he had convinced the right people that he knew all about fossils, given himself a fake degree and then found a job in a prestigious museum. Most people would never have noticed the mistakes he made, but my father was a genius. He knew more about fossils than anyone I have ever met. He was bitterly disappointed when he learned the truth about his mentor, the man he looked up to.

"He confronted him, pointed out the mistakes he had made and told him that he knew everything. He said he would tell the university authorities if Dr Browning did not confess himself. The hypocrisy of Dr Browning still rankles me now! He had no university education, just like my father, but he had always told my father that he would never achieve a name for himself because of that lack. All the time he had been playing the role of a doctor without a degree!

"My father told me all about this, made me promise to keep it a secret. I think he was worried. I think he saw how dangerous a man Dr Browning really was. And the next night he died, he was murdered and people kept saying it was some intruder who had come to steal exhibits. But I knew better! I knew Dr Browning had killed him! No one would listen to me, I was just a boy, and all these years I have hated him. And then my mother died and I..."

Sam crumpled back on the bed and hung his head, his hands flopped between his legs and he sagged like a ragdoll.

"I wanted to frame Dr Browning for murder. To bring justice to my father. Maybe you would even look into the Germany case again, but even if you didn't, Dr Browning would hang and he would see the irony, if no one else did."

"You murdered a stranger to get justice for your father?" Park-Coombs was appalled as he spoke. "An innocent man was nearly in danger of being tried for that crime. You destroyed a stranger's life to get revenge?"

"You don't understand," Sam coughed as tears started to overwhelm him. "No one ever understands. My father was a good man. I had to bring him justice."

Clara had heard enough.

"Because of you a woman is widowed," she said coldly. "John Morley might not have been the nicest of men, but he meant something to her. You had no right to take his life for such a callous reason. What would your father have thought of that?"

Sam clutched his head in his hands and began to sob. There was nothing more Clara wanted to say. She walked from the cells and Park-Coombs followed.

"Well, we solved it," he said to her as they reached the front desk. "We know who killed John Morley."

"And we know why," Clara said without any satisfaction. "The world is wicked."

"Men are wicked, Clara, the world just happens to be the place we all live in," Park-Coombs shrugged.

Clara shook her head, all she wanted right then was to go home.

~~~*~~~

Clara drifted about the house for the rest of the afternoon, mulling over what Sam had told her about Dr Browning. He was right when he said no one could imagine Dr Browning as a killer. Did that mean they had been blind to what he had done? Had he really killed Sam's father? They had no proof other than the son's suspicions and he hardly appeared reliable after his own involvement in a murder to frame Dr Browning. Clara could not help but wonder, however, if she had looked a murderer in the eye and not recognised him for what he was.

She was distracted from her thoughts by the sound of raised voices. Clara headed towards the parlour where Annie was in tears and Tommy was trying to console her.

"Whatever is going on?" Clara asked.

"He has bought a fancy necklace for that woman!" Annie declared furiously, pointing to the jewellery box Tommy had bought earlier. "I found it in his sock drawer when I was putting away some clothes."

"Annie won't believe me when I say it is for her!" Tommy snapped, looking irate that he was being called a liar.

"What would I do with that?" Annie demanded of him. "I don't wear jewellery, it is the sort of thing that Miss Holbein would wear!"

"I have no interest in Miss Holbein! I have spent most of the week trying to get rid of her!" Tommy threw up his hands and stormed out of the room.

"Annie," Clara took her friend by the arms, "I was with Tommy when he bought the necklace. It is for you. All right, I admit it is not quite your cup of tea, but it was meant as a gift."

Annie wiped at her eyes and looked rather abashed.

"Really?"

"Yes. You are being much too harsh on Tommy, he loves you to pieces. Why have you become so silly over this misunderstanding with Miss Holbein?"

Annie sniffed.

"I just…" she shook her head. "I don't know, I just have this terror he is going to realise one day that I am just an ordinary girl. I'm a good cook, but what else am I? You are so clever Clara, and Tommy is too. I sometimes think he deserves someone more interesting than me. What can he see in me, after all?"

"I see a good heart and a kind soul," Tommy said softly from the doorway.

Annie and Clara both turned towards him.

"That necklace is damn awful," Tommy continued. "I was going to take it back, that's why I shoved it in the sock drawer. It wasn't what I wanted to buy you at all. What I really wanted to buy you, was this."

Tommy presented his hand with a cube-shaped velvet box perched on his palm. Annie's eyes widened. Tommy stepped towards her and sank down on one knee.

"Annie, you are the only woman I want in my life, excluding Clara, of course," Tommy said.

"I'm just your sister, I don't count," Clara grinned, taking a pace back to give them room.

"Annie, I would be deeply honoured if you would marry me," Tommy opened the box and a diamond ring sat in the cushioned interior. "Unless, that is, you still think I am interested in that terrible Holbein woman."

Clara kicked him lightly with her foot.

"Don't spoil it!" She scolded him.

Annie had put her hands to her face and looked like she might faint. After a moment she took a ragged breath through her clenched teeth.

"Oh!" She groaned.

"That isn't precisely a yes," Tommy said. "Also, my legs aren't entirely happy with me kneeling like this. If you could perhaps come to a decision."

Annie snapped out of her astonishment.

"Get up you silly man," she grabbed his arm and helped him lever his legs back to straight. "Of course, I will marry you!"

She kissed him on the cheek and Clara cheered. Tommy took the engagement ring from the box and slipped it onto Annie's finger. It was a dainty, pretty thing, not elaborate but all the more delightful for its understatement. Annie sighed as she looked at it, then she turned to Clara and popped up onto her toes.

"I'm engaged!" She cried.

Clara laughed and hugged her. Then she grabbed Tommy and hugged him too, smiling and crying all at the same time.

"What would I do without you two?" she said, wiping away a tear.

"Life would be a lot simpler," Tommy teased.

Clara shoved him.

"I don't need simple," she declared.

~~~*~~~

The exhibition left Brighton on schedule. The Earl of Rendham was satisfied, though he probably would be less pleased when he read the article Gilbert was working on concerning his 'new' fossil discovery. Gilbert was digging deep into the Earl's archaeopteryx and from what little he had been prepared to tell Clara, it seemed he had come across some disturbing information about the supposedly genuine find. Gilbert thought he was onto something big. Clara was happy to let him deal with the matter. At the end of the day, she had solved the murder and that was that.

Clara watched the lorry that transported the exhibits being loaded from across the road. She saw Wallace Sunderland leading the packing. She had not told anyone about the letters he had written, but upon the understanding that he would desist. She did not feel like losing him his job, not when the Earl was really behind the threats. She had passed all that information to Gilbert too, to do with as he wished.

Then there was Dr Browning. The doctors wanted him

256

to rest, but his life revolved around the fossils in the exhibition and he refused to abandon them. He had discharged himself from the hospital just so he could leave town with the exhibits. Clara watched the weary old man, hunched up over a walking stick as he supervised the loading of the lorry. From time to time he coughed hard and pressed a hand to his chest. Clara did not think he was long for this world. Perhaps, after all, some sort of justice was catching up with him. She did not know if he was a murderer, but it played on her mind that he might be, that she might have been fooled by his façade of homely innocence.

Clara liked to think she had good instincts for people, but in this instance she felt uncertain. Had she been in the presence of a cold-blooded killer and never even realised it? Worse, had she felt sorry for a killer?

Not that it was an excuse for Sam Gutenberg's actions. It was just a consideration. Sam would hang for killing John Morley, while the possible killer of his father continued to walk free. Though Clara felt the Grim Reaper already had his hand on his shoulder and Dr Browning would soon be facing the only justice they could all expect one day. Death was the great equaliser, as it was said.

Clara turned and walked away. She could not solve an old murder that happened in Germany, but she had solved the riddle of John Morley's death. That would not bring peace to Ruby, who was lying at death's door in her brother's house, but it did mean Harry Beasley was truly free from suspicion. Crazy to think that all this trouble had been sparked by a lot of stones. Who knew that an ancient bird could be the source of so much mischief and heartache? It was truly remarkable what people would kill over. As Clara set off her home, she mused that humanity was truly a complicated creature – the only beings on the planet who would kill over a fossil that had been in the ground millions of years.

Utterly astounding, yet also utterly alarming.

Printed in Great Britain
by Amazon